Virginia Steffens
October 28, 2023
October 31, 2023
Happy Halloween

TIMELESS
Victorian
COLLECTION

A Grand TOUR

A Grand Tour

Anthea Lawson

Jennifer Moore

Heather B. Moore

Mirror Press

Interior Design by Cora Johnson
Edited by Jennie Stevens, Haley Swan, and Lisa Shepherd
Cover design by Rachael Anderson
Cover Photo Credit: Richard Jenkins Photography

Published by Mirror Press, LLC

ISBN: 978-1-947152-75-5

Timeless Victorian Collections

Summer Holiday

A Grand Tour

Orient Express

Timeless Regency Collections

Autumn Masquerade

A Midwinter Ball

Spring in Hyde Park

Summer House Party

A Country Christmas

A Season in London

Falling for a Duke

A Night in Grosvenor Square

Road to Gretna Green

Table of Contents

A Lord's Chance

-Anthea Lawson-

Southern coast of Spain, October 1852

The smell of deck tar warming under the Mediterranean sun made Miss Isabelle Strathmore smile beneath the brim of her second-best bonnet. She was shipboard once again and in the climate she loved best. Despite the memories lodged within her like hard pebbles, she could not help but surrender to the dry light and warm air as the steamship *Floramay* turned south, toward Morocco.

Even her stalwart companion, Mrs. Hodges, had given a satisfied harrumph at their first sight of orange groves reaching down to the sea, the heady fragrance borne offshore so that the air was a mix of salt and sweet.

"Look there." Mrs. Hodges pointed toward the shore with the tip of her ever-present black umbrella.

In the distance the white buildings of Cadiz shone in the sunshine, the pale towers of the cathedral clear against the blue sky.

Isabelle turned her back to the railing, her mood dimming.

"I shall not recall it."

Five years ago, she had argued with her cousin in those very streets, her foolish heart set on a course for disaster.

But she was older now, and wiser, moving through the world with a guarded heart and open eyes. *This* journey to the Mediterranean, she would not fall in love, nor suffer the awful consequences of that emotion.

"At least the sea has learned to behave, instead of plunging up and down in a most nauseating fashion." Mrs. Hodges frowned at the water.

"I'm glad you've found your sea legs at last," Isabelle said.

During their last trip out, her companion had often been laid low by seasickness. But despite her curmudgeonly exterior, Mrs. Hodges possessed the soul of an adventurer. Why else had she agreed to accompany Isabelle on a Grand Tour culminating in Greece?

"I don't know if your family will ever be done gallivanting about the globe," the older woman had said. "What with your father's scientific inclinations, I'm sure he'll end up traveling to the farthest reaches of the globe before he's done. Botanists!"

Isabelle had not suggested that Mrs. Hodges stay at home instead of accompanying her on this trip, of course. It would be rather an insult, and besides, Isabelle was still of an age where a companion was necessary.

Maybe in a few more years, Isabelle herself would take on the role of companion or governess to some gently bred young lady. She'd never marry, of course. Even though her parents enjoyed a happy life together, she knew that path was not for her.

She let out a quiet breath and turned back to the railing,

staring pensively down at the glittering waves. The sea was as impenetrable as her own future—the surface clear, but the depths beyond quite impossible to look into. Nothing but blue-green shadows shading into black.

"Miss Strathmore!" A man's voice rang out across the deck.

Isabelle glanced up to see a sandy-haired fellow striding toward her. It was Lord Weston, who, upon coming aboard in Lisbon, had commenced flirting outrageously with her. While she found it a bit annoying, he was an amiable gentleman and harmless enough.

He was accompanied by the dark and quiet Lord Jasper, who, like a shadow, seemed to follow his friend about as though he had no choice in the matter. Where Lord Weston was a boisterous, happy retriever, Lord Jasper was an aloof black cat who hardly deigned to glance at the humans among whom he found himself.

"Good day," Isabelle said as the gentlemen joined her at the railing.

"It very much is, now that we have discovered you in it," Lord Weston said. "Are you planning to go ashore this afternoon? I most fervently hope you say yes so that we might accompany you." He shot a look at his friend, who was staring at the water and seemingly paying no attention to the conversation at hand. "What do you think, Gav? A jaunt to Morocco will be just the thing."

"Certainly." Lord Jasper flicked a disinterested glance at Isabelle, his dark-gray eyes barely resting for a moment on her face before he looked away again.

What an irritating fellow!

While she was not overfond of the fawning attentions of Lord Weston, at least she was accustomed to such regard. It was unpleasantly novel to be treated as though she were scarcely there.

She'd gathered that Lord Gavin Reed, the Earl of Jasper, was traveling with his friend in the wake of some unfortunate personal circumstance. Unlike Mrs. Hodges, he apparently had not been softened in the least by the sunshine and balmy air.

"When we dock in Tangier, we'll be sure to look for you," Isabelle said to Lord Weston, pointedly ignoring his friend. Two could play that game, after all.

And if Lord Jasper's dark good looks reminded her too much of a certain other lord on a certain other journey, then it was all to the good that they had as little to do with each other as possible. The last thing Isabelle needed was another reminder that her heart could never be trusted.

Gavin Reed, the Earl of Jasper, frowned at his friend Lord Weston as they returned to their elegantly appointed cabin.

"In my opinion, you should stay away from that young lady," Gavin said. "A fortune hunter if ever I've seen one, and she's old enough to be getting desperate."

William Tuttle, who bore the title of Viscount Weston, laughed. "You're just afraid that any pretty young lady is after your money and title. Which, considering your last *affaire de coeur,* I can understand. But not all women are Rosalie."

"Or Amanda? Or Faith?" Gavin couldn't help the edge in his voice.

Will's smile turned wry. "It's true, you have the worst luck with women. You're simply too handsome, more's the pity."

"Not to mention rich. What is that so-called universal

truth . . . that I must be in want of a wife?" Gavin shook his shoulders, trying to dislodge the notion.

He strode the few paces to his bunk and stood there, balancing against the gentle rolling of the ship. The porthole showed blue, and paler blue, and blue again as the sea and sky traded places in his view.

"When I let you talk me into this jaunt," he said, "you promised no romantic entanglements."

"For you!" Will removed his hat and hung it on the tiny bentwood stand. "I'm perfectly happy flirting with any pretty girl who comes my way. That doesn't mean you have to."

"Yes—but I don't like having to watch as some young miss sets her claws in you."

"Miss Strathmore is perfectly delightful," Will said. "And you are too suspicious. I know that the young women you've encountered of late are less than ideal, but at some point you're going to have to take a chance on one of them."

Gavin crossed his arms. It was useless to argue with his friend. The whole conversation was stirring unpleasant emotions, and he'd come on this trip to try and get away from such things.

And if he were being quite honest, he was, in fact, more than ready to settle down, take up residence at his vast country estate, and run it, he hoped, as deftly as his father had.

He wanted a companion—very well, a *wife*—who could take on the management of the household and bear him heirs. His mother had hinted quite strongly that she was not growing any younger and greatly desired grandchildren to dandle upon her knee.

He could have had a wife by now if he'd been less particular.

But the obvious graspings of the Rosalies and Amandas of the nobility had, quite frankly, turned his stomach. He could not see any of those greedy young women as suitable mothers of his children. Not to mention that the act of creating such children would feel like a duty, not a pleasure.

So here he was, embarked on a tour of the Mediterranean with his friend Will and not finding much to enjoy about it. His failure to find a wife perched on his shoulder like a black crow, claws digging into his skin every time he turned his head.

The luncheon bell interrupted his unhappy musings, signaling it was time for the passengers to gather for their next meal.

"Don't look so glum," Will said. "The world's full of delightful young women just waiting to meet you. We'll find you the right one yet, mark my words."

Gavin did not bother to reply to this transparent attempt to cheer him up and merely gestured for his friend to precede him to the dining room.

The ship's horn sounded, summoning passengers to the deck, but Isabelle and Mrs. Hodges were already there, watching their approach into Tangier. The city spilled down to the bay in a rumpled collection of white and cream buildings with a few red and yellow houses providing a splash of color.

Isabelle turned her attention to the passengers collecting near the stern. Among travelers there seemed to be certain characters one could always spot. There, the studious older man—a scholar or writer, no doubt. The group of matrons off on a well-deserved holiday, giving reproachful glances to the clot of boisterous young men and their harried-looking tutor.

And there, echoing herself and Mrs. Hodges, another young lady with her unsmiling companion. Isabelle watched as they made their way forward. The girl glanced about with a fresh, curious expression, while her companion seemed even more humorless than Mrs. Hodges appeared to be.

The young lady fetched up at the railing next to them and turned her open smile upon Isabelle.

"Hello," she said. "Isn't this exciting! I've never been to Africa before. I'd love to see Egypt, too, but—"

"Ahem." The companion stepped forward. "I apologize for my charge—she is a bit outspoken. Allow me to introduce ourselves. This is Miss Sarah Taylor, and I am her governess, Miss Primm."

Isabelle swallowed a laugh. The governess was aptly named, and she wondered whether the woman had always had such a tight-lipped and disapproving expression or whether she'd decided to grow into her name at a later date.

"Lovely to meet you," Isabelle said. "I'm Miss Isabelle Strathmore, and this is my companion, Mrs. Hodges."

"A pleasure, I'm sure." Miss Primm inclined her head. "As you have no doubt guessed, this is our first journey abroad. Am I correct in thinking the two of you are seasoned tourists?"

"We have been to the Mediterranean before," Isabelle said.

"I guessed as much." The governess gave her a slightly superior look, as if to imply that there was something unbecoming about being an experienced traveler. "I'm certain we'll benefit from your wisdom. Though no doubt this will be our only excursion. Miss Taylor comes from an excellent family and is merely getting a touch of polish before she goes home to England to make a brilliant match."

Mrs. Hodges's bushy eyebrow twitched up the merest fraction.

"I expect that travel will be good for both of you," she said in a dry voice. "It does tend to broaden the mind."

Miss Primm's expression became even primmer, but her charge, Miss Taylor, grinned.

"No matter what my governess says, I don't want to get married. Not yet, anyway. There's so much of the world to see!"

She waved at the port they were rapidly approaching, the colorful fishing boats docked along the smaller piers. Above the turquoise waters, dun-colored medieval walls enclosed the old city, while newer buildings spilled around the edges on either side, some of them dome topped, others with doors painted so brightly that the colors were clear even at this distance.

As they were admiring the view, Lord Weston arrived at the railing with Lord Jasper in tow.

"We meet again, Miss Strathmore, Mrs. Hodges," Lord Weston said. "We are looking forward to accompanying you into Tangier."

Miss Primm eyed the gentlemen, her expression moving to grudging approval as Isabelle made the introductions.

"A viscount and an earl," she said. "How marvelous. And how gallant of you gentlemen to offer to escort Miss Strathmore and her companion into the city. I must admit, I'm a trifle apprehensive at the prospect of setting foot in Morocco without the company of the stronger sex."

Miss Taylor rounded on her governess. "But you *promised* we could go."

"I did not promise." Miss Primm's lips thinned. "I said we might go on deck to observe the ship as it made port, then see what transpired."

The *Floramay* docked with a soft bump, men on deck and the dock below making quick work of securing the ship. The smell of frying onions and spices drifted past, and Isabelle sniffed appreciatively. She'd always been adventurous in her tastes and looked forward to reacquainting herself with the delicacies of North Africa.

"Stand back from the railing," the purser called. The buttons on his uniform shone as he bustled up, three deck-hands behind him.

The crowd shifted back, and the sailors ran the gangway down to the dock with a rattle and bang. Once it was secured, the ship's bell rang out crisply.

"You have the entire afternoon to sightsee," the purser said from his station at the head of the ramp. "Return to the ship by sunset, however. While Tangier is safe, we do not recommend that our passengers remain onshore after dark."

"Oh," Miss Taylor said in a soft voice.

"Have no fear." Lord Weston made her a slight bow. "Nothing would please us better than to accompany all four of you ladies into Tangier to see the sights. Don't you think so, Gav?"

He nudged his friend with his elbow. Discreetly, but Isabelle still saw the motion.

Lord Jasper glanced at Lord Weston.

"Certainly," he said, his tone as dry as the sere hills rising above the city.

At least he was too much of a gentleman to argue. Even if he was dismissive of most people he met.

She shouldn't be glad that the earl had looked at Miss Taylor with the same studied disinterest he displayed toward her, yet she had to admit it had brightened her mood a bit. Not that she cared what Lord Jasper thought of her, or of anyone. His opinions were none of her concern.

Miss Taylor bounced up and down on her toes. "You'll let us come with you? Thank you so much! I would have perished from envy if I'd been trapped aboard the ship while everyone else was off exploring Morocco."

"Then it is a good thing we happened upon you, to avert such a dreadful fate." Lord Weston offered her his arm. "Shall we?"

While Isabelle was relieved he'd transferred his attentions elsewhere for the time being, it unfortunately left Lord Jasper to be her escort.

He did not seem delighted with the prospect either. Mouth set, he held out his elbow to her.

"I don't bite," she murmured, a bit stung, as she set her hand on his forearm.

"Indeed." His voice was as chilly as his eyes.

"Unless provoked to it," she could not help but add.

This made him glance at her. "Dare I ask what would provoke you?"

They stepped down the gangway behind Mrs. Hodges and Miss Primm, and Isabelle cocked her head, considering how forthright she might be. On the one hand there was no need for impoliteness—though Lord Jasper had skirted that line with his dismissive behavior toward her. On the other hand, she possessed the hard-won courage to speak the truth to scoundrels. No gentleman should be able to act callously and escape unscathed.

Lord Jasper had not been callous, however. At least, not yet—but perhaps it would be wise of her to put him on notice, seeing as they were now forced into each other's company.

"Being treated as though I were a speck of dirt upon your coat would certainly cause me to bare my teeth a bit," she said.

"Then I am to consider them bared in my direction, I suppose?"

She smiled at him, letting her lips part to show her teeth. To her surprise, a glint of amusement sparked in his eyes—so quickly tamped down that she wasn't even sure she'd glimpsed it.

"I shall consider myself warned," he said.

Mrs. Hodges let out a cough. No doubt her keen hearing had caught the entire conversation. There was not much her companion missed, and Isabelle now considered Mrs. Hodges as much a friend as a chaperone, despite the disparity of years between them.

"Sarah," Miss Primm called to her charge as they stepped onto the dock, "do put up your parasol. We must preserve your complexion." This last was said with a pitying glance at Isabelle.

For a moment, Isabelle wished she could actually growl at the governess.

But to be fair, despite the fact she wore her bonnet today, she'd been careless in the past about shading her face—as the smattering of freckles across her cheeks attested. It had been rather freeing to let go of the notion she must remain beautiful at all times in order to catch a husband, and to instead let the warm sun touch her skin as the mood struck her.

"Where to?" Lord Weston paused on the wharf and let the rest of the party catch up. "I admit, I'm unfamiliar with the sights of Tangier."

"We certainly should go to the *medina*—the old town," Isabelle said. "The market there will be well worth visiting. And while we're there, perhaps a viewing of the *casbah*—the sultan's palace. Though it is unlikely that foreigners will be admitted without a prior appointment."

"The sultan." Miss Taylor gave a little shiver of excitement. "We truly are far from home, aren't we? Which way do we go?"

Isabelle gestured to the right, where the crenellated walls of the fortified palace could be seen rising above the nearby buildings. The city sloped up from the harbor, and several men with donkey carts were lined up on the far side of the docks. They called out in French, exhorting the new arrivals to purchase a ride up the "terrible, steep" streets in order to avoid injury.

"You seem to know a great deal about the city," Miss Primm said, a note of censure in her voice, as though such knowledge were unladylike.

"I believe in being informed about one's ports of call," Isabelle said.

"Not to mention that we have already traveled in North Africa," Mrs. Hodges said. "One gains a certain familiarity, even though Morocco is not Tunisia."

"You've been to Tunisia?" Lord Jasper glanced at Isabelle.

"Yes, five years ago." She kept her tone brisk, as though her soul had not been completely crushed at the end of that journey. "My father is a botanist, and our family accompanied him on several expeditions when I was younger. Now, might I suggest we hire a donkey cart to convey us up the hill?"

After a bit of haggling between Lord Weston and one of the drivers, the party was soon ensconced in a cart and jolting up the steeply ramped street into the old city of Tangier.

Sunlight gleamed on the indigo water of the bay, and the pale beach seemed quite inviting, with gentle waves lapping up and down the sand. Isabelle wiped a trickle of perspiration from her temple. Miss Taylor looked a bit flushed, despite the shade of her parasol, as did her governess. Mrs. Hodges, in her usual stoic fashion, seemed unmoved by the heat beneath her black umbrella.

Somewhat to Isabelle's annoyance, Lord Jasper had not broken a sweat, either, though Lord Weston had already mopped his forehead twice with his handkerchief.

The donkey cart passed through the thick walls encircling the *medina* and into a hubbub of veiled women, darting children, brightly garbed men in long tunics, and the cries of vendors. The driver halted before a market square, and the party disembarked.

Miss Taylor turned in a circle, eyes wide, and Isabelle wondered if she herself had ever been *quite* that much of an innocent. Luckily, neither of the gentlemen accompanying them seemed the type of scoundrel ready to prey on such naïveté. Harmlessly flirtatious and irritatingly dour, perhaps, but she'd kept company with worse.

They meandered for a time through the market, pausing to admire a bit of jewelry here, bright mounds of colorful spices there. Thin silver fish, so fresh they had not begun to smell, glinted in a rough-hewn wheelbarrow. The gentlemen took a bit of time at a knife vendor, discussing the merits of the various shapes of blades. In one section, the rugs and scarves draped so thickly overhead that the narrow street felt more like a tent than an alley open to the sky.

They emerged into another square, and Isabelle bought a selection of fruits from the date vendor there, choosing a sampling from the array ranging from pale brown to nearly black.

"Are they safe?" Miss Primm asked, giving the packet of sticky fruit a suspicious look.

"Of course they are. Try one." Isabelle held the dates out, pleased to see that both gentlemen did not hesitate to take a fruit.

Neither did Miss Taylor, though the young lady did strip off her glove before selecting a date—a practical touch that Isabelle quickly emulated. Even Mrs. Hodges took one, though she was not a particular fan of sweets.

Miss Primm kept her gloves on and her hands firmly folded.

"If the lot of you want to court sickness, then it's upon

your heads. Sarah, I'm disappointed. I thought you had better sense than to devour random native offerings."

The young lady in question simply grinned and took another date. "They're delicious—but now I'm terribly thirsty."

"Tea seller, yonder." Mrs. Hodges tipped her umbrella to the low tables set up beneath a bright yellow awning.

They had already passed a number of tea vendors, the ornate teapots and finely decorated glasses unmistakable. Indeed, there seemed to be even more people drinking tea in Morocco than coffee. Small, strong cups of the bitter brew had been the staple drink in Tunisia, though Isabelle had never acquired a taste for it.

Mint-flavored tea, however, was another matter.

"Come, Miss Primm," Lord Weston said. "You can see they boil the water over the braziers. I'm certain it's perfectly safe to drink."

The governess sniffed, but when they were all settled on the rugs and cushions beneath the awning, she agreed to have a glass.

The proprietor hurried up and bowed, then began the preparation of the tea, mixing hot water with dried tea leaves and fresh mint and, at the end, a cone of sugar. He poured them each a glass, holding the pot up very high as the tea frothed into scarlet glasses covered with scrolled gold decoration.

"It seems a bit odd," Miss Taylor said, "to be drinking a hot beverage when the air is so very warm."

She held her glass up to the light, the liquid inside the cup glowing like a ruby.

"And yet, it's most refreshing," Isabelle assured her.

"Perhaps it's similar to the Indian habit of eating highly spiced foods," Lord Weston said. "Somehow it triggers an interior cooling mechanism in the body."

Mrs. Hodges let out a harrumph, and Lord Jasper looked amused for a brief second before taking a swallow of his tea.

"Not bad," he said, as if he'd expected much worse.

"Are you feeling cooled, my lord?" Isabelle could not help asking. For some reason—possibly that of being an older sister—his standoffish façade made her want to poke at him until she got a reaction.

"Indubitably," he replied, the barest edge of humor in his dry tone.

"As I said." Lord Weston drained half his glass and gave a satisfied nod. "Invigorating."

Even Miss Primm unbent enough to admit that she did not mind the sweet mint-flavored tea. High praise coming from someone who seemed determined to dislike everything about travel abroad.

After they finished their tea, they went to look at the *casbah.* As Isabelle had expected, the gates were closed to tourists. They caught glimpses of ornately tiled courtyards with merrily splashing fountains and the Moorish arched doorways that had become so familiar in Tunisia.

"The sun's starting to go down," Miss Primm said as they returned to the main street leading away from the palace. "We must make all haste back to the ship."

"Never fear," Lord Weston said. "We'd never let you ladies come to any harm. Besides, we have plenty of time before dusk falls."

Isabelle glanced at the shadows sifting into the sky and then at the tall walls enclosing the *medina.* Luckily, the way out was simple enough. They kept to the road at the edge of the wall, and every few cross streets she could see sunlight slanting off the water below.

Miss Primm hurried ahead, exhorting Miss Taylor and Lord Weston to keep up, but Isabelle felt no need to sprint back to the harbor. Mrs. Hodges strode out a bit faster, with a single look over her shoulder as if to advise Isabelle to make good use of her moments alone with Lord Jasper. Isabelle tried not to roll her eyes at her companion in return. Mrs. Hodges was not in the habit of pushing Isabelle to spend time with eligible gentlemen, but there were exceptions. Apparently Lord Jasper was one. Perhaps Mrs. Hodges recognized a kindred spirit in his irritable nature.

Oh, but that was unkind to her companion. And possibly to Lord Jasper as well.

"Have you been much abroad, my lord?" she asked him.

"I made the compulsory Grand Tour with my tutor several years ago, though we did not set foot in North Africa. You have an adventurous spirit, Miss Strathmore."

"Perhaps I do. Or perhaps, since my family traveled so often, I have simply fallen into the habit of it and not gotten out again."

"No." He said the word firmly. "You strike me as a young lady who makes her way confidently in the world."

She blinked at him. "That's rather an extraordinary statement to make on such short acquaintance. I did not take you for an idle flatterer."

"I'm not."

Still a bit distracted by his words, Isabelle scarcely noted the robed fellow coming up on her right side—until he tore her reticule from her grasp and dashed away down a nearby alley.

"Stop!" she cried, shocked by the boldness of the theft.

Lord Jasper pivoted and sprinted down the narrow street after the thief. Isabelle followed, outrage fueling her steps as she ran over the clay bricks. How dare he? In all her time in Tunisia she had never once been accosted in such a manner.

It was difficult to keep the fellow in sight, but Lord Jasper was adept at following the thief's twists and turns. Isabelle managed to keep Lord Jasper's dark-blue coat in sight, and finally, in a courtyard covered in chipped green and white tiles, he caught up to the pickpocket.

Panting, Isabelle arrived in time to see her escort grab her reticule back and give the man's shoulder a rough shake.

"I'll haul you to the authorities for this," Lord Jasper said, his voice low and full of threat. "Understand?"

The man blurted out something in Arabic and then thrashed about in Lord Jasper's grip. Cloth tore, and a moment later the thief was free. Ripped robe flapping, he whirled and dashed out of the courtyard, leaving Isabelle and Lord Jasper standing alone in the quickening twilight—alone and quite unfortunately lost in the dangerous heart of the old city.

Isabelle glanced up at the sky hemmed in by the buildings surrounding the shabby courtyard. The air had turned the drab gray of a pigeon's wing, and her anger cooled to a chilly apprehension. Whatever were they to do now?

"Here." Lord Jasper handed her the reticule, his voice tight.

"Perhaps we shouldn't have chased the thief." She looked down at her bag. "There's really not much of value inside."

"Why didn't you stay with your companion?" he asked. "I had the matter well in hand."

"I . . ." She stared into his eyes, noting the unmistakable flash of displeasure in their depths. "It's my regrettable spirit of adventure, I suppose."

In truth, it hadn't occurred to her to stay behind, though most gently bred young ladies would have. She'd been too much on her own, perhaps, accustomed to acting for herself without always deferring to a gentleman.

And now it had landed her in a spot of difficulty—though she did have company.

"You'd still be lost in the *medina*, even if I weren't here," she said, a bit tartly.

"I'm not lost. And it's safer for me to be on my own than it is to have to protect you."

She didn't have a ready response to that. Besides, there was no point in wasting time arguing with Lord Jasper when they really needed to be getting back to the ship.

"If you're not lost," she said, gesturing to the alleyways opening off the courtyard, "then, by all means, lead the way."

With a quick glance at the twilight sky, he nodded to their left. "This way."

Not the choice she would have made, but she bit her tongue and followed. There was not enough room in the narrow stone-walled passageway for her to take his arm. And if it came to a fight, it was probably for the best that he had his hands free.

After a few twists and turns, she was quite certain they were losing themselves even deeper in the maze of the old city. The smell of garlic frying in oil drifted from a nearby doorway, and a child watched them go past, wide-eyed and silent.

Lord Jasper hesitated at a cross street. Isabelle tasted dust at the back of her throat and took a moment to catch her breath.

"Are you sure you know the proper direction?" she asked.

"Yes."

A clatter of stone on tile came from behind them, and she shot a quick glance over her shoulder, her heartbeat leaping. There was nothing to be seen—but that didn't mean menacing figures weren't skulking invisibly in the shadows, hands resting on long, curved knives, waiting to leap out . . .

As if sensing her fear, Lord Jasper reached back and grabbed her hand. Not for comfort, as it turned out, but in order to pull her along at a faster pace.

"We're losing the light," he said.

"I'm well aware of the fact." The sky had turned from ashes to coal dust, the scattering of stars overhead little caring what fate befell the mortals scurrying below.

Just when Isabelle was ready to give in to despair, they burst out of an alley onto the wide street leading down to the harbor. Light rushed back into the sky, reflected from the silver mirror of the bay, and she let out a deep breath of relief.

"I told you I knew where I was going," Lord Jasper said, a hint of smugness in his tone.

She glanced at his strong profile silhouetted against the twilight. "How?"

"I've always had an excellent sense of direction, even as a child. Not to mention the ability to find lost items. My mother is the same way and believes it to be a function of keen perception of the world around us." He shrugged.

"However you want to explain it, I'm very grateful."

"I will not say it was my pleasure, Miss Strathmore." His teeth gleamed momentarily in an unexpected smile. "Still, you must admit it was an adventure. I understand you're partial to such things."

"Only up to a point. I'd prefer not to risk life and limb in the depths of an unknown city."

He sobered. "I wouldn't have let any harm come to you."

His words sent a pleasant shiver down her spine, and she belatedly realized their hands were still clasped.

Oh no. She must not do something so foolish as to lose her senses over a gentleman. Especially not one as darkly handsome as Lord Jasper. She pulled free of his grasp and straightened.

"High time we returned to the *Floramay*," she said briskly.

Remember, she told herself fiercely. *Remember what happened last time.* She would never make that mistake again.

In the light of the fitful lamps lining the street, Gavin studied Miss Strathmore. She marched forward, pert nose pointed into the air, golden curls peeking from beneath her bonnet.

Despite himself, his interest was piqued—and oh, wouldn't Will find that amusing, after Gavin's assurances that he intended to steer clear of women for the time being? But there was something about the young lady by his side—her self-assurance, her fortitude while they had been navigating the twisty streets of the old city—that he found intriguing.

Yes, she was a bit impulsive, but contrary to his first impression, she did not seem to be a fortune hunter.

Of course, he'd thought that of the other young women whose clutches he'd narrowly escaped too. Still, Miss Isabelle Strathmore wasn't displaying any avaricious tendencies toward him. In fact, she'd let go of his hand so quickly he wondered if there was something the matter.

When they reached the harbor, Gavin saw a clot of people had gathered on the dock below the *Floramay*. As he and Miss Strathmore approached, he identified the local authorities, the ship's captain, Will, and Miss Strathmore's doughty companion. Clearly a party was preparing to come in search of them.

"Isabelle!" Mrs. Hodges called, catching sight of them. "There you are."

In a moment, he and Miss Strathmore were the center of a hubbub, everyone exclaiming and firing off questions.

"Whatever happened?" Will asked. "We feared you'd gotten into a spot of trouble."

"We're all right," Gavin said. "Miss Strathmore's reticule was snatched. We chased the thief down and retrieved it, then returned to the harbor."

"Was that wise?" Mrs. Hodges shot her charge a dark look.

"Not particularly," Miss Strathmore said. "And I must say, Lord Jasper is being too modest. His impeccable sense of direction saved us from being lost for hours in the *medina*."

"Excellent!" Will clapped Gavin on the shoulder. "Always a good man in a pinch."

Miss Strathmore said nothing more, but the warm look she shot him conveyed her thanks well enough.

The leader of the local authorities shouldered forward. "Tell us more of this pickpocket."

Gavin gave him a brief description of the thief, but he doubted anything would come of it. Especially as the steamer was departing in the morning, the witnesses to the crime bound for Athens.

"If you've no more need of Miss Strathmore," her companion said, "we're going aboard."

"I advise that all my passengers return to the ship," the captain said, nodding to Gavin and Will. "Best that everyone is on board, safely tucked into their cabins. I want no more scares this evening."

At the top of the gangway, Miss Strathmore turned to Gavin.

"Good night," she said.

"To you as well." He inclined his head. "I hope your dreams are peaceful."

She let out a laugh. "Thank you, but I suspect they'll be full of twisty passages and inescapable mazes."

"Then you must imagine I am there to guide you out," he said.

"Perhaps I shall." The smile she gave him was a trifle crooked.

As she and her companion made for the stairs, Will rounded on him, a twinkle in his eye.

"The devil! That was outright flirtation, Gav. Whatever did you and Miss Strathmore get up to while you were lost in the city?"

"Nothing, I assure you. All our thoughts were bent on getting out before full dark."

"Not even one stolen kiss? A quick embrace in a shadowed doorway?"

"Sorry to disappoint." Gavin shot him a look. "Anyhow, I thought you had designs upon Miss Strathmore."

"You know my interest was mostly idle flirtation to help pass the time. In this case, I yield the field to the better man." He made Gavin a crisp salute.

"Stop it. I've no intention of courting Miss Strathmore, as you well know. I'm on this journey to keep you company and put women out of my mind. They are nothing but trouble—as witnessed by my adventures this evening."

"If you say so." Will stuck his hands in his coat pockets. "Some of the other gentlemen are getting up a game of whist in the men's lounge tonight. Are you in?"

"Certainly." It would be a welcome distraction, a chance to armor himself once more against his unfortunate tendency to attract unsuitable members of the opposite sex.

And was Miss Isabelle Strathmore unsuitable? Given his recent experiences, the answer was probably yes. At any rate, he did not intend to find out.

Despite Gavin's resolve not to entangle himself with Miss Strathmore, he couldn't help approaching her two days later as she strolled about the deck with Miss Taylor. Neither of their companions were to be seen, which was just as well. He did not much care for the sour Miss Primm, and Mrs. Hodges was, quite frankly, a trifle intimidating. He'd no doubt she would bash him across the shins with her ever-present umbrella if she thought he was misbehaving.

"Good afternoon, ladies," he said, tipping his hat.

"Hello, Lord Jasper." Miss Strathmore gave him a guarded smile.

"How pleasant to see you." Miss Taylor was less restrained in her greeting. "Oh, do say you and Lord Weston will be attending the shipboard ball tomorrow night. The purser says sometimes there are too many ladies without a dancing partner, since the gentlemen shirk their duties. Which, you must admit, is rather appalling."

"Most ungentlemanly," Gavin agreed, though he had planned to do that very thing. "I shall endeavor not to disappoint."

"I think the notion of a ball on deck beneath the stars is quite romantic." Miss Taylor gave a little sigh.

"If one is inclined to such things," Miss Strathmore said. "And as long as the sea remains calm. One would hate to go overboard in the middle of a mazurka."

"Certainly there's no danger?" Miss Taylor's eyes widened. "Do you really think we might fall off the ship?"

"I was teasing," Miss Strathmore said gently. "Besides, I'm sure if there is any possibility of rough weather, they would cancel the ball. You know how the captain likes to shoo us all below decks the moment the wind rises."

"Then we must hope for the best," Miss Taylor said. "Lord Jasper, I'll save a dance for you."

"I would be delighted." He made her a slight bow, then could not help glancing at Miss Strathmore, who was watching him with a thoughtful expression. "And of course, I would not neglect you either, Miss Strathmore."

"Thank you," she said, "but I wasn't planning to attend."

"Oh, but you must!" Miss Taylor grabbed her hand and gave her an imploring look. "Please, Isabelle. You're my only friend aboard. I can't go without you."

"Well." Miss Strathmore darted another inscrutable look at Gavin, a shadow darkening her blue eyes. "I suppose I might come, at least for a few dances."

"I knew I could count on you," Miss Taylor said with a broad smile. "It will be lovely, I promise."

"No doubt." Miss Strathmore glanced at the pocket watch pinned to her bodice. "It's been lovely chatting with you, Lord Jasper, but I believe it's time for us to go below for tea. Good day."

"Cheers!" Miss Taylor gave him a jaunty wave.

A moment later Gavin was alone on the deck. The warm breeze curled about him, twisting softly like his thoughts. What a curious young woman Miss Strathmore was turning out to be, and not at all what he'd expected.

Perhaps her behavior was a ploy to capture his interest, but considering the wary way she'd regarded him, he thought not. She hadn't leaped at the opportunity to dance with him, either. It was altogether outside his experience to see a young lady having to be coerced into attending a ball.

Speaking of coercion, he'd have to rope Will into coming too. They could suffer through the first half, then make their escape to the men's lounge after the requisite dances with the ladies, and no harm done.

Isabelle stabbed a topaz-encrusted comb into her hair. Her eyes were bright, but not with excitement for the ball that evening. No, the young woman who stared back at her from the mirror was upset, color high in her cheeks, eyes glinting like polished sapphires.

I did not ask for this, she thought fiercely. Not her attractive features and golden hair, her blue eyes, her smile which had, at various times, been compared to sunshine, honey, and rose petals.

She would prefer to be fog, lemon, and stones.

And she was growing rather weary of being Miss Isabelle Strathmore, who had once upon a time fallen foolishly in love with a handsome, black-haired lord.

I will not make that same mistake. She jammed another comb into her hair, the teeth scraping her scalp painfully.

"Drat it!"

Mrs. Hodges glanced up from her knitting. "What is the matter?"

"Nothing." Isabelle blew out a breath. "Everything."

It was unfair of her to be angry—with herself, with Miss Taylor, who had trapped her into attending the ball, with Lord Jasper, who appeared—on the surface—to be a perfectly respectable gentleman, despite his brooding tendencies.

Lord Reginald Huntington had seemed much the same. He'd danced with her beneath the Mediterranean stars, stolen her heart, and then betrayed her, putting everyone she loved in peril.

She turned from the mirror to face her companion. "I simply don't have any desire to go to the ball, let alone dance, this evening."

"Are you quite sure?" Mrs. Hodges gave her a penetrating look. "Or is it that you do, in fact, want to attend? That you would like to dance with Lord Jasper but wish you did not?"

Isabelle winced. Her companion's words were too close to the mark, and she could not deny the bitter truth of it.

"I've no business feeling any sort of attraction to Lord Jasper," she said after a moment. "It's not wise in the least."

Mrs. Hodges set her knitting down.

"We passed Tunisia earlier," she said mildly. "Did you notice?"

"Yes." Though Isabelle had not bothered to go out on deck to watch the coast fall away, as the purser had suggested to the ladies at tea.

"It is behind you, Isabelle. In every sense. Not all the black-haired gentlemen in the world possess black hearts. Perhaps you might give Lord Jasper the benefit of the doubt."

I don't want to.

It was far safer to continue on as she had been. There was danger in the balmy night air, in the bright stars overhead, in the prospect of being in Lord Jasper's arms.

"He's only interested in my pretty face," she said.

"No, I believe that would be his friend, Lord Weston."

Mrs. Hodges began to knit again, needles clicking with brisk efficiency. "Consider this—you've had five years in which you might have been seduced by some scoundrel, and nothing of the sort has happened."

"That's because I've guarded my heart well." Isabelle pivoted back to the mirror, her temper rising again.

Mrs. Hodges was perceptive, true, but her attempts at understanding often fell short. Isabelle knew that, for herself, falling in love could only result in disaster.

A knock from the corridor signaled the arrival of Miss Taylor and Miss Prim, and Isabelle rose, grateful for the distraction.

"Oh, don't you look beautiful," Miss Taylor said as Isabelle opened the door. "I wish I could wear that color gold, but it washes out my complexion dreadfully."

"You look lovely yourself," Isabelle said. "Periwinkle blue suits you very well."

Mindful of their wide skirts, they mounted the stairs to the deck. Miss Primm and Mrs. Hodges followed, ready to catch them if they stumbled backward. Truly, ball gowns were impractical on board a ship. Especially one like the *Floramay*, which had been built before enormous crinolines became the fashion. Luckily, they managed to reach the deck without mishap.

"How delightful." Miss Taylor clasped her gloved hands together in approval.

Small candle lanterns had been strung up on the port side, delineating a dance floor, and tables of refreshments were set out, more candles glimmering in glass bowls.

A string trio seated near the stern was playing, and a few couples promenaded about under the star-spangled sky.

"This seems a rather informal event," Miss Primm said, a note of disapproval in her voice.

"One could hardly demand more," Mrs. Hodges said. "We're on board a ship, after all. But I'm sure that, under your watchful eye, everyone will behave as they ought."

Isabelle smiled at her companion's dry humor, which no doubt was completely lost upon Miss Primm.

"There they are." Lord Weston swept up to them, Lord Jasper at his side. "The loveliest ladies at the ball."

Not that there were all that many to choose from. Aside from Isabelle and Miss Taylor, there were perhaps three other eligible young misses aboard. The other attendees of the ball were mostly older couples and the cluster of matrons, who seemed ready to drink punch and gossip all evening long.

"Lovely indeed," Lord Jasper said.

To Isabelle's delighted dismay, his gaze seemed to linger on her a moment too long.

"I'm so glad you promised to come," Miss Taylor said to him. "Otherwise, I'm afraid Miss Strathmore and myself would be quite the wallflowers."

"We certainly could not allow that to happen," he said. "Would you like to dance now, Miss Taylor?"

"Why, yes." She set her gloved hand in his, a faint blush coloring her cheeks.

"An earl," Miss Primm murmured to Mrs. Hodges. "How fortuitous."

Lord Weston turned to Isabelle. "Would you do me the favor of granting me a dance?"

"It would be my pleasure."

She allowed him to lead her to the area marked for dancing. The trio, seeing the two couples approach, struck up a schottische, and it did not take long for a few others to join them in the lively figures of the dance.

It was pleasant, she had to admit, to be dancing in the open air and not the stuffy confines of a ballroom. The warm breeze ruffled her skirts and blew a pleasant breath over the nape of her neck, exposed by her upswept hair.

Isabelle tried not to notice how very much Miss Taylor seemed to be enjoying herself as she danced with Lord Jasper. Really, it was none of her concern whether or not the young lady's laughter rang out merrily into the night.

When the set ended, Lord Weston returned her to Mrs. Hodges and went to fetch them each a cup of punch. Lord Jasper did the same, and Miss Taylor watched him stride away, her eyes shining.

She leaned toward Isabelle.

"Isn't he the handsomest fellow?" she asked. "It's quite amazing that we are all on the same ship. Think of the chances! We might never have met."

Oh dear. It seemed Miss Taylor had fallen rather quickly into the throes of an infatuation.

"As I told you earlier," Miss Primm said to her charge, "you must make sure to catch his eye at every opportunity. Wouldn't that be a coup, to snag the Earl of Jasper while out on a Grand Tour?"

Mrs. Hodges cleared her throat. "I don't think the earl is the least bit interested in getting himself snagged."

Miss Primm flapped her hand at the older woman. "None of them ever are. It's up to us ladies to make sure to set the hook."

Snags and hooks—Isabelle was glad she had no need to dwell upon such things. There were some advantages to having decided against marriage.

The gentlemen returned, a serving man behind them carrying six cups of punch and a sampling of canapés on a silver tray.

"What a pleasant evening picnic," Miss Taylor said as

they settled around a grouping of small tables. "One could get used to dining *alfresco*."

"Not at home, of course." Miss Primm shot her charge a reproving look. "That's why we have dining rooms, after all."

"Tell me, Lord Jasper," Miss Taylor said, cupping her chin in her hand. "Do you possess a very elegant dining room? I feel you must."

He blinked at her with what Isabelle thought was a flash of alarm. "It's the usual sort of dining room, I suppose. Table, chairs."

"Crystal chandeliers? Aubusson carpet?"

"I suppose," he said stiffly. "I've never much noticed."

"Sarah, do stop prying into the details of Lord Jasper's life," Miss Primm said, though her tone was approving. "If he would like you to see his dining room, perhaps he will invite us to dinner once we return to England."

An awkward silence fell, though Lord Weston looked as though he might burst out laughing.

"No escape, Gav," he said quietly to his friend.

Lord Jasper sent him a dark look.

"We make port in Athens in two days," Isabelle said, trying to ease the tension. "What is everyone looking forward to seeing in Greece?"

"The Acropolis, surely," Miss Taylor said.

"As long as you avert your eyes from certain portions of the statues," Miss Primm said. "The ancient Greeks had no notion of what was suitable."

"Or, ahem, normal," Lord Weston said, and Isabelle wondered if he'd been spiking his punch. "Unless their depictions are accurate. In which case, I feel sorry for the poor Greek women."

"William." Lord Jasper gave his friend a quelling look. "Do recall there are ladies present."

Luckily, the string trio struck a chord, distracting them all from the lurching conversation. In a heartbeat, Lord Jasper was on his feet, offering his hand to Isabelle.

"Might I have the pleasure?" he asked.

"Of course." Isabelle rose, trying to ignore Miss Taylor's crestfallen expression.

The young lady's face cleared somewhat as Lord Weston stepped into the gap—though a viscount was not quite as suitable as an earl, of course.

Heavens, the machinations of the *ton* were enough to give one a headache. Isabelle had been hoping to escape such things on this journey. She'd neglected to consider that, wherever there was a gathering of her countrymen, status would always be a concern.

"You seem pensive," Lord Jasper said as he led her to the corner of the makeshift dance floor.

"Just considering the sights of Greece," she lied. "I've never been there."

"We'll have to explore it together," he said. "Along with Mrs. Hodges, of course."

She gave him a close look. "Lord Jasper, are you planning to use me as a shield against Miss Taylor's attentions? How unflattering."

The faintest flush colored his cheekbones. "No, Miss Strathmore. Primarily, I would like to see Greece in your company because I find that company interesting."

The words were not delivered in a flirtatious manner, and the sincerity in his voice set her quite off-balance. She wanted to find reasons to dislike the man, not stumble deeper into attraction.

The trio finished their introduction and launched into a waltz. Of course it had to be a waltz. It seemed fate was conspiring against her. The more distance she desired from Lord Jasper, the more closely they were thrown together.

He gathered her into his arms, one hand at her waist, the other clasping her gloved hand. They fit together distressingly well. When he stepped out, she followed, discovering that their paces were equally well matched.

Lord Jasper danced with restrained confidence—much the same way as he moved through the world. His steps were not as lighthearted as Lord Weston's or as ostentatious as some of the other gentlemen she'd danced with in the past, but she rather preferred his style.

"I await your answer," he said. "Will you see the sights of Greece with me?"

She could refuse to accompany him, of course, but that would leave him to Miss Taylor. While the young lady was harmless, Isabelle would not put it past Miss Primm to engineer a situation where Lord Jasper was forced to propose to her charge.

And, in truth, he was not such bad company as she'd first thought.

"You scarcely know me," she said at last.

"True enough. But I do know of your family. After you mentioned botanical expeditions and Tunisia, I recalled that I've attended a few of your father's lectures at Kew Gardens. He's Sir Edward Strathmore, is he not?"

"He is."

"And you were on the expedition to Tunisia where he discovered that new species of flower?"

"Yes." There was no reason to elaborate.

"How extraordinary, for all of you. I'd be interested in hearing your account of that journey."

He whirled her into a spin, and her mind whirled as well.

It was difficult to think clearly with the warm air wafting around her and Lord Jasper holding her a touch too near.

"It was not a . . . pleasant trip for me," she said once they were traversing the deck again. "I prefer not to speak of it."

He gave her a thoughtful look. "Allow me one question, if you will?"

She should say no. Still, she owed him a kindness in return for their adventure in Tangier, which had been, after all, her fault. No doubt he was curious about the discovery of the flower.

"Very well," she said. "Just one question."

"Was there a gentleman associated with this unpleasantness?"

She drew in a quick breath. Lord Jasper was far more perceptive than she'd given him credit for, drat him. But she had agreed to answer.

"Yes, there was," she said quietly.

His expression hardened, but not toward her. "I know we are newly met, Miss Strathmore. But if there's anything to be done about the fellow, I hope you will consider calling upon me."

She blinked up at him, finding his concern both touching and discomfiting. "That's very gallant of you. However, I dealt with the gentleman myself some time ago—with assistance from Mrs. Hodges."

They were waltzing past her companion at that very moment. Lord Jasper glanced at Mrs. Hodges, then back to Isabelle.

"I would not like to be on the receiving end of your companion's ire," he said. "Or yours, for that matter. Forgive me if I've been presumptuous and offended you, Miss Strathmore. It was never my intention."

The music slowed, and he swept her into one last turn.

She held to his shoulder and could not help but lean back into the warm strength of his arm, experiencing for just a moment that which she could never truly have.

It's all right, she reminded herself. *I'm perfectly content ending up as a spinster.*

Somehow, though, a stubborn corner of her heart refused to listen.

Gavin was not certain what it was that drew him the most to Miss Isabelle Strathmore. Her self-assurance, certainly. Her wry humor, which matched his own. Her expressive mouth, which he found himself wishing to drop kisses upon . . .

Not that he had any business doing so.

"Would you like to take a turn about the deck?" he asked, curiously unwilling to let her out of his arms.

She glanced up at him, hesitating, and he cursed the unknown fellow who had, if he was not mistaken, broken her heart. The wounded look in her eyes when she spoke of the botanical expedition had roused a strangely protective feeling in him. Most unexpected, and he was not entirely sure he welcomed the sensation.

"Very well," she finally said. "A short stroll."

He tucked her arm beneath his own, and they promenaded toward the bow of the boat, passing Miss Taylor and Lord Weston. Will gave him an open wink, which Gavin ignored. His friend had already spent the hour before the ball laughing at him.

"To think—you were convinced that Miss Strathmore was yet another fortune hunter. Now you've developed an interest in her, and it seems she does not return the feeling. The irony!"

"It's not amusing," Gavin had said, though he had to admit it was a bit of a contradiction.

He'd selected a freshly pressed dress shirt, glad to see that the valet he and Will were sharing was skilled at his job. Not only were all of the clothes correctly pressed, their shoes had been freshly polished and their neckties starched to perfection.

"Are you going to pursue her?" Will cocked one eyebrow at him. "Do you even know how to do anything except run away?"

"Stop it, or I'll throw my shoe at you." Gavin brandished his left dress shoe. "You know my aim is excellent, and you'll have a mark on your forehead all night. That should put the ladies off."

Will sobered. "Look, Gav, it's just a bit unusual for you. Are you certain you're not attracted to Miss Strathmore *because* of her disinterest?"

"I've considered it, and no. I've never felt the need to pursue young ladies who aren't falling at my feet, just to prove a point. In fact, Miss Strathmore's reticence only demonstrates that she's not on the hunt for a husband. Given my recent past, that is a quality I do find appealing—but that is not her primary attraction."

"An excellent speech!" Will applauded. "One cannot help notice that Miss Strathmore is quite pretty."

"Some people value more than appearances." Gavin gave his friend an exasperated look.

"Well, yes." Will grinned. "But you wouldn't want to marry an ugly girl now, would you?"

"I'd like to think that if I were sufficiently drawn to a woman's character, her beauty or lack thereof wouldn't be a concern."

"But it doesn't hurt to have a lovely face to go along with

her attractive personality. Though personally, I find Miss Strathmore too forthright for my tastes."

"She is rather self-assured," Gavin agreed. "I like her confidence, and her obvious intelligence, and her—"

"Clearly you've given the matter of Miss Strathmore a great deal of thought." Will began rummaging through his neckties. "Should I be worried for you? Perhaps travel abroad has shaken something loose in your head."

"If it's shaken anything, it's my belief that I'd find a suitable wife among the *ton*. My horizons have broadened."

His friend gave him a solemn look. "If you're serious, then try not to scare her off. But on to more important things . . ." He held up two neckties. "Which one, the striped or the black?"

Now, walking about the deck with Miss Strathmore on his arm, Gavin found himself at a loss for words. Will was right—he was not particularly adept at wooing. Or the art of idle flirtation, which seemed to come so easily to his friend.

Miss Strathmore did not seem to mind, however, and the silence that fell between them was a companionable one.

As they rounded the ship's prow, she halted and stared up into the sky. Gavin followed her gaze to where a bright cluster of stars hung above the dark horizon.

"The Pleiades," he said, just as she murmured, "The Seven Sisters."

They looked at each other and smiled.

"Are you a stargazer, Lord Jasper? I wouldn't have thought it."

"When I was a boy, my father and I would look at the stars at night from the lawns of our country estate. He taught me the names of the constellations. I've never forgotten them."

"What an excellent father. Mine only taught me the Latin

names of every plant we passed. Much more prosaic, and I don't think I remember even half."

"But you know the names of the stars."

She glanced up again. "My brother was given a book of Greek myths by his tutor, which I promptly stole. When I learned that many of the tales had to do with constellations, I spent the summer sneaking out on the terrace, trying to figure out their places in the sky. Mostly I remember the tragic ones."

"Like the Seven Sisters."

"Yes, and below them, the Hyades." She pointed slightly to the right. "Another group of sisters turned into stars to escape their terrible fate. It must be pleasant to float serenely in the night sky, out of reach of earthly troubles."

"But rather dull after a while, don't you think? Looking down but never experiencing anything."

"Well." She turned her head and gave him a wry smile. "The first century or so must be rather nice."

"Not all of the constellations are tragic, you know. Andromeda and Perseus get to spend eternity side by side in the sky."

"A star gazer *and* a romantic," she said softly. "I never would have guessed. Alas, I never learned how to find Andromeda."

He braced his legs and lifted his face to the stars. Find Taurus, then up and over to Perseus, and then further to the bright stars at Andromeda's shoulder and ankle.

"There." He took Miss Strathmore by the shoulders and gently turned her to face the proper direction. "Do you see that bright star at about eleven o'clock?"

She tilted her chin up. "Um. I'm not sure." She pointed. "That one?"

He crouched down a bit, following the direction of her finger. "No, that's in Pegasus."

Without thinking, he took her arm and guided it upward. "There—that's Andromeda's foot."

"Where's the rest of her?"

She sounded a trifle breathless, and he belatedly realized that he'd tucked her up against him, their faces close together. He could smell the flowery scent of her soap, and for a moment his voice was frozen in his throat.

Breathe, he reminded himself. She had not pulled away. On the contrary, she'd asked him to finish showing her the constellation, and he wondered if she knew just how much she'd let down her guard. He blessed the sheltering darkness of the night, that she felt safe enough to do so.

Carefully, he moved her hand, helping her find the princess hidden in the stars.

"Up so, to her shoulder, do you see?"

"Yes." The word was barely a whisper.

He could feel her ribs moving with her breath. Despite his urge to pull her in even closer, he held her lightly, letting her know she was free to step away at any time. *Try not to scare her off.* Will's words echoed in his mind.

But there was a clamor in him, a fierce yearning he'd never felt so intensely before. The longer she stayed in his arms, the harder it was not to turn her about and kiss her until all memory of the stars was burned away.

It was sweet torture. He could not bear to put her away from him, nor could he act upon his desire. He was Perseus, suspended in the sky, almost touching Andromeda, but unable to brush his lips against hers or tangle his fingers through her hair.

Miss Strathmore let out a sigh, so forlorn it twisted his heart. She took two steps forward, and he let his hands drop to his sides.

"Miss Strathmore, why are you still unmarried?" The

moment he spoke the words, he wished he could haul them back.

Her silhouette stiffened against the diamond-dusted sky.

"I am not fit for it," she said, all softness gone from her voice.

"I would argue otherwise."

"You know nothing of it. Or of me."

She made to go, and he reached toward her.

"Please, wait," he said. "At least allow me to escort you back to the others."

There was a moment of chilly silence, and then she set her hand on his forearm, light as a moth that would take flight any second.

"You've said twice now that I don't know you," he said. "And that is true enough. But I would like to become better acquainted."

"I'm not the least bit interested in being courted." She sounded as distant as the stars.

"Do you not think we might be friends, at least? Just for the duration of the trip?"

She pulled in a shocked breath, and he hastened to reassure her.

"I'm not suggesting anything improper, Miss Strathmore. I'm not that type of gentleman. But, as you noted earlier, I am in need of, well, a buffer between myself and Miss Taylor. And you did agree to see the sights of Greece with me."

She let out a low breath, and her hand rested a fraction more heavily upon his arm.

"I suppose I did."

It was a small victory, but Gavin was determined to be contented with it. Even he, unskilled as he was at wooing, knew enough to take things one step at a time.

As soon as Lord Jasper returned Isabelle to the others, she bade them all good night and fled to the safety of her cabin.

Once she gained that small sanctuary, she lit a single lamp, then sat on her bunk and squeezed her eyes tightly shut. Her insides whirled with dread.

This was terrible. History was repeating itself.

"No," she said, trying to impose order on the chaos of her thoughts. "I am not smitten with Lord Jasper. I refuse."

The words were hollow, and she could not force herself to believe them. In the span of a few minutes, looking at the stars together, something inside her had cracked open, and she had no notion how to repair the armor around her heart.

She wrapped her arms about herself, as though she could somehow return to the safety of who she had been before the journey.

I should never have come. Trips to the Mediterranean were her undoing.

"Isabelle?" Mrs. Hodges stepped into the room and closed the door softly behind her. "What happened?"

"I looked at the stars with Lord Jasper." Isabelle caught her breath on something very like a sob. "And it was lovely, and it was horrible, and now I've no notion of anything."

"Oh, my dear." There was more sympathy in Mrs. Hodges's voice than Isabelle had heard there in a long while. "It's painful to come out of the cocoon."

"I feel . . . broken."

Her companion nodded and settled beside her, giving her back a pat. "What do you think happens to the chrysalis when the butterfly emerges? It breaks. It is destroyed—but only in the process of becoming something new and better."

Isabelle summoned up a crooked smile. "Are you saying I was a worm before?"

"Of course not." A note of brusqueness crept back in Mrs. Hodges's voice. "One can only take a metaphor so far. Just remember, transformation can be an awkward state."

Isabelle felt beyond awkward. If she truly were turning into something else—the thought of which was rather terrifying—she could not see what she might become. She felt limp and useless, all her self-assurance gone.

Mrs. Hodges gave her back one last pat, then stood. "Nothing to do but move forward, eh? I'm for bed, myself."

Sleep sounded better than anything else—a warm, dark place for Isabelle to escape to, with no sea, no sky, no stars. No self-possessed lords bewildering her at every turn. Just the comfort of the black.

Gavin was relieved to see Miss Strathmore appear in the ship's dining room for luncheon the next day, though she did seem paler and more subdued than usual. He deliberated whether or not he should go over to greet her, but in the end he could not help himself.

"Good day," he said, pausing at the table where she sat with her companion. "I noticed you weren't at breakfast, Miss Strathmore. I hope you are feeling well."

She looked up at him, her expression reserved, and he missed the customary bright sparkle of her eyes.

"I am well enough," she said.

"Sit, Lord Jasper." Mrs. Hodges tapped an empty chair with the tip of her umbrella. "Keep us company."

"I wouldn't want to intrude," he said.

"Nonsense," Mrs. Hodges said. "We'd welcome your company."

Miss Strathmore glanced at her companion but didn't protest as Gavin settled across from her at the table.

"I'm sorry if I upset you last night," he said, keeping his voice low. "It was never my intention to cause you distress."

"You did not." She lifted her cup of tea as if it were a shield between them.

"Tell us about yourself, Lord Jasper," Mrs. Hodges said. "Have you any siblings?"

"A younger brother, who is at Oxford. He is the scholar of the family. I gather you have a younger brother as well, Miss Strathmore?"

She nodded. "Richard is studying piano at the Leipzig Conservatory. It keeps him out of trouble."

"Barely." Mrs. Hodges let out a harrumph. "I must say, Lord Jasper, the two of them were nothing but mischief growing up. Riding about bareback like wild savages, creating explosions in the kitchen, digging up the ornamental shrubbery in search of treasure. I scarcely survived the experience."

A spark of animation returned to Miss Strathmore's face.

"We weren't as bad as all that, truly. I believe Mrs. Hodges likes to remember only the worst escapades. Have you forgotten the plays we'd put on or the book we spent an entire summer writing?"

"What was it about?" Gavin asked, his curiosity piqued.

"Why, the adventures of a brother and sister of course, who sailed the high seas, fought pirates—eventually becoming pirates themselves—adventured in America, and finally discovered the lost golden city of a hidden tribe deep in the jungle." She smiled. "Our cousin Lily helped with the illustrations. It was a magnificent work."

"I admit," Gavin said, "your childhood sounds much more entertaining than my own."

Miss Strathmore smiled at him. "Mrs. Hodges would say it was because our parents were too lenient."

"Indeed." Her companion gave her a stern look, but

Gavin could see the humor lurking in her eyes. "Verging on the Bohemian—your father, especially. It's a good thing I was there to infuse a bit of civility into your lives."

The servers came around with their meal, and Gavin was glad that no one else joined their table. Mrs. Hodges kept the conversation going with pithy remarks and pointed questions to Gavin about his own parents, his schooling, his interests. It was a grilling of the first degree, but he did his best to turn the same questions back on Miss Strathmore.

By the end of luncheon, they had, he hoped, moved a bit closer to something resembling friendship.

As the other diners began trickling out of the room, he took a last swallow of lemon-flavored water and turned to Miss Strathmore.

"We make port in Athens early tomorrow," he said. "What time would you like to go ashore?"

Her smile tilted a bit, and she glanced at her companion. Mrs. Hodges's arm moved slightly, and Gavin guessed she was poking her charge beneath the table with her umbrella. For whatever reason, the curmudgeonly companion seemed to have become his advocate, and he was thankful for it. Winning over Miss Strathmore was not going to be an easy task.

Not that he was going to let that stop him.

He'd woken at dawn, the surface of the sea turning to liquid gold outside the porthole by his bed. The hazy notion that Miss Isabelle Strathmore was, quite possibly, the right woman for him had solidified overnight into a clear conviction.

It was difficult to explain why he felt so strongly, and no doubt Will would continue to laugh at him, but Gavin couldn't help feeling that he'd met a kindred spirit in her. Not only was he deeply attracted to Miss Strathmore, he could envision spending the rest of their lives together. As friends, as helpmates, as lovers.

They were both wary of love, true, though he was quickly changing his mind where she was concerned.

He hoped that he could help change hers, as well.

"I suppose we could go directly after breakfast," Miss Strathmore said at last. "Before the heat of the day grows too heavy."

"An excellent plan," Mrs. Hodges said. "Join us for that meal, sir, and we can discuss the itinerary. In fact, join us for dinner as well."

"It would be my pleasure."

He rose and took his leave, his steps lighter than they had been in years.

The Acropolis was smaller than Isabelle had expected, hemmed in by the squalor and bustle of Athens, though perched above it on a rocky promontory. There was little shade. Wild thyme clung to the crevices, and scrappy alliums sprouted between the cracks in the rough paving as she, Lord Jasper, and Mrs. Hodges wandered up the path leading to the *Propylaea*—the official gate—located partway up the hill.

Somewhat to her regret, Miss Primm and Miss Taylor also accompanied them. Lord Weston was along, too, but she did not mind his presence, as he was a helpful buffer. The rest of the party had joined herself and Mrs. Hodges at dinner the night before and had been, perforce, included in the sightseeing plans.

"How ramshackle it all is," Miss Primm said, shading her eyes as she looked at the Parthenon perched overhead. "The Greeks really ought to take better care of their artifacts."

"And the English ought to stop vandalizing them," Lord

Jasper said. "I support the view that Lord Elgin did irreparable damage when he removed so many of the friezes and sculptures from the building."

"My father would agree," Isabelle said. "During our travels abroad, we saw too many instances of harm done by foreign looters."

"But Lord Elgin was not a looter, surely?" Miss Taylor turned her innocent gaze on Isabelle. "Think of how many more people are able to enjoy the beauty of Classical Greece thanks to the fact that he sold the marbles to the British Museum."

"It's too lovely a morning for argument," Lord Weston said, stepping forward. "Regardless of how you feel about it, the Acropolis is here and ready for us to explore. Come."

He gestured, and the rest of the party followed, taking their time on the tumbled blocks of the stairs leading up through the crumbled gateway.

"Look." Miss Taylor pointed to one of the sculptures carved into the frieze—Athena reaching down to adjust her footwear, the drapery of her robes astonishingly fluid. "Even goddesses had to fix their sandals."

At last they reached the flat, high plateau where the Parthenon stood. The city of Athens tumbled below, the white buildings interrupted here and there by islands of green and the bumps of other hills. The blue water of the Mediterranean glowed, just visible, in the harbor beyond.

"We should visit the sacred olive tree of Athena," Isabelle said. "I believe it is located yonder, at Athena's temple." She gestured at the smaller building to the left of the Parthenon.

Miss Primm sniffed. "I don't hold with such pagan beliefs."

"Some people could use a visit from the goddess of wisdom," Mrs. Hodges replied with a pointed look.

Isabelle ducked her head in order to muffle her laugh and caught Lord Jasper's eye. He, too, was trying to hide his smile, and the moment of camaraderie warmed her. Perhaps it was not so terrible, after all, to be friends.

"My father," Isabelle said, "being a botanist, gave me a list of important flora to visit on our travels. The olive tree here being foremost among them."

"Then by all means, let us make a visit," Lord Weston said. He'd clearly appointed himself their guide for the day despite having little knowledge of the place.

The old temple, despite being in a worse state of ruin than the Parthenon, nonetheless held a quiet grace and beauty that Isabelle appreciated. The olive tree growing at its side was gnarled; the silvery green leaves contrasted against the white marble blocks of the building.

Beside the tree, the entryway soared up, graceful columns supporting a broken ceiling.

After paying their respects to the olive tree, the party made their way to the Parthenon, and Isabelle found she preferred Athena's temple. Or perhaps it was that there had been some foliage there, while the columns of the bigger building rose starkly into the hot, blue air.

Miss Primm pulled a fan from her sleeve and began waving it vigorously. "This climate is a bit warm for my tastes, I must say. England is much more civilized. Thank heavens Athens is the farthest point on our tour. Travel is all very well, but I can scarcely wait to return home."

Lord Jasper leaned closer to Isabelle.

"I hope she and Miss Taylor will not choose to go on our next outing. The ship docks next at the island of Kíthira, I believe?"

"Yes," Isabelle said. "The *Floramay* anchors there tomorrow afternoon. It's hard to believe that our trip is halfway over."

"And are you also eager to return to England?" he asked, his tone serious.

"No." She answered him honestly. "I'd be happy to float about in the Mediterranean for several centuries more."

Once she set foot back on English soil, she'd have to face her future. Increasingly, it felt rather bleak.

He gently touched her arm. "I'd be more than glad to keep you company. I could teach you all the constellations."

Stop it, she told her foolish, treacherous heart as it leaped into her throat.

She might have emerged from a chrysalis, as Mrs. Hodges wanted to believe; but if so, the wet, limp things on her back could hardly be trusted to carry her aloft. Far more likely that, like Icarus and his makeshift wings, she'd end up plunging into the sea and drown.

Isabelle stood at the railing and watched the isle of Kíthira approach. Brown hills dusted with green rose above buildings white as a smile on the shore. Beneath the ship's bow, the sea shaded from indigo—*wine dark* as Homer would say—to azure, to turquoise. The perfect crescent harbor ahead was pale aquamarine, but the *Floramay* was too large to anchor in those waters.

Instead, a fleet of colorful fishing boats was already underway to meet the steamer. The sailors' laughter echoed over the water as they called to one another in Greek, each captain no doubt making boasting claims about being the first to reach the prize.

To Isabelle's relief, the Misses Primm and Taylor would not be going ashore. They had contracted indigestion after eating the lobster bisque at dinner the night before—a fact Isabelle found rather ironic, as Miss Primm had forbidden her charge from eating any of the Athenian street food on offer earlier that day. They had watched, the governess with folded arms, Miss Taylor with an envious expression, while Isabelle,

Mrs. Hodges, and the gentlemen had enjoyed skewers of spiced meat from the bustling marketplace. The skewers had been quite delicious, though Isabelle was careful not to inquire too closely as to the animal of origin.

With a rattle and clank, the ship's anchor splashed into the bay. Mrs. Hodges, seated in a nearby deck chair, tucked her knitting away in preparation to disembark.

"Good afternoon," Lord Jasper said, joining Isabelle at the railing.

It was—the October air still balmy, the sunshine warm and sparkling off the sea.

"Is Lord Weston not joining us?" she asked.

"Alas." He gave her a look that showed no hint of regret. "Will insisted I go as a vanguard. He'll join us later."

She turned back to the view, trying to hide the flush of pleasure this information gave her. While she did not dislike Lord Weston, she had to admit she liked Lord Jasper far better.

"Which boat shall we take to shore?" Isabelle asked as the little fleet pulled up to the *Floramay*.

"That green one there, with blue trim." Lord Jasper gestured to the boat in the lead. "It looks well kept up, and it's the fastest."

"As long as it's not prone to tossing about too dreadfully on the waves." Mrs. Hodges came to peer at the boat in question.

The purser rang the ship's bell, then called for all interested passengers to gather near the stern. They would be lowered down by means of the ship's chair or, in the case of the more agile gentlemen, use the ladder on the boat's side to reach the smaller vessels.

Perhaps because of the lobster bisque, there were not many people gathered to go ashore. Isabelle and Lord Jasper judged their moment and managed to secure three places in the green boat. Soon they were skimming the waves, the white sail belled out above them.

The little boat pulled up deftly beside the pier, and Lord Jasper jumped out, offering his hand to the ladies. Isabelle assisted her companion with a discreet push from behind, then followed Mrs. Hodges out of the boat.

"The isle of Kíthira, birthplace of Aphrodite," Lord Jasper said. "A goddess born of sea-foam and sunlight."

"How very poetic." Isabelle raised her brows. "I believe the Mediterranean climate is making you a bit soft in the head, sir."

He smiled at her, and for a moment she wondered how she could have ever thought him dour and standoffish.

They explored the little town curving about the harbor. At the far end, Mrs. Hodges declared she was ready for a rest and shooed Isabelle and Lord Jasper off to stroll along the beach.

"Just stay where I can see you," she said, settling on a rough-hewn bench and unfurling her umbrella with a *whap*.

"Of course." Isabelle set her hand on Lord Jasper's arm. "Shall we?"

"It would be my pleasure."

They strolled down the sandy crescent, the waves running up and down the beach, never quite high enough to threaten the tips of their boots. A rocky hillside jutted up to one side, rising high above the harbor. Wild grasses grew along the side of a trail leading to the summit, and the smell of wild marjoram drifted on the breeze.

Just when they'd gone far enough that Isabelle judged they should consider turning around, Lord Jasper paused. He turned to face her and cleared his throat.

"Miss Strathmore," he said. "Isabelle."

Her pulse jumped in alarm at his use of her given name.

"Lord Jasper," she said. "I beg you, do not make a fool of yourself. Or of me."

"I cannot keep silent any longer," he said. "Surely you can see that I've formed an affection for you. More than an affection, if I may be clear."

"You hardly know—"

"I know you well enough to appreciate your wit and intelligence and to recognize the spark of humor in your eyes. I've seen your intrepid spirit and how reticent you are in matters of the heart."

"Then you should know better than to speak to me of this."

The beauty of the day was gone, the sun suddenly too harsh upon the water, the waves glinting like knives, the air rasping the back of her throat with every breath.

"And yet, I must take this chance. I must speak." He took her hands in his, so gently.

She looked up at him: that black hair, the guarded eyes that now gazed at her, full of such honesty she could not bear it.

"Wait," she whispered.

"I cannot. Isabelle, I promise I will never hurt you. I will be your willing friend and companion as we walk through this world together. Would you do me the very great honor of consenting to be my wife?"

She squeezed her eyes shut against the horrible brightness of the sky.

"What of love?" she asked through the brambles edging her voice.

"That is simple enough. I love you. Please, Isabelle, open your eyes and tell me you feel the same."

She lifted her lids and stared at him. The stark emotion in his gaze cut her to the heart.

A heart that trembled, and shuddered, and could not bear this moment any longer. It was too soon; she was still too broken.

"Do you . . . love me?" he asked, doubt finally filling his eyes, sunshine giving way to night—dark and cold and inevitable.

"I do not," she said, the words leaving her lips like stones.

Ignoring his stricken expression, she tore her hands from his, whirled, and ran toward the path leading away from the beach.

"Isabelle," he called.

"Leave me alone," she called over her shoulder. "Please."

To her relief, he did not follow as she ascended the hill. Finally, a stitch in her side forced her to stop for breath, and she glanced back down at the white curve of sand. He stood where she had left him, hands open at his sides.

Mrs. Hodges, umbrella folded closed, stalked down the beach toward him. Good. Her companion could be depended on to tell him to go away and never bother Isabelle again. She turned back to the path and kept climbing, driving herself to the very top of the rocky hill.

Away, her heartbeat thumped. *Away, away.*

Still breathless, she gained the summit. The little town and harbor looked surprisingly small below; the hill was higher than she'd thought. Two figures walked on the beach, almost out of sight from where she stood. She hoped that Mrs. Hodges was talking sense into Lord Jasper.

Now, if only Isabelle could find some peace for herself. She perched on a boulder and tried to quiet her pounding heart, which seemed to be shaking the very ground beneath her.

No. Dear heavens, the earth was moving, the stones about her rumbling. She stood in alarm, suddenly aware of the very steep drop down to the restless water. The hillside began to slide out from under her, and she scrabbled at the rocks, trying to catch herself.

"Isabelle!"

She scarcely heard the rough shout from below as, with horrible slowness, she lost her balance and tumbled down and down into the sea.

Gavin had gambled everything—and lost. He could scarcely believe it as he watched Isabelle run away from him, her boot heels kicking up little sprays of sand until she reached the path winding up the hillside.

What a fool he'd been! Groaning, he put his head in his hands. The bridge of friendship they'd built between them was not, after all, strong enough to withstand weighty declarations of love.

"Here now," a gruff voice called. "What have you done?"

He glanced behind him to see Mrs. Hodges approaching at a brisk pace.

"I was an idiot," he said when she reached him. "I asked Miss Strathmore to marry me."

"Confound it," she said, her mouth twisting.

"I'm sorry—"

"Don't blame yourself, sir. Isabelle is the source of my aggravation." Mrs. Hodges shaded her eyes with one hand, looking up to the flash of pale-blue skirts where Isabelle still climbed. "I had hoped . . . Well. There's no undoing what has been done."

Misery gnawed at him. Once again, he'd failed, though this time it was not because he wanted to escape matrimony but rather embrace it.

"Clearly I misjudged her emotions," he said.

"And your own?" Mrs. Hodges raised a brow at him.

"Not at all," he replied, stung. "I am firm in my affections for Miss Strathmore."

The matron gave a satisfied nod. "It might still be salvaged, then."

They both looked up to where Isabelle had nearly gained the crest of the hill, almost around the corner from their view.

"Should I go after her?" he asked.

"Not quite yet." Mrs. Hodges squinted. "She needs time to sort out her own mind—and heart. Try to be patient, Lord Jasper."

He nodded, his gaze never leaving the distant figure of Isabelle as she settled on a boulder, far too near the edge of the hillside for his comfort.

Without warning, Mrs. Hodges stumbled against him. Gavin caught her, at first fearing she'd suffered some kind of fit, but then the beach went to pudding beneath his feet, the waves frothing and turbulent.

"Earthquake," Mrs. Hodges gasped out.

Chest constricting, Gavin looked up once more to where Isabelle perched high above the sea.

"Isabelle!" he cried, knowing it was far too late to reach her.

In horror, he watched as the stones about her shook and tumbled, and then—dear gods no—Isabelle Strathmore plummeted into the ocean.

Before his mind could grapple with the horrible image of

her falling, his body was in action. His feet dug temporary divots into the sand as he raced back toward the harbor.

It was the opposite direction from where Isabelle had fallen, and yet, deep in his bones, he knew it was the fastest way to reach her.

A boat.

He must commandeer the first available vessel and head for Isabelle by water. She could swim, he hoped—but her petticoats would drag her down, and her corset would restrict her breath. He prayed to every deity he could think of, but especially to Aphrodite, whose island this was, that he could reach her in time.

With a smack, Isabelle hit the water—painful as a slap from some gigantic hand. She barely had time to gulp in half a breath before her head went under. The sound of the waves filled her ears, and the once-clear sea churned, disorienting her until she did not know up from down.

But she must have air.

Lungs burning, she kicked, hoping desperately that she was pointed toward the surface. Her full petticoats dragged at her, the cotton flounces turned to anchors, pulling her down.

She had to breathe.

She had to get free of her skirts.

Clamping her lips together to keep from gasping in saltwater, Isabelle tore at her undergarments. The sodden ties were knots beneath her fumbling fingers as the sea shoved her back and forth. She was probably dangerously near the rocks, but that did not matter if her clothing drowned her first.

After several thundering heartbeats, her body screaming for air, she managed to strip off her petticoats and kick upward again. The last bit of air escaped from her mouth, silvery bubbles swept away. She must remove her boots, too, but not now. She had to *breathe*.

A black spot formed in her vision, growing larger, larger, until suddenly the restless ceiling over her head broke.

Air.

She pulled in a great, gasping breath, then swallowed seawater and went under again, lungs convulsing.

Something bumped against her head and spun away, and she flailed out blindly. Eyes burning from salt, she forced herself to scan the murky blue landscape.

There. A black shape, bobbing overhead.

It took all her strength to kick, kick, kick, until she was close enough to grab the thing. Wild creature or bit of flotsam, she did not care. Only that it floated and would bear her up.

Her head emerged from the water again, and she wrapped her arms around the thing. It turned out to be the trunk of an olive tree torn from the ground, branches broken, gray-green leaves sodden.

It was hardly buoyant enough to bear her weight. When Isabelle tried hoisting herself further onto the trunk, it spun and dipped below the surface, and she lost her grip.

Panicked, she thrashed after it while the sea tried to slurp her down. Finally, she caught the tree again and hooked one elbow over the rough wood. It abraded her skin, but she did not care.

The choppiness of the waves abated, and Isabelle looked up to see that the current had carried her some distance from the rocky hill where she'd fallen. The curve of the harbor was quite hidden from view. Nothing to be seen but the empty shore of Kíthira and the endless blue of the Mediterranean.

She had never felt so alone.

And hopeless.

For a moment, she rested her head against the rough bark

and concentrated on breathing. The sea was cool. Not horribly chilly, but if she were swept away from the island, she was not certain how many hours she would last.

But she could not give up. They had seen her fall, Mrs. Hodges and Lord Jasper.

He'd called her name, his voice rough and desperate, and all she could see was his face. The way his mouth had tightened with despair, the color blanching from his high cheekbones when she'd told him she did not love him.

Ah, but it had been a lie. Aphrodite herself had punished her for it, for spurning the gift of love, and thrown Isabelle into the ocean.

It was, almost, a tragic Greek myth; but there would be no ascending to the stars for her, no constellation glimmering with the memory of her name. She was merely human. And she had let the worst mistake of her life lead directly to the second. Instead of learning, she had simply blundered into new heartbreak.

It was not *love* that she should have been afraid of but choosing unwisely. That had been the lesson she had not grasped.

Until too late.

Her boots were lead weights encasing her feet, and she did not have the energy to pry them off. Below her, the black mouth of the sea stretched wide—not dark as wine, not the roadway upon which adventurers sailed, but hungry and implacable. It would eat her soon.

Soon, the little wavelets whispered, running up against her arms.

She did not want to die.

She did not want to die alone off the coast of the isle of Kíthira.

Most especially, she did not want to die without telling Gavin she loved him.

She caught her breath on a sob. Grief swept over her, numbing her grip. Or perhaps that was the effect of the water, cooling her body until her fingers loosened their hold and she slipped soundlessly into the sea.

No. She shook her head, her hair sticking to her cheek. Her bonnet was long gone, ripped from her head in that first plunge into the water.

I am Isabelle Strathmore, she thought fiercely. *I survived Lord Reginald, and bandits, and fire, and I will survive this, too.*

And when she next looked into Gavin's eyes, she would tell him the truth.

She took a new breath, careful not to inhale any seawater. Then she pointed the broken olive tree toward Kíthira, and slowly, kicking with weary legs that would scarcely obey, began the long journey back to shore.

"Go back?" the Greek fisherman asked Gavin, gesturing toward the pier behind them.

It had been nearly impossible to coax the man out in the first place. The harbor had been full of milling sailors, boats knocked about by the quake, and general chaos and confusion. Luckily, the green-and-blue fishing boat was still seaworthy and, by dint of a hefty number of coins, Gavin had convinced the captain to raise the sail.

Though, clearly, he hadn't conveyed the urgency of the fact that they were going on a rescue mission. Gavin gritted his teeth at the knowledge that this was all his fault. If he hadn't so badly misjudged the moment, Isabelle would not have run away from him. Or climbed the hill. Or fallen into the sea.

His heart cracked again at the memory of watching her plummet, blue skirts billowing about her. She had not screamed.

Hold fast, Isabelle. I'm coming.

"Not back." Gavin pointed to the hill rising above the

shore and made a circling motion with his hand. "We go around. Around."

It was all he could do not to rip the tiller from the man's grasp, but he had never been much of a sailor—to his everlasting regret.

The fisherman shrugged but obediently turned the little boat so that it would skirt the shoreline.

"Faster," Gavin said. "Can we go any faster?"

He had half a mind to dive into the water, but the wiser part of him knew that, despite appearances, the sailboat was going more quickly than he could swim. To keep from going completely mad, he leaned over the bow, fists opening and closing, and scanned the churning blue waves.

Isabelle was out there. She must be.

The boat rounded the promontory, and the captain glanced at Gavin.

"Now go back?" he asked.

"No." Gads, Gavin wanted to shake the man. He let out a short breath and tried once more to explain. "A lady fell. Down. Into the sea. We must find her."

"Is no lady." The man swept his arm out.

It was true. Ahead of them lay only the silver spangled waves of the Mediterranean, the innocent-looking hill, a few swallows weaving and darting nearer the shore.

For a moment, utter blackness threatened to swallow Gavin. He had found his lady and lost her, and he could not imagine any reason that he should not leap into the sea and let his bones join hers on the ocean floor.

But he was not one to give up. And the strange kernel of *knowing* inside his chest told him that Isabelle still lived. He closed his eyes, calmed his thoughts, and listened to that part of him that knew its way home.

There.

Eyes still closed, warm sun and the cooling breeze on his cheek, he turned until he faced the right direction.

He opened his eyes to see the darting swallows, white bellies flashing against the shadows on the hill.

"There." He pointed. "Go that way."

The fisherman turned the tiller and adjusted the sail, seeming to have given up arguing with the crazed Englishman for the time being.

A glimpse of lighter blue—not froth or glimmer. Gavin's heart squeezed with hope. With fear. He grabbed a nearby line to steady himself and leaped up on the railing.

"Mister!" the captain cried in protest.

"Keep going."

His breath failed, then he gasped as he identified what he was seeing on the water.

It was her.

Alive, thank all stars in the sky. Alive. Gavin nearly fell off the boat in relief at the sight. She had not yet spotted them and was kicking doggedly toward shore with the determination he had come to expect of her. *Isabelle. Dear, dear Isabelle.*

He jumped down and began unlacing his boots, then shrugged out of his coat and vest.

He carefully removed his father's gold pocket watch from one trouser pocket and his wallet from the other. The fisherman watched, the look on his face implying he would never understand the whims of foreigners.

But that did not matter.

"Closer," Gavin said, then hopped back up, the wood of the railing smooth beneath his bare feet.

"Isabelle!" he called toward the spot of lighter blue upon the water.

From the middle of that splotch, an arm rose and waved back and forth.

"Ahh," the fisherman breathed, peering from beneath the brim of his blue cap. "A lady."

He adjusted course a little and let out more of the sail, and soon the boat had drawn up to where Isabelle Strathmore floated, a pale, half-drowned mermaid clinging to a sodden bit of tree.

"Hello, Lord Jasper." Her voice was hoarse. "You took your time about finding me."

"I came as soon as I could."

He dove into the water, letting the coolness rush over him and wash the tears from his face. A heartbeat later he emerged next to her, wanting nothing more than to pull her into an embrace. But one look at her face told him she was nearing the end of her strength. He had no right to take her in his arms, other than to help her to the side of the fishing boat, which he did.

The captain leaned over and grabbed her wrists, and Gavin boosted her up, cursing the weight of her waterlogged dress. She collapsed in a heap on the deck, then lifted her head as he swung over the side.

"Bring the tree," she said. "It doesn't deserve to drown. And it saved me."

Without a word, he plunged back into the water, snagged the broken trunk, and hauled it aboard. The captain's brow furrowed, but he simply shook his head at this further proof of Gavin's insanity.

"Ouzo," he said, producing a flask from beneath his coat. "Drink."

Gavin took it, pried open the stopper, and held the strong-smelling liquor to Isabelle's lips.

"It will help," he said. "Carefully, now."

She took a small sip, and then another. When he urged a third swallow upon her, she shook her head.

"That's quite enough." Her voice was a touch stronger.

He handed the flask back to the fisherman, who took a deep swig before capping the bottle and tucking it away. One hand still on the tiller, he flipped open the lid of a nearby box and pulled out a rough blanket.

Gavin took it, and, despite the fact that it smelled strongly of goat, vowed to give the man more money as soon as they reached the harbor.

"Let's get you warm," he said, wrapping the rough fabric around Isabelle's shoulders.

She reached up and clasped his hand, her fingers cold.

"That would be grand," she said, a shiver running through her.

He knelt and pulled her against him, trying to infuse his warmth into her body. Trying to tell her, without words, how very sorry he was.

The little boat rocked over the waves. The blessed heat of the sun shone down, and slowly, her shuddering ceased.

"Almost back," the fisherman called.

Isabelle took a breath and stirred in Gavin's embrace.

"Lord Jasper," she whispered. "Let me go."

He almost could not bear it, knowing that he would never hold her again, but he forced his arms to open.

She swiveled to face him, her cheeks still pale but her eyes nearly as bright as the sky.

"When I was in the water," she said, "I made a promise. I vowed to live, because I could not bear . . ." She glanced at the white sail, the blue sea, then back at his face. "I hurt you, and I did not tell you the truth."

The world stopped for a moment, the ticking seconds suspended. He was falling into the sweet blue of Isabelle

Strathmore's eyes, his heart suddenly so hot within him that he feared it would scorch right through his chest, leaving a burn mark.

"What truth was that?" His own voice sounded very far away.

Her lips tilted up into that wry, wise smile of hers, and he was lost.

"The truth is, I love you, Gavin."

Her words smote him, and he was forced to blink back tears. No seawater to hide them this time. He took her hand.

"I feared I'd lost you," he said. *And I couldn't bear it.* "But are you quite certain, Isabelle? This is not some emotion born of gratitude because I rescued you?"

She laughed—a fraction of her usual mirth, but a laugh all the same. "I was rescuing myself, if you hadn't noticed. Though I suppose it was because of you. I couldn't leave you like that, after all."

"Like what?"

She stared into his eyes. "Like a man whose heart had just been broken."

It had, though he could scarcely admit the fact.

"Thank you," he said, dropping a kiss on her knuckles. He felt like a prisoner freed from the gallows, a blind man suddenly restored to sight. "Thank you for coming back to save me."

"I suppose we've saved each other." She tilted her head. "Now tell me, Lord Gavin Reed, Earl of Jasper—will you do me the very great honor of becoming my husband?"

He let out a laugh, then pulled her back into his arms and kissed her on the lips. Cool, and sweet as honey. He even swore he could hear bells.

They kissed until the fisherman let out a self-conscious cough. When Isabelle pulled away, Gavin realized bells *were* sounding, ringing out from the little church beside the bay. The captain had guided them so smoothly back, Gavin hadn't even noticed their entry into the harbor.

"Well?" Isabelle took his face between her palms. "Will you give me an answer, sir?"

"Yes," he said, as the boat docked. He stood and scooped her up in his arms. "Yes, Miss Isabelle Strathmore, I will surely marry you."

"Good," she said.

And there, in front of Mrs. Hodges and a half-dozen Greek sailors, she kissed Gavin with enough heat to curl his toes and make him want to carry her off to some secluded olive grove.

He resisted the notion, though it wasn't easy. When he finally set her back on her feet, he found that they were surrounded by a crowd of smiling villagers.

They applauded, and two wreaths were produced and placed upon their heads.

"Myrtle," Isabelle said, giving his a quick look. "Sacred to Aphrodite, I believe."

"Of course."

Nothing else would suffice, then, but that a feast be thrown to celebrate the engagement of the two English—and the fact that the earthquake had passed with little damage and no lives lost.

"I think the Greeks simply want an excuse to dance and drink and eat," Mrs. Hodges said, though she did not sound particularly cross at the thought.

A boat was sent to the *Floramay* to explain the situation, and the captain of the steamer gave his permission for a few of his passengers to remain onshore until later that evening.

"We were scheduled to anchor here overnight, anyway," Isabelle said. "So it's not as though the itinerary is changing."

To Gavin's surprise, Miss Primm and Miss Taylor ventured ashore to congratulate them. And if the governess looked a bit sour and Miss Taylor slightly teary eyed, well, that was not Gavin's fault. He'd learned not to apologize or take responsibility for every expectation of matrimony slung in his direction.

Will came ashore, too, of course, and could not help gloating.

"Well done, old fellow," he said, clapping Gavin on the shoulder. "I never thought you'd take a chance on Miss Strathmore, after your first impression, and look at you now! Engaged to be married. What've you done for a ring?"

Blast.

"I hadn't planned to go quite this far," Gavin said.

"Harrumph." Mrs. Hodges materialized at his side. "Gentlemen. Never ready. Here."

She thrust a small velvet bag into his hand.

Blinking, Gavin peeked inside to see a silver band set with a single aquamarine. It was lovely in its simplicity, the gem nearly the color of Isabelle's eyes.

"It's perfect," he said. "But wherever did you get it?"

"The market in Athens, yesterday." Mrs. Hodges pursed her lips at him. "I could see you weren't thinking, and someone had to. It's the right size."

"Of course." Gavin made her a bow. "I'm in your debt."

"Yes you are." She poked him in the chest with her umbrella, punctuating each word. "And don't forget it."

As she stumped off, Will's muffled laughter grew louder.

"Oh, she's a rare one, that companion," he said. "If she were two decades younger, I'd marry her myself."

"You would not." Gavin tucked the ring into his pocket. Some time that evening, he'd find the opportunity to slip it onto Isabelle's finger.

Throughout the feasting, and the dancing, and the drinking of ouzo, Gavin watched Isabelle carefully. She seemed to be recovering from her ordeal, the color returning to her cheeks, the bright spark to her eyes.

Brighter, even, than before. The guarded wariness of her past had fallen away, scrubbed clean by the Mediterranean sea and Aphrodite's blessing. Or perhaps Athena's. In either case, he wasn't going to argue, and drank a silent toast to each goddess, just to be sure.

Much later, as the great bonfire on the beach burned down to embers and the festivities quieted, he strolled with Isabelle to where the inky waters lapped the shore.

"I have a ring," he said quietly.

She gave him a surprised look, and he smiled, a little sheepishly.

"Mrs. Hodges gave it to me," he confessed, pulling it from his pocket.

"She prides herself on being prepared," Isabelle said. "Oh, it's lovely."

She held her hand out, and he slid the ring onto her finger. As promised, it fit perfectly, the polished gemstone winking in the last firelight.

They settled together in a warm hollow in the sand, and after several sweet, lingering kisses he tucked his soon-to-be bride close against him.

"Isabelle," he said, as the stars shone brilliantly overhead, bright myths whirling though the sky, "I promise that I will never lose you again."

And he never did.

A *USA Today* bestselling author and two-time RITA nominee, **Anthea Lawson** was named "one of the new stars of historical romance" by *Booklist.* Her books have received starred reviews in *Library Journal* and *Publishers Weekly. A Lord's Chance* is the newest novella in her Passport to Romance collection.

Anthea lives with her husband and daughter in sunny Southern California, where they enjoy fresh oranges all winter long. In addition to writing historical romance, Anthea plays the Irish fiddle and pens bestselling, award-winning YA urban fantasy as Anthea Sharp.

Find out about all her books at anthealawson.com, and join her mailing list, tinyletter.com/AntheaLawson, for a FREE STORY, plus all the news about upcoming releases and reader perks!

For more sweet Victorian romance by Anthea,
try the following novellas:

A Countess for Christmas
A Duke for Midwinter
A Prince for Yuletide
To Wed the Earl
A Lady's Choice

For more romantic adventure set abroad, the *spicy* full-length novel *Fortune's Flower* reveals Isabelle's past, as the Strathmore family adventures in Tunisia in search of a fabled bloom.

Falling in Rome
-Jennifer Moore-

Rome, Italy, 1879

The Trevi Fountain stood in all its shining marble and travertine glory, radiant white against an azure blue sky, looking every bit as magnificent as the drawings Eleanor Doyle had seen in her father's books. She stepped from the carriage, taking the driver's hand without a glance, her eyes captured completely by the striking sculptures, the classic architecture, and the flowing water shimmering in the pool beneath. Though she'd studied renderings, ink and paper were unable to convey the full grandeur of Nicola Salvi's creation.

"Oh, it is glorious." Lillian Blakely exited the carriage and moved up beside her teacher, turning pages in her drawing book. "I shan't be able to rest until I sketch it."

Eleanor hid a smile at the younger woman's words. What she lacked in artistic talent, Lillian made up for with enthusiasm. Over their four-month tour of the continent, Lillian had filled page after page in her sketchbooks with depictions of everything from French masterpieces to Swiss mountain vistas.

Lillian found a shady bench near the edge of the piazza, chose a charcoal pencil, and set to work, brows drawn together in concentration. Eleanor sat beside her. Lillian's excitement was endearing . . . and completely unshared by her younger sister, who was last to exit the carriage, of course.

Rosalie Blakely huffed as she flounced onto the other end of the bench, pink ruffles and blonde curls bouncing. "It is so dreadfully hot." She waved a fan in front of her face. "We really should return to the *pensione*. I still haven't chosen a gown for the ball this evening." Her blue eyes were wide, and her pink lips pulled into a pout. Though only a year apart in age, the two young ladies could not have been more different.

"The hour is not yet noon." Eleanor assumed her most patient smile—one she employed often when speaking to her students, this one in particular. "You've so many new gowns from Paris; I'm certain you will have plenty of time once we return this afternoon to find just the right one."

Rosalie's response was the perfect combination of a moan and a whine that only an eighteen-year-old young lady can produce. "But I still do not know which slippers or jewelry to wear. And how shall I arrange my hair?" She lifted blonde curls from her neck with the back of her hand to allow some air circulation.

Both young women wore their hair down in curls over their shoulders—one head fair and the other dark. They favored parasols to hats, which Eleanor found extremely impractical, especially in this heat. She herself preferred to keep her hands free for writing and her heavy hair pulled up beneath a sensible head covering.

Lillian shifted to keep her sketchbook from being bumped as her sister flipped her curls and pouted.

"And how long must we remain here?" Rosalie asked. "We've seen the fountain, so can we leave? I can hardly breathe this hot air."

Eleanor pushed down a flash of irritation. This morning was the first time she'd convinced her young charges to see any of the city's sights. They'd not even visited St. Peter's and had only seen the Colosseum in passing. "Just a bit longer," Eleanor said. "We've only just arrived. I told the carriage driver to fetch us in an hour."

"How shall I bear the heat for so long?" Rosalie huffed out a breath, planting her elbows on her knees and her chin into her hands.

"Perhaps if you think about something else," Eleanor said. "Do you realize the Trevi is the largest Baroque fountain in the world?"

Rosalie rolled her eyes, her typical reaction to any attempt Eleanor made to teach her about the amazing things they had seen these last four months. The girl was determined to be bored, but Eleanor was even more determined to make sure she went home with some improved cultural refinement.

Eleanor continued as if she hadn't noticed the reaction, waving toward the cluster of sculptures at the center of the fountain. "Look there. Tell me, what do you see?"

"An ugly man with an unfashionable beard and no clothes on." Rosalie folded her arms and shrugged.

Eleanor smiled. "Yes, well, who is he?"

"Neptune?" Lillian asked from behind her book.

"A good guess," Eleanor said. "But typically we see Neptune with a trident and a dolphin at his heel. This man symbolizes the ocean—the water that flows all over the earth. And do you see the two horses pulling his chariot? One represents the calm of the sea and the other the unpredictability and violence. And behind Ocean, you can see other sculptures depicting . . ." She let her voice trail off. Lillian had returned to her drawing, and Rosalie was looking around the piazza, a bored expression on her face.

Eleanor stood. "Well, I'd like a closer look. Would either of you care to join me?"

Neither moved to accompany her, so Eleanor left them in the shade and descended the large curving steps leading down to the pool. The brilliant design made the entire piazza feel as if it were part of the fountain.

She walked slowly around the edge of the large basin, her hand trailing along the lip as she took it all in. The fountain and the façade surrounding it were awe-inspiring—a perfect blend of functionality, architecture, and sculpture. She would never fail to be amazed at the skill of an artist who could create such wonders as movement and texture from a slab of stone.

The sound of flowing water dulled the conversations around her as she passed small clusters of people, turning their voices into a distant hum, and the pool cooled the air comfortably. For a moment, the weight of her responsibility pertaining to her charges seemed lighter. She breathed deeply, allowing the calm sensation to settle over her.

They'd arrived in Rome two weeks earlier, and the young ladies were much more interested in the city's society than its historical import. Eleanor, on the other hand, didn't care a fig about dinner parties or morning visits. She'd dreamed of visiting this city since she was a child and her father had told her tales of the ancient Roman Empire. If not for this opportunity to chaperone the Blakely sisters, she would never have had the chance to see it. If only she could pique their interest in the remarkable history Rome held.

She let her gaze travel over the carvings, noticing new details from this angle, then move upward, reading the Latin inscriptions. She took her notebook and a pencil from her reticule and recorded her impressions of the work and philosophical considerations that occurred to her as she studied it. She would have time to ponder later. Her father had taught her to take these kinds of notes, and though he'd passed on years ago, she still did a thorough job. *Striking, as the sculptor intended. Thought-provoking as one considers the belief of water as a gift from—*

As she wrote, a voice caught her attention—an Englishman's voice. She glanced to the side, noting three young gentlemen at the edge of the pool gathered around a man she guessed must be their teacher. The young men listened closely, their expressions pensive as their teacher described the fountain's history, the pope who commissioned it, and the architect and sculptors responsible for its construction.

Eleanor didn't consider herself to be the type of woman to eavesdrop on another's conversations, but something about the man's voice held her interest. The younger men seemed enthralled as well.

The teacher was perhaps in his early thirties, only a few years older than herself. Eleanor recognized the trappings of a scholar: wire-rimmed spectacles, a pencil poking from behind his ear, and in his hand, a worn leather-bound book. But there was more to him than a mind filled with facts and dates. The man was a born teacher—a person whose words could capture and hold the interest of a group. His own enthusiasm for the subject projected outward, spreading to those who listened and infusing them with the same passion. She'd known others like him and envied their natural ability to make even the most mundane topics appealing. Teaching in this way was a skill that couldn't be learned. Again, her mind turned to her father. He had been such a teacher.

"And there is also a legend pertaining to this fountain,"

the teacher said. "If you toss in a coin, the belief is that you will one day be fortunate enough to return to Rome."

"I wouldn't say no to another visit," one of the young men said, fishing a coin from his pocket and tossing it into the pool. "If only for the tiramisu."

"Hear, hear," his friend said, tossing in his own coin. "And the sorbet."

"If I do return, I hope it will be in the winter," the third said, flipping a coin into the water. "Not when it's so blasted hot." He glanced to the side and grimaced when he noticed Eleanor. "Pardon my language, ma'am. I didn't see you there."

She smiled. "It is hot today."

He smiled in return, excused himself with a polite bow, and tugged on the brim of his hat as he passed. His friends followed.

Eleanor returned to her notebook.

The teacher stood a moment longer, staring at the fountain, apparently unaware of the exchange. He took a hand from his pocket and flipped a coin into the water. When he turned and saw Eleanor watching, he inclined his head. His eyes were a deep brown, and when he smiled the corners crinkled.

A funny feeling moved through Eleanor's middle, and she glanced toward the water, speaking quickly to cover her discomposure. "You didn't tell them about tossing a second coin."

His eyes crinkled further, and the feeling increased. "You're English."

She nodded. "As are you."

"Professor Russell Kendrick at your service, miss."

She inclined her head. "Eleanor Doyle. A pleasure."

His smile remained as he spoke. "As for your question, Miss Doyle, I didn't mention the second coin because I don't think my charges need to worry at present about the promise of finding true love. They are still very young and should focus on their education."

His brow furrowed and he frowned, looking toward the water for a moment. "I suppose I still haven't fully rejected the possibility." Then he tossed in another coin, following it with his eyes. When he looked up, his smile had reappeared, looking a bit sheepish. "What about you, Miss Doyle? Don't you wish to return to Rome?"

"I do very much." She opened her coin purse and selected a coin. She tossed it into the water, watching as it sank into the pool.

"Only one?" His voice held a tease.

She turned toward him. "I'm a teacher, Professor Kendrick, soon to be a research assistant. My course is set and my future decided." She snapped the coin purse shut and dropped it back into her reticule.

The furrow returned but disappeared quickly. "And what brings you to Rome?" he asked.

"I'm escorting two young women on their grand tour."

"We've more in common than I realized. I myself am shepherding a group of young men."

The sound of laughter drifted across the piazza. Eleanor recognized Rosalie's voice, and she suspected, by the male intonations that followed, that the professor's young charges were the reason for it. *That girl could find a man in a convent!*

Eleanor hurried up the stairs and toward the group without excusing herself. Rosalie had already been involved in one scandal, which had been hushed up quickly and was the impetus for the young lady's quick departure from London. Her parents, as benefactors of the new university, had set events in motion to provide Eleanor with a permanent situation as a research assistant in the Archaeology and Ancient

History department once she returned from escorting their daughters. In only a few months, Eleanor would have the position she'd dreamed of, and Rosalie's reputation would be repaired. Additionally, Eleanor would have completed a tour of the continent—something few women of her station ever had the chance to do. Though it had not been stated outright when the opportunity was offered, she understood that one misstep by Rosalie or any negligence on Eleanor's part could destroy both their futures.

"Lillian, Rosalie . . ." Eleanor spoke politely as she crossed the final steps, but there was no mistaking the reprimand.

Rosalie's smile was unconcerned as she brushed a mass of blonde curls over her shoulder. "Miss Doyle, do come and meet our new friends."

Eleanor raised her brow. Although Rosalie had no qualms about speaking with strangers, she was surprised Lillian had allowed an exchange. And what of the young men's manners? It was highly improper for these gentlemen to presume to acquaint themselves with young ladies they'd not been introduced to.

Lillian set aside her sketchbook and extended a hand toward one of the men. "This is Mr. Adrian Curtis of Surrey. Mr. Curtis and I became acquainted at Lady Wimbley's house party last summer."

"A pleasure," Eleanor said. So they had been acquainted before. Well, she still wasn't pleased, especially when she noticed Rosalie's overly wide smile and fluttering lashes.

The young man she had spoken to at the fountain bowed and smiled, flashing white teeth. "Miss Blakely, I must say, was my saving grace that week."

"It's true. Lord Wimbley was a bit . . . long-winded," Lillian said. A blush covered her cheeks. In social situations, the young woman was a bit shy.

"Indeed, he was," Mr. Curtis said. "And who could forget—"

"Croquet!" the two of them said at the same moment. They shared a laugh at a joke to which only they were privy, then Lillian immediately returned to her sketchbook.

One of the young men cleared his throat.

Mr. Curtis stepped to the side and motioned toward his friends. "Mr. Caleb Darrington and Mr. Harlan Reid." The two men bowed in turn. "These chaps have been my closest friends since our first year at Eton," Mr. Curtis continued. He glanced behind Eleanor. "Oh, and of course our bear leader, Ken."

Eleanor glanced to the side and saw that the professor had followed her. "Yes, Professor Kendrick and I met." She introduced the young men's teacher to Lillian and Rosalie.

"Delighted to make your acquaintance," the professor said. "And how do you like the fountain?"

"Marvelous," Rosalie answered. "And isn't it the perfect day to enjoy it, Mr. Reid?"

Eleanor was speechless.

The young man with dark curls, thick side-whiskers, and a fondness for tiramisu smiled. "Indeed."

"And you, Miss Blakely?" Mr. Kendrick said to Lillian.

"Breathtaking. I could not wait to sketch it."

"Glad to hear it." He nodded, apparently satisfied that the young people had been suitably impressed by the aqueduct's termination. "I planned to continue today's tour at a nearby church, *Santi Vincenzo e Anastasio*. Would you ladies care to join us? It has quite an interesting history."

Rosalie clapped her hands. "We would love to, wouldn't we, Lillian? Miss Doyle?"

Eleanor raised a brow. Rosalie hadn't shown this much

enthusiasm since she'd flirted with the handsome curator at the Louvre museum. "Very well," Eleanor said after a pause.

"You'll like Ken's stories," Mr. Reid said, offering his arm to Rosalie.

She slipped her hand into the bend of his elbow, and the pair followed Professor Kendrick to the far corner of the piazza.

Eleanor walked at the rear of the group, turning over the situation in her mind. Rosalie obviously fancied Mr. Reid and was not subtle about it. Eleanor's instinct was to take her away and forbid her from seeing him—perhaps leave Rome altogether. Lillian would agree with the decision, and Mr. and Mrs. Blakely would have no qualms about Eleanor removing the young lady from a potentially disreputable situation, even if it cut their time in Italy short.

On the other hand, the pair was supervised by not one, but two chaperones. And after months of pouting and complaining, Rosalie was willingly attending an educational tour. The mere presence of the young gentlemen had completely changed her attitude. And they had come to Rome to further the young women's cultural education.

They arrived at the base of the tall columns, and Mr. Kendrick held open the wrought iron gate, allowing the others to enter.

"And isn't this happy news?" Rosalie proclaimed to Lillian as they climbed the steps. "Mr. Reid, Mr. Darrington, and Mr. Curtis are all coming to Lady Aberline's ball tonight!"

Eleanor met Professor Kendrick's gaze as she passed, returning his smile. She was surprised to find herself looking forward to the ball as well.

That evening, Ken stood at the balcony above the villa's atrium. The large space below was open to the sky with four pool-style fountains set into the mosaic tile of the floor. Anciently, the pools would have taken up the majority of the room, leaving smaller walkways filled with potted plants and benches. A villa of this size would need the larger pools for cooling during the hot summer months. However, Lord and Lady Aberline had decided a sizeable dance floor was more important than their comfort.

Placing a hand on the rail, Ken looked over the edge at the orchestra playing below and the refreshment table serving finger sandwiches, cakes, punch, and tea. *Tea.* In this heat. He considered himself as English as the next man, but the idea of a hot drink brought sweat to his forehead. He dabbed at it with a handkerchief and noticed flashes of white as others around the ballroom and surrounding balcony did the same. Even at this late hour with servants operating large fans to move the air, the night was stifling.

If there was one consistent aspect of the English, it was

that they continued to be English no matter the setting. Whether in an Indian jungle, African safari, or outback ranch house, English routines and traditions were adhered to as strictly as if one were on holiday in Sussex. Ken considered it a pity not to fully immerse oneself into the customs of the local culture. Ambrose's saying, "When in Rome," was tossed about with a laugh among the tourists, but tonight, standing in a formal coat listening to a minuet while tea was served, the irony was nearly absurd.

He ran a finger around the inside of his collar, thinking how pleasant an airy toga would feel and couldn't help his grin at the gasps of shock it would incite.

In spite of the discomfort of his cravat and wool coat, however, Ken was quite enjoying the ball. The setting was magnificent. Built in the style of an ancient Roman home, the villa showcased manicured gardens, tile mosaics, and an art collection that would make most museums envious.

He watched couples turning about on the dance floor, carefully avoiding a misstep into a pool, and his gaze moved to the entrance. He'd thought Miss Doyle and her young charges would have arrived by now. The fact that he stood in this spot with such a view gave him pause. Was he waiting for them? For her? The realization came as a surprise. But, his actions were justifiable, he told himself. Quite some time had passed since he'd associated with a woman of his own age, or close to it. He guessed Miss Doyle was perhaps five years his junior. And the fact of the matter was, he liked her. He'd enjoyed the day spent in her company.

Miss Doyle was clever and thoughtful as opposed to the silly young ladies she accompanied. She'd shown genuine interest in the church and even jotted down notes as he'd explained some of the building's history. Her questions showed a real understanding and an insightfulness that was refreshing.

And she was quite pleasant to look at.

He glanced around. Though he knew no one could hear his thoughts, he'd been told his feelings were easily read on his face. And these feelings would be cause for particular embarrassment should they be revealed.

When he looked back toward the entrance, Miss Doyle and the Blakely sisters stepped into the ballroom as if his thoughts had conjured them.

Miss Doyle's gown followed her figure tightly in the bodice, then spread into flounces or ruffles or one of those words men were not taught. There was lace and some pearl-colored buttons, and ribbons in her hair. Though he could not describe the details of her dress with any amount of accuracy, he could confirm that it was yellow. And she looked radiant.

Ken took a step back, not wanting to be seen staring. He continued slowly around the balcony, occasionally glancing down.

Harlan Reid, apparently in youth not having the same scruples as his teacher, walked directly to the ladies and, a moment later, escorted the younger Miss Blakely toward the dance floor before Ken had even reached the stairs.

The dark-haired sister pointed toward something on the far end of the room and excitedly turned pages in her sketchbook as she and Miss Doyle crossed the atrium. They moved beneath the balcony, and Ken lost sight of them.

He took his time walking along the railing, studying the sculptures and paintings on display as he made his way to the stairs. He wondered if Miss Doyle might be interested in the collection and then wondered how long he should wait before asking her.

Half an hour later, after straightening his cravat in the

men's washroom, Ken found the two women. Miss Blakely was situated on a bench, facing a potted fern of all things. Her face was tight in concentration as she glanced back and forth between the plant and her book.

Miss Doyle sat beside her but rose when Ken approached. She moved behind the bench to join him. A smile lifted her cheeks and brightened her eyes, calming Ken's worries. He held a glass of punch toward her.

"Thank you," she said, her voice hardly audible so near to the orchestra.

Ken stepped closer, tipping his head toward her. "I'm glad to see you made it, Miss Doyle."

She sipped the punch and turned to speak closer to his ear. "Isn't the villa wonderful?"

"Extremely so." He glanced at Miss Blakely's drawing pad, then looked back again, squinting as he tried to make out what exactly he was seeing. The drawing was horrendous.

Miss Doyle leaned toward him. "Lillian loves to draw," she said, a brow ticking upward and a nearly indiscernible smile pulling at her lips.

He leaned forward. "Lovely work, Miss Blakely."

The young woman beamed up at him, then returned to her drawing.

"Miss Doyle, there is a gallery above the atrium." He gestured upward with a lift of his chin. "If you'd care to accompany me. Lord and Lady Aberline have collected some of the most outstanding ancient pieces I've ever had the privilege of seeing. Many are uncommonly well preserved." He took her empty glass and offered his elbow.

She glanced back at the dancers. "I should keep watch over Rosalie," she said.

"The balcony gives a fine view of the dance floor." Was she searching for an excuse to turn him down?

She looked upward and then to the dance floor, considering. "I . . ." An immense relief filled him when she slid her hand into the bend of his elbow. "I should like that very much."

They climbed the stairs and strolled slowly along the balcony, pausing to study each sculpture. No conversation was necessary as they admired the ancient carvings and occasionally bent down to read a discreetly hidden plaque with information about the piece.

They moved along in a comfortable silence until Miss Doyle stopped, drawing in a breath and letting it out in a sigh. "Oh, it's beautiful."

Ken looked at the piece she was admiring. A smallish, not particularly impressive woman's head and one shoulder were all that remained of the sculpture. It sat on a pedestal, the better to be viewed. He couldn't understand why she was so taken with it. "What is it that you admire about this particular work?" he finally asked.

"Look at the detail, the lovely face." She moved to the side to study the back of the stone woman's head. "From the Augustan period, I believe."

Ken leaned down and read the inscription, his eyes widening when he saw that she was correct. "How did you know?"

Miss Doyle continued to admire the carved fragment. "Her hairstyle, parted in the middle with a roll in the center . . ." She glanced up. "My father taught me."

"I confess that I am not an expert of sculpture," Ken said.

"Nor am I." She smiled, and for the first time, he saw shyness in her expression. "But I do know a bit."

He lifted a hand toward the sculpture, indicating that she should continue. "Please, I'd love to hear what you have to say."

Miss Doyle hesitated, but only for a moment. "Father said Greek statues were created as a tribute to the idealized human form, but the Romans were more interested in documentation, preserving a person's true appearance without any exaggeration."

He nodded, and so she continued, pointing toward the sculpture. "Hair styles and clothing fashions changed over time, helping researchers date when a sculpture was made, as well as identify the subject's age, marital status, and position in society." She moved toward another statue, holding out her hand toward the head. "For example, this woman here might be assumed to be a Vestal Virgin by her *seni crines* hairstyle, but the flowers in her hair identify her as a bride. On her wedding day, her hair would have been parted by a ceremonial spear—" She stopped speaking. "I am talking too much. I apologize."

"If you think identifying ancient sculptures to be a topic I find tiresome, you obviously have not met many professors of ancient history, Miss Doyle."

She smiled. "I knew one very well. My father."

Ken felt a shock. How had he not seen it? "James Doyle, Professor of Ancient Languages and Antiquities at The University of London."

She nodded, her eyes lighting up. "Yes. You knew him."

"I should have realized." Now that he looked closer, he could see the similarity—slight though it was. Miss Doyle hardly resembled a plump, middle-aged man with thinning hair, but her eyes held the same depth, the same thirst for knowledge. Professor Doyle had been brilliant. All these years later, Ken still remembered insights the man had shared, his meticulous research methods, and above all, the way he genuinely cared for his students' welfare. Professor Doyle was larger than life—more of a symbol of the kind of teacher Ken wanted to become than an actual memory. Perhaps that was why he didn't recognize the man's daughter sooner.

"He was an exceptional man and gifted scholar," Ken said. "One of the finest instructors I ever had." He took her hand, tucking it beneath his arm and leading her around the balcony. "I attended his funeral. What was it, fifteen years ago?"

"Fourteen."

Ken remembered Professor Doyle's young daughter sitting in the church pew. A shy-looking child twisting a handkerchief in her lap. His heart had ached for her then, and now . . . here she was, a confident intelligent woman.

Miss Doyle remained quiet as she contemplated another sculpture.

"He would have been proud of you, Miss Doyle. The way you've followed in his footsteps."

A small smile flickered over her lips.

"You said you're taking a position as a research assistant," he said, thinking he should change the topic, but not wishing to stray too far. "Is that why you've come to Italy?"

"Partly." She darted her eyes at him, then moved closer to the railing, her gaze moving around the open area beneath until it lighted upon Rosalie Blakely at the far side of the room, conversing with Harlan and Caleb. Miss Doyle turned, craning her neck to see Lillian sitting beneath the other balcony, still working on her drawing. Mr. Curtis sat beside her, looking as if he was trying to start a conversation, but Lillian was engrossed in her drawing.

"The Blakelys are on the board of the new Royal Holloway College, an affiliate of the University of London," she said. "They submitted my name and qualifications, and of course the two of them have quite a bit of influence with the school."

Ken raised his brows. “Impressive. I’d not heard of the University of London hiring female instructors.”

Her cheeks reddened. “Well, of course I wouldn’t be an *instructor.* Only a research assistant. And officially, my name would be ‘E. Doyle.’ Without my father’s reputation and the Blakely’s recommendation, per my success in shepherding their daughters through Europe, this appointment wouldn’t even be considered.” She glanced up at him. “As a woman, my options are rather limited.”

Her admission bothered him. If she was indeed qualified to instruct, it was a pity that her gender should hold her back. But of course, a woman would not have been permitted to attend university in the first place, so qualification as an instructor wasn’t actually possible. He didn’t know whether the idea of her being granted a position based on her father’s merit bothered him more, or the fact that a clever person such as herself was denied higher education.

“A university instructor is your choice of occupation, then?” he asked, curious about her aspirations. “If you were allowed any vocation, with no restrictions based on funding or gender, this is what you would select?”

“If I could choose any career, it would be archaeology,” she said without hesitation. “Reading about discoveries or studying artifacts in a museum isn’t the same as seeing firsthand where they come from. I’d like to understand the lives of the people who lived long ago, instead of looking at their former possessions in a museum or book.”

Her answer surprised him. He wasn’t sure what he’d expected, but he didn’t think one woman in a thousand would have chosen archaeologist as their ideal vocation.

“And what of yourself?” she asked. “What would you aspire to if no limitations existed on your dreams?”

“Truthfully, I would choose archaeology as well. But as

you know, it's a rich man's hobby." He shrugged, wishing he didn't feel the familiar heaviness when he thought of it. If he could get funding . . . His research was sound, but still not original enough to persuade the university. If he was lucky, however, this trip would change things.

He cleared his throat and tapped his fingers on the railing, watching but not truly seeing the dancers below. "Two years ago, I spent some time studying beneath Professor Giuseppe Fiorelli at the University of Naples. He's since been appointed head of the excavation of two ancient cities near Mt. Vesuvius. The cities were buried when the volcano erupted in AD 79." He glanced at her. "Of course, you've probably heard of them."

"Pompeii and Herculaneum. It is so fascinating," Miss Doyle said. "Think of all there is to discover beneath the ashes."

Her cheeks were flushed and her eyes bright. The hand on his arm was clenched. Ken grinned. The prim school mistress was quite a different person when she spoke of unearthing devastated civilizations. And he knew exactly how she felt. To be a part of something of this magnitude . . . He couldn't imagine wanting anything more.

He bumped his arm into her shoulder, then shrugged. "Perhaps one day a common man can make a career out of archaeology, and if that is possible, why not a woman too?" He grinned and winked. "Maybe we shall be partners, Miss Doyle, wearing work boots and bucket hats, unearthing an Egyptian mummy."

She laughed and opened her mouth to respond, but was interrupted.

"Professor Kendrick. Thought I saw you from down below."

They turned together as a portly man with a monocle hanging from his waistcoat approached.

"Mr. Bodkin." Ken smiled, inclining his head in a bow. "Miss Doyle, if I might make an introduction."

She nodded.

"This is Mr. Alastair Bodkin, patron of the English Historical Society and my dear friend." He clapped a hand on Bodkin's shoulder. "And Alastair, it is my pleasure to introduce you to Miss Eleanor Doyle. Perhaps you remember her father—"

"James Doyle. Of course I remember him. Brilliant man. Fine speaker. Went to listen to him on many occasions. Professor Doyle had a way of holding an entire auditorium captive with his stories."

"That he did," Ken agreed.

"And it is my great honor to meet his lovely daughter." Bodkin bowed as deeply as his rotund belly would allow.

"A pleasure, sir."

Bodkin straightened and took a handkerchief from his pocket to dab his forehead. His face was redder than usual, Ken noted. The heat wasn't agreeing with him. Or perhaps it was the climb up the stairs. He motioned to a servant to bring his friend a drink.

"Now tell me, Miss Doyle. What brings you to Rome?" Bodkin asked, taking the drink with a nod of thanks.

"I'm chaperoning some young ladies on their grand tour."

"Excellent. Glad to hear it."

The three talked as they strolled around the balcony, commenting on the heat wave and the various art pieces, and Bodkin told Miss Doyle where to find the very best sorbet in the city. At Bodkin's inquiry, she told him about the young ladies and their tour up to this point, as well as their plans to stay in Rome at least another few months. They stopped at their original location near the top of the stairs.

Miss Doyle looked over the balcony, her gaze moving between her two charges.

Bodkin took a drink. "Ken and I had discussed a trip to the Colosseum and Forum excavation site with his young gentlemen. I hope Friday is agreeable? I hired a local guide to show us around."

"Friday will be perfect," Ken said.

"Excellent." Bodkin turned back to Miss Doyle, leaning in as if confiding a secret. "Heaven knows I've no idea what all the piles of broken rocks mean—Ken's the expert. " He dabbed his forehead again. "If you're interested, you and your young ladies are welcome to accompany us."

Miss Doyle smiled. "Mr. Bodkin, what a thoughtful invitation. I know I speak for the others when I say we'd be thrilled to join you."

"Capital." Bodkin grinned and shook Ken's hand. "Then it's settled. Friday morning at the Colosseum, nine o'clock sharp."

"I wouldn't miss it," Ken said.

"Now, if you'll excuse me, I'm off in search of another cold drink and a cool breeze," Bodkin said and descended the stairs.

"What a pleasant man," Miss Doyle said.

"Very amiable," Ken agreed, leaning back against the railing. "I thought you'd like him."

"I think it would be impossible not to." Her smile turned into a grin. "His good cheer is contagious."

"That it is."

"And to meet two people who knew my father in one day . . ." She smiled wistfully. "This evening has been quite a pleasure."

She moved to join him at the rail, watching the guests mingle below. "Did he say you're an expert on the Colosseum?"

"Not exactly. He was referring to—"

Miss Doyle grabbed his arm. "Professor, where are they?"

Ken stared at her. "They?"

"I can't see them anywhere." Her brows pinched together. "Where are Rosalie and Harlan Reid?

Eleanor rushed down the staircase, cursing the yards of ruffles she had to lift out of her way to do so. She scanned the faces in the crowded room as she passed, but didn't see Rosalie or Harlan Reid among them. Panic tingled her fingers as she hurried past the fountains and refreshment table to where Lillian sat on the same bench, still intent on her drawing. Behind, she could hear Professor Kendrick's footsteps.

Near the orchestra, Eleanor slowed. She must find out if Lillian had seen her sister without letting on that Rosalie was missing. Lillian had no patience for her sister's lack of common sense, especially since the resulting shame would impact her own reputation, as had the scandal that had sent both of them away from London. She would be quick to write to her parents, and their tour would end, along with the promise of Eleanor's new position.

Eleanor glanced over the dancers one more time, then sat down beside the young artist. "How do you like the ball, Lillian?"

Lillian looked up. "Oh. You startled me." She glanced at the professor standing behind the bench.

"Have you been enjoying yourself?" Eleanor asked.

"Quite a lot. This fern is so intricate, and the design on the pot will take quite some time if I wish to get the shading just right."

"Did . . . ah . . . have you visited with anyone?"

"Mr. Curtis sat with me for a bit. He brought a fairy cake and some punch."

"Oh, isn't that nice?" Eleanor unclenched her hands and laid them softly in her lap. "And did you speak with anyone else?"

"No, I've been quite occupied with my art," she said, holding up a thumb in front of one eye as she studied the fern.

"I can see. You've done a lovely job." Eleanor spoke the words automatically without looking at the sketchbook.

"Thank you." Lillian glanced around. "Where is Rosalie? I should like to show her this pot."

"Dancing," Eleanor said. "When I see her, I'll tell her you're asking for her."

Lillian nodded, focused again on her drawing.

Eleanor bid her farewell and hurried away, intending to make a circle of the room before looking elsewhere—perhaps find and question the other young men.

"Miss Doyle," Professor Kendrick said from behind her.

She didn't pause. As she moved through the crowd, she forced herself to breathe steadily.

"Miss Doyle," he called again.

She shook her head, hurrying past the orchestra. Talking to him, forgetting her duty, was the reason she was in this situation in the first place. With every passing second, she felt her future slip away.

"Eleanor." He held her elbow, stopping her. "Please wait."

His use of her Christian name made her pause. "I can't. I must find Rosalie."

His brow was furrowed as he studied her face. "I understand. We'll find her, but—"

"You *don't* understand. We must find her now." The words came out harsher than she intended.

"Very well," he said, releasing her arm carefully, as if she might hurt him, or herself.

She knew she was behaving rudely, but there was more riding on this than he could possibly know. Turning away quickly, she hurried around a fountain pool and nearly crashed directly into Mr. Curtis and Mr. Darrington.

Mr. Curtis reached out a protective arm to keep her from falling into the water. "Good evening, Miss Doyle."

Mr. Darrington bowed. "Bodkin said you and the Blakely sisters will be joining us Frid—"

She cut off his words. "Rosalie, Mr. Reid, have you seen them? Where are they?"

Mr. Curtis gaped, taken aback by her rudeness. Mr. Darrington glanced at his friend, then at his teacher, but Eleanor didn't care if she was making a poor impression.

"I believe they've gone to walk in the gardens," Mr. Curtis said.

Without excusing herself, Eleanor changed her path, heading toward the far side of the room, away from the entrance. The passageway from the atrium was wide, leading down stone steps into the gardens. She paused, glancing over the park, trying to decide which direction a young man and woman might have taken.

"Eleanor, wait," Professor Kendrick said, following her

once again. "Let us think through this logically. There is no reason to panic."

"There is every reason to panic." Her voice was sharp. "A young lady's reputation is at risk."

"You don't know that," he said. His calmness made her even more angry. He wasn't taking this seriously. "They may be simply taking a stroll."

"Alone? Just the pair of them? We must find them."

She started out into the gardens, passing elegantly trimmed shrubs and columns holding pots of trailing flowers. Gas lamps cast halos on the ground, illuminating sections of the path but leaving pockets of darkness.

"Eleanor, listen to me. I don't know Rosalie, but I teach young men Harlan's age every day. Reacting in anger and forbidding them from spending time together is the quickest way to ensure that they will want to be together. Nothing is as exciting to young lovers as a forbidden romance. Look at Romeo and Juliet."

"You don't . . . understand." She was panting, her tight corset not allowing her to draw a full breath.

"Then tell me. I want to help."

"If you want to help, keep your young men in line. Did you even watch them tonight? Know what they were doing?" She knew she was directing her anger at the wrong person, but she couldn't help it.

"Harlan's a gentleman." His voice wasn't angry, but it was no longer gentle and full of understanding. "He's a good young man. They all are."

"It's not just Rosalie's future on the line." Eleanor turned down another garden path. It was only a matter of time before Lillian discovered that Rosalie was gone or someone found the two young people alone together and spread gossip. Rosalie's fragile reputation couldn't take one more blow.

The sound of giggling came from a side path. Eleanor veered in that direction, recognizing the voice immediately. "Rosalie!"

She came upon the pair of them, standing beneath a gas lamp, Rosalie's hand on Harlan's arm.

"Miss Doyle," Harlan said, inclining his head. "Nice to see you."

Eleanor's face was hot, and her head felt like a steam engine filled with pressure. "Rosalie, come. It's time to leave."

"Leave?" The young woman looked between the three of them. "But the night's only begun."

Eleanor could feel herself trembling, both from relief and anger. "Rosalie."

"Harlan, I believe the ladies need to speak privately." Professor Kendrick jerked his head to the side, and a confused Mr. Reid followed him back toward the party.

Eleanor clasped her hands together to keep from shaking the younger woman. "Rosalie, what were you thinking?"

Rosalie looked at her with wide eyes. "I didn't do anything wrong. Mr. Reid and I were just walking."

"Alone? In the dark?"

A wrinkle appeared between her brows. "But nothing happened."

Eleanor took a calming breath and let it out slowly. She rubbed her brow, feeling a headache coming. "You know better. You know how quickly gossip can spread."

Rosalie pouted, looking as if she might start to weep at any moment.

"Do you think of no one but yourself?" Eleanor continued. "What of Lillian? A scandal would blight her name as well."

She didn't answer, but Eleanor could see Rosalie wasn't defiant, and that diffused a bit of her anger. She softened her voice and moved closer, laying a hand on the younger woman's arm. "Rosalie, you promised to behave yourself around young men. You promised all of us, your parents, Lillian."

Rosalie sniffed. "But Mr. Reid is a gentleman, and I am so very fond of him."

Eleanor nodded. "I know he's handsome and polite, but you just met him today. Give it time. And please remember the rules. You mustn't allow yourself to even appear to be in a compromising position. Rosalie, it is more important than you can imagine."

Rosalie leaned against her, and Eleanor wrapped her arms around the young woman, compassion overriding her other emotions. Though she was thoughtless and impulsive, Rosalie was still just a young woman.

"Are you going to forbid me from seeing Mr. Reid?" Rosalie spoke in a small voice.

Eleanor thought of Professor Kendrick's words. *Nothing is as exciting to young lovers as a forbidden romance.* The last thing she needed was for Rosalie to sneak away to meet her Romeo. "I am not going to forbid it. But you must remember to follow the rules. With him and with all gentlemen. If you do not, we shall have to return to London immediately."

"And you won't tell Lillian what happened tonight?"

"No."

Eleanor felt the young woman go slack with relief. She held her a moment longer, then stepped back. "Come, let's fetch your sister."

A few minutes later, the pair sat on the bench admiring the sketch of a potted fern.

"And we really must leave? Already?" Lillian asked.

Rosalie pressed a hand against her stomach and glanced

at Eleanor. "I'm sorry. I must have eaten something that disagreed with me."

"A pity," Lillian closed her sketchbook and put her pencil into its case. "I'd hoped to sketch Lady Aberline's candelabra."

They walked through the atrium and to the entrance to await the carriage.

"How do you feel, Rosalie?" Lillian slid an arm around her sister.

"Not well."

"Mr. Curtis tells me we're to meet the group and a friend on Friday morning for a tour of a dig site and the Colosseum," Lillian said.

Rosalie straightened, a hopeful smile lighting her face. "Are we going, Miss Doyle?"

Eleanor's insides drew together into a tight knot. She'd forgotten about Mr. Bodkin's invitation. Thinking of how she'd acted to Professor Kendrick made her ill. But should she have acted differently? Allowing herself to develop a friendship with the man had kept her from her assigned task. When she thought of all that could have gone wrong tonight, she didn't regret reprimanding him for his lack of supervision. But she hadn't chosen her words well. There was no excuse for her rudeness.

She'd promised Rosalie that she'd not forbid her from seeing Mr. Reid, and she'd promised Mr. Bodkin they'd join him for the tour. And, even though she didn't like to admit it, she owed Professor Kendrick an apology.

"Yes," she finally said. "If Rosalie's health is improved, we will join the gentlemen on Friday."

Ken stood in the shade of an archway in the Colosseum's outer wall with his three charges, Bodkin, and the hired guide, Signore Celino. He tapped his foot against his heavy satchel, watching with some surprise and a fair bit of apprehension as a carriage stopped in the Piazza del Colosseo and the ladies stepped out. Truth be told, he had doubted whether Miss Doyle would come at all.

The young men and Bodkin hurried forward, exchanging greetings and smiles with the ladies, but Ken hung back, unsure of exactly how to conduct himself.

Miss Doyle's words and behavior at the ball had left him feeling as if he should apologize. But for what? Not following adult men around a party like an overprotective mother hen? His pride protested that he'd not done anything wrong. If he hadn't seen her reaction with his own eyes, he'd not have believed a person could become so upset over a mere possibility that something improper *might* have happened. In the days since the ball, he'd felt a fair bit of anger over this, not to mention defensiveness when it came to his friend. Harlan Reid was a respectable young gentleman, and to make an assumption without any provocation felt unjustified.

But as he'd calmed and considered the situation from Miss Doyle's position, he'd realized her responsibility when it came to the young ladies was immense. While he, as bear leader, ensured that his young gentlemen didn't get swindled by a fortuneteller or find themselves on the wrong train, Miss Doyle had much more to be concerned about. The society abroad was very much the same as in England, and gossip, whether true or not, could ruin a young lady's character in the blink of an eye. He thought it a shame that a woman feared her own countrymen's misplaced words over the other dangers that might befall a traveler in a foreign land.

"Miss Doyle, I can't tell you how pleased I am to see you this morning." Bodkin's voice echoed through the piazza.

"And you as well," she said. "Thank you again for the invitation." She glanced over his shoulder, her gaze meeting Ken's. She winced, her cheeks reddening, and looked away.

He supposed her discomfort was a good sign. At least it wasn't impartiality. But returning to their former ease would take some work, and possibly time, he thought, rather discouraged.

Bodkin and the young ladies were introduced, and of course the man had them smiling in seconds. Everyone loved Alastair Bodkin. He offered his arm to Miss Doyle and led her toward the entrance. The others followed, Lillian gazing with wide eyes at the enormous ancient structure, and Rosalie gazing with wide eyes at Harlan.

Ken straightened as they approached. "Miss Doyle, Miss Blakely, Miss Rosalie." He inclined his head to each lady in turn. "Might I introduce our guide, Signore Celino?"

The Italian man bowed in greeting. "Ah, to have beautiful

women on the tour, what a delight." He gave an elegant bow. "Shall we begin?" Seeing that he had the attention of the group, he cleared his throat. "In 80 anno Domini, Emperor Vespasian's son, Titus, gifted the Flavian Amphitheater to the Roman people. The grand opening was celebrated with one hundred days of games such as gladiatorial combats and wild animal fights." He paused, ensuring his audience was suitably impressed before continuing. "The Colosseum, as it was later called, is an entirely free-standing structure, unlike Greek theaters built into hillsides. The outer wall contains over one hundred thousand cubic meters of travertine stone, set with three hundred tons of iron clamps." He flourished his hand toward the outer wall. "The structure is composed of three levels and an attic. The arches in the upper levels housed statues of heroes and gods."

As one, the group leaned back, looking toward the upper levels. Even though Ken had visited the Colosseum multiple times, the enormity of the amphitheater never failed to impress him.

"Eighty entrances ring the ground level. And as you can see, each has a number, which would correspond to the number on a spectator's purchased ticket—a tessera made from a shard of pottery—directing him to the correct section and row to find his seat."

Ken looked over the group. The guide's speech was rehearsed, but interesting, and his accent gave the experience a touch of the dramatic. He didn't mind playing tourist with the students and Bodkin. Though he'd visited the arena multiple times, he still couldn't fail to be impressed by the enormity and history of the ancient structure, but today he was anxious to get through the Colosseum and onto the Forum's excavation site. He glanced down at his satchel. The research he hoped to do at the site could set his work apart in the academic world, legitimize his studies, and hopefully earn the attention and funding he needed to further his career.

Signore Celino swept his hand toward the entrance. "Please, ladies and gentlemen, follow me as we step back in time."

He led them into the barrel-vaulted passageway that ran around the ground floor with stairs and ramps radiating from it, leading up to the various seating sections. Their feet tapped on the stone floor, echoing through the vast space. Inside the building, the air was cool and damp—part of the reason visiting the site at night was discouraged. The building and the surrounding area posed a risk for malaria, also known as Roman fever.

Miss Doyle released Bodkin's arm to write in her notebook, and the young people craned their necks, admiring the stonework of the high passageway.

"Imagine you are a citizen of ancient Rome and have come to the arena for a day of entertainment." Signore Celino's voice boomed, causing the younger ladies and a few of the gentlemen to startle. "Perhaps it is a holiday, a celebration of a military victory, or maybe you are hoping to see your favorite gladiator in battle. If you're lucky, you may even catch a glimpse of the emperor."

Ken's mind wandered as the guide continued speaking. He watched Miss Doyle, wondering what she was writing. Her own impressions of the place? Was she recording the statistics the guide had mentioned? Questions to ask later? What did she think of the Colosseum? Was she astonished? How could she not be?

Signore Celino led them through an archway and down a short flight of crumbling steps into the arena itself. The stadium floor was dirt, in places mud, littered with piles of rock and broken columns. Vines and other greenery grew over the seating area and spread across the ground, giving the impression of Mother Earth reclaiming her territory.

In the center of the space stood a large wooden cross, surrounded by smaller monuments representing the Stations of the Cross. Over the last centuries, the site had been consecrated as holy. The reasoning was that it was a location where Christians were martyred, though Ken had found no evidence to support this—likely anti-pagan propaganda. But, between the games and executions, many people had died here, he reasoned. Some must have been Christian.

At first glance, the arena was unchanged from the times Ken had seen it over the years, but he remembered there had been talk of restoration, and when he looked closer, he could see a few sections of the arena floor had been excavated, the walls of the underground passageways visible, and a grouping of white stone fragments were arranged neatly along one side. He wondered if they were an attempt to reconstruct inscriptions.

Intrigued, he set down the heavy satchel and started toward the stones.

"Professor Kendrick?" Miss Doyle called as she walked toward him.

He stopped.

"I owe you an apology," she said. Her cheeks pulled in a grimace. "The other night, I allowed my fears to become anger, and I should not have directed it toward you."

Ken was surprised by her admission, but not unpleasantly so. He'd worried he'd have to be the one to seek her out and negotiate a peaceful settlement. "You've no need to apologize."

"I behaved very rudely. To you and to—"

Ken held up a hand. "I understand."

Her brows pulled together. "You understand? What do you understand?"

"You said it was not just Rosalie's future on the line," he said. "By that, you meant that any blotch on her name affects her sister by association, and yourself as well. I imagine the benefactors of the university would not continue to sponsor a potential candidate who allowed their daughter's reputation to be damaged."

She looked down, her hands twisting together. The tension hadn't fully abated, but Ken could feel it lessening. "It sounds so selfish. I promise I am not only looking out for my own interest."

Ken touched her arm, and she looked up. "You care about your charges, that is obvious. But you are also a woman trying to make a place for herself in a field where your sex is an impediment."

She nodded. "Understanding the reasoning behind it does not excuse my rudeness."

"Then I will accept your apology on one condition."

Miss Doyle tipped her head. "Condition?"

"Well, two conditions actually." He grinned. "No, make that three."

"Three conditions? That seems rather excessive." Her expression softened.

He took his hand from her arm and held up a finger. "First of all, you must accept my apology as well."

"You've no reason to apologize."

"These are *my* conditions, Miss Doyle." Ken waggled his finger in reprimand, but he smiled to show he was teasing. He grew serious. "I apologize for not taking your concerns more seriously. I've spoken with my charges, and I will do better in my responsibility toward them and the young ladies they associate with."

She gave a small smile and a curt nod. "Thank you. I accept your apology."

Ken raised a second finger. "The next condition is that you and I become friends again. I have spent the past days worrying that you were angry with me and I wouldn't have the opportunity to see you again." He spoke lightly, but he hoped she could hear the truth in his words. He had missed her, missed their conversations and banter, missed the feeling of victory when he learned something new about her or when her eyes twinkled in a shy smile, exactly as they did this moment. The smile was accompanied by a pink color in her cheeks that was very attractive.

"I should like that. To be friends."

"My friends call me Ken," he said matter-of-factly, keeping an innocent face even though his bold words bordered on impudence.

Her eyes went wide. "Is that the third condition?"

He shook his head and raised a third finger. "The third condition is this: If you and I ever find ourselves at a ball again, I should really like to dance with you, Miss Doyle. Or may I call you Eleanor?"

A blush exploded on her cheeks. This time, his words had been presumptuous, but the shyness in her smile had given him a surge of confidence, and he'd been unable to help himself.

She looked down at her hands, then across the stadium, and back to a clump of grass, as if her gaze didn't know where to settle. "Professor, I . . ."

"Ken." He grinned, feeling satisfied. He quite enjoying flustering the proper woman, but he knew he shouldn't push her too far into discomfort. He offered his arm. "Tell me, *friend*, what is your impression of the Roman Colosseum?"

"Magnificent. More than words or drawings can

convey." After a brief hesitation, she took his arm, and they continued in the same direction, toward the arrangement of stones.

Bodkin and some of the young people were walking around the edge of the arena. Adrian sat beside Lillian, who was sketching something or other in her book. Reassuring himself that their charges were behaving, Ken continued the conversation. "I agree wholeheartedly," he said. "This place, this city, is so steeped in history, sometimes I feel as though the very stones can talk." He felt silly speaking so romantically, but he'd allowed himself to be vulnerable, and here, in this place, with this woman, it felt right.

Eleanor looked up at him and smiled wistfully. "I feel that way, too. So many famous stories and important events happened in this very spot. But then, there were also regular people—parents, friends, children. And I want to know about them, as well."

He patted her hand where it rested on his arm. She understood perfectly.

When they reached the stones, he saw they were indeed covered with inscriptions. Some contained just parts of carved letters while a few were filled with writing.

An attempt had been made to put a long collection of words in order. He imagined the text must have, at one time, circled the stadium, declaring the supremacy of one emperor or another or proclaiming the latest Roman victory. He found a few completed words among the fragments. One stood out: *invictissimi*, meaning "never defeated," a favorite among the Romans, and a date.

"Fifth century," he muttered. "During the reign of the corulers."

Eleanor crouched down, making notes in her book as she studied an inscribed block that was nearly complete, save for a broken corner.

"Ah, Miss Doyle, you've found quite a treasure," Bodkin said.

Ken had been so intent upon the carvings, he hadn't noticed Signore Celino and Bodkin approach.

"Sì, this stone is very important," the guide said, crossing himself. "It tells of the great tragedy that befell Christian martyrs under the reign of the emperors."

Eleanor frowned, looking at the man, then back at the stone. She opened her mouth, then closed it again, as if she'd changed her mind about speaking.

Ken rolled his eyes. The stone most certainly said nothing of the kind. Roman stonecutters didn't carve tragic tales that never happened. The stone likely told of an emperor's latest conquest or praised a powerful senator who sponsored a winning fighter.

The guide clicked his tongue, shaking his head sadly. "A pity, is it not, Miss Doyle?"

"Yes," Eleanor said. "A pity." She looked at him for a moment, then stood and moved away to another stone.

"Oh, I think you may have upset her," Bodkin said, his voice filled with concern. "Ladies can be sensitive about these things."

Ken didn't think Eleanor had been upset by the story. She had seemed more bothered by the guide's inaccuracies, but was it because she didn't believe the stories of Christian martyrdom? Or had she read the tablet and been bothered by Signore Celino's incorrect interpretation? He shook his head. It must be the first. Ken had never known a woman to understand Latin, so she couldn't have read it. He joined her, speaking low so the others couldn't hear.

"Eleanor? What is wrong?"

She shook her head. "Nothing is wrong."

"You look upset."

"No, I'm not upset. Just a bit confused." She gave an unconvincing smile and turned back to look at a different stone.

Ken walked back to read the first tablet she'd been studying, finding it difficult to interpret. There was no punctuation or spaces between words, and the carver seemed to feel a need to conserve space by cramming as many letters as close together as possible. Ken concentrated, finding words he recognized and making a rough translation. He'd been correct in his initial assumption. The tablet made no mention of Christian martyrs. Signore Celino must have known exactly what tourists wished to hear and not have bothered to learn the actual translation.

In his periphery, Ken saw Eleanor turning the pages of her notebook. She read for a moment, then looked back at the stone, frowning. He walked toward her, but she didn't notice. She looked back through her notebook, turning the pages quickly, as if searching for something.

"Eleanor?" he asked.

She blew out a breath, brows pulled together tightly. Clearly, she was frustrated.

"What is the matter, my dear?" Bodkin said, coming to stand beside her.

She looked between them. "I . . ."

"Go ahead, Miss Doyle." The plump man patted her arm and gave an encouraging lift of his brows. "Tell us what is bothering you."

Eleanor took a deep breath and pointed to the engraving. "It says here that the patrician, Decius Marius Venantius Basilius, funded the repairs of the arena after a dreaded movement of the earth during the Theodoric reign. Does this refer to the great earthquake of 443? Because as I understand it, Valentinian III celebrated his twenty years of rule in 444. Theodoric the Great would not rule until eighty years later."

The three men stared at Eleanor Doyle. Ken's mouth actually dropped open like an actor in a comedic performance.

She flipped through the pages of her notebook. "Perhaps there was another great quake."

Bodkin stepped close and looked over her shoulder at the notes in her book, then down to the inscribed stone. "My dear, do you read Latin?" He sounded utterly flabbergasted, which was how Ken felt. Not only had she read the words on the inscription, she was fitting them into historical context.

Eleanor nodded, looking like she'd been caught doing something illegal. "I do."

Bodkin waved Ken closer. "Is she correct?"

Ken studied the inscription, running his fingers over the letters. He read the words and found it was just as she'd said—all of it. "She's correct." He looked up. "Eleanor, I had no idea."

She blushed. "You know my father, sir. Are you surprised he insisted I learn Latin?"

Bodkin laughed. "Miss Doyle, what a delight. A woman who reads Latin. Capital. As far as your question, I've no idea about earthquakes or anything of the sort. And I imagine Signore Celino doesn't either."

The guide shrugged apologetically.

"But luckily," Bodkin continued, "the expert on the matter is right here. The historic society often consults Ken about emperors and the workings of the Roman Republic. I'm sure he can answer any question you might have."

"Oh, I had no idea," Eleanor said.

Ken shrugged, feeling his own blush. "Well, I wouldn't say *any* question."

"Come, sir, you're far too modest." Bodkin leaned toward Eleanor. "He's writing the definitive work on Julius Caesar as we speak. Knows more about the man than Julius's own mother."

Ken imagined Aurelia Cotta would take offense at the claim, but he didn't correct his friend.

"I'm afraid I don't know the answer to your question, Eleanor," Ken said. He looked toward his book-filled satchel. "But, if you're interested in doing a little research, I imagine we could find out."

Eleanor shifted on the picnic blanket and turned a page of the old volume resting in her lap. She couldn't remember enjoying a day more than this one. A breeze carried the scent of freshly turned earth, and birds chirped in the trees above. The group had set up a picnic luncheon on a shady patch of grass, and while the others ate and visited, she and Ken searched through his books for mention of a second Roman earthquake. She couldn't have been more delighted in the conversation or the company.

Over the years, she'd come to realize her father's pleasure in a daughter's accomplishments had been an anomaly. Men typically didn't care for a woman's thoughts on topics they considered out of her realm of concern. She'd learned to remain quiet instead of correcting an instructor, even when he was unquestionably wrong, and found her proficiency in ancient language to be a hindrance when it was discovered. The talents her father praised her for became a source of shame. Eleanor had been called unladylike or a bluestocking often enough that it was easier to feign ignorance.

But today, that had all changed. Ken had been impressed with her skill, not threatened by it, and when they discussed ancient texts, he'd spoken to her as an equal, and she felt a swell of pride that had been absent since her father's death.

She sighed contentedly and pushed the heavy book from her lap. She'd been reading long enough. She looked around the partially excavated site to locate the other members of her party who had dispersed around the wide space while she'd been engrossed in the book. A short distance away, Mr. Darrington, Mr. Curtis, and Mr. Reid walked with Rosalie alongside a line of uneven columns.

Eleanor stood and stretched, then walked to where Lillian sat beneath a tree, sketching a broken piece of statuary. Bodkin was reclining on the grass beside the younger girl, complimenting her artistic skill. His praises were so convincing that Eleanor wondered whether he was the kindest man on earth or simply a terrible critic of art. Bodkin moved to rise when she approached.

"No." Eleanor held out her hands. "Don't get up. I'm looking for Ken. Do you know where he is?"

Bodkin grunted as he pulled himself into a sitting position and squinted, looking over the hills of the site. "Can't have gone far now, can he?"

Eleanor gazed across the space as well, looking between broken columns, past muddy pits, and over rocky mounds. Since the unification of Italy a few decades earlier, the new government had turned its thoughts to preserving its ancient history, and in spite of protests, archaeological work had begun on the hill that was once home to the Imperial palace and the area below where the Forum had stood.

"Is that him over there?" Bodkin pointed toward a distant figure in the center of the site.

"I believe it is," she said. She bid the pair farewell and

crossed the uneven ground toward Ken, taking care not to disturb anything that may be important to the restoration of the ancient site.

Ken held an open book, consulting it as he walked around a particular area in the Forum. When she drew near, she slowed and then stopped, waiting a small distance away, not wanting to disturb his concentration. He lifted his gaze from the book and looked around as if to get his bearings, then walked in a different direction, but eventually stopped, shook his head, and returned to the same area.

Finally, Eleanor's curiosity won out. "Looking for something?"

Ken spun, his frown of concentration turning into a smile. "I suppose I'm just trying to figure out this map." He nodded toward the book and held it toward her.

She stepped beside him and looked closer. She recognized it right away. It was a copy of the *Forma Urbis Romae*, a stone map commissioned by Septimus Severus. Eleanor knew the stone carving had been severely damaged in the middle ages, and a large part of it was lost. This version depicted the original map, but it appeared someone had attempted to complete it. She wondered what drew Ken to this particular spot, and tried to find it on the map, but between the speculative images on the paper and the very few landmarks around them, fixing their location was difficult.

She handed the book back to him. "I'm sorry. I'm a terrible map reader."

"You, Eleanor? I didn't realize there was anything you did not do well."

She searched his face for mockery, but it appeared he was paying her a sincere compliment. Her heart warmed. "I also darn socks very poorly."

"Ah." Ken shut the book with a snap. "You should have

probably told me that sooner." He winked. "That seems something a person should know right away when they begin a new acquaintance."

Eleanor wanted to laugh at his teasing, but ever since his words inside the Colosseum, she felt something different when he spoke to her. She didn't know whether his way of speaking had changed or just her perception. His words felt *more* somehow—even the simple ones—and she didn't quite understand the reason. It left her feeling unsettled and at the same time warm and dreamy. She fingered the strap of the reticule on her wrist, thinking of something to say in order to turn the conversation away from herself.

"This entire day, you've not spoken once about Julius Caesar." She pretended to be offended. "I was told you're a leading expert on the topic."

Ken sat on a large block, stretching his legs in front of him. "What would you like to hear about him?"

Eleanor settled onto the remains of a brick wall near him. "Why don't we begin simply? What is your opinion of the man?"

"I've studied Caesar for nearly a decade, so you can imagine my opinion can't be summed up in a few simple sentences. Perhaps if you had a few hours . . ."

"Then tell me your view on the classic question: Was Julius Caesar a hero or a villain?"

He grinned. "I'd say the answer is extremely complicated."

Ken seemed to be enjoying himself, which she found odd. If he was such an expert on Julius Caesar, why was it so difficult to get him to speak about it? Perhaps he knew once he began, it would be difficult to stop.

"What is *your* estimation, Eleanor? Hero or villain?"

She raised a brow.

"Ah, let me guess. You read Shakespeare's rendition, were moved by Mark Anthony's famous speech, and consider Julius Caesar to be the evilest of villains."

She nodded. "That is all true. I do think him a villain, and I have read Shakespeare's play. But I've also read Suetonius, Tacitus, and Plutarch."

"Plutarch." Ken smiled, shaking his head. "I should have known Professor Doyle's daughter reads ancient Greek as well as Latin."

She shrugged, though she felt flattered at the admiration in his voice. "That is neither here nor there." She twisted around to face him. "The question concerns Julius Caesar, the murderous dictator who brought about the fall of the Roman Republic." She spoke the words as a challenge.

If Eleanor hadn't seen it with her own eyes, she'd have thought it impossible for Ken's grin to grow any wider, and yet that's exactly what happened.

"All of that is true," he said, looking like someone had just handed him a Christmas gift. "But you must understand him in the context of his time. He was an unparalleled military commander who treated his soldiers well and increased their pay. He created jobs, improved roads, and fought for the rights of the plebeians at a time when the government was mainly controlled by the wealthy, who gave little thought to the lower class."

"He started a civil war and sold millions into slavery," Eleanor countered. "He seized power from a democratically elected senate and tried to make himself into a god."

Ken nodded. "All true. By today's moral standards, he would be considered a homicidal monster, but he was a product of his time. The world then was ruthless, and violence was a political tool, and Caesar wielded it better than anyone."

"He overthrew his own country and declared himself dictator for life." Eleanor crossed her arms.

Ken nodded. "But Caesar didn't attack Rome to gain personal wealth or power. He already had both. He did it to further the cause of the Populares, the party that largely supported the labor class, and to prevent the more conservative Gnaeus Pompey from taking power." He moved his hands as he spoke, becoming more animated. "Julius Caesar was a champion of the people. A self-made man who was ferocious in battle, yet forgave his enemies."

"I agree with that," Eleanor said. "But a tyrant should not be forgiven just because he lives in a world where tyranny is acceptable."

"A very good point. And that is why this question cannot have a definitive answer. The time period is a factor, but men are never fully moral nor are they completely evil. A person is complex and fickle and . . ." His voice trailed off.

"And?" Eleanor prompted.

He studied her face, his contented grin still in place, his eyes gentle. "Eleanor Doyle, I quite enjoy arguing with you." His soft voice sent shivers over her skin.

"Oh." She wished she could control the heat spreading through her cheeks. The unsettling feeling returned, and she looked around for something to say—something to change the topic or distract them from the way the air thickened around them. Her gaze lit on the book Ken had set on a rock beside his leg, and understanding registered.

"I know what you're looking for," she said.

He looked startled. "I—Pardon me?"

"*Templum Divi Iulius.* The Temple of the Divine Caesar."

He lifted the book and nodded. "I am, indeed."

"It would lend so much distinction to your work on

Julius Caesar," she said, feeling excited at the prospect. "Finding his burial site would be . . . unprecedented."

"Exactly. The excavation of the Forum, I'd hoped, would offer the perfect opportunity to discover the temple's remains, or at least where it once stood. But . . . " He waved his hand toward the chaos of the site. "It's proving more difficult than I'd thought."

Eleanor scrutinized the area around them. It seemed that for all the reports of cleaning this area, not much had actually been excavated. Irregular columns rose from the dirt at random intervals; many shallow pits had been started, and then abandoned; shovels, pickaxes, and other tools lay haphazardly around the site. Workers dug in a few locations, though she couldn't see any rhyme or reason to how the excavation was being carried out.

She looked farther afield. Of course, there were the triumphal arches, still standing strong after centuries. The temple of Antonius and Faustina had been repurposed over the years and was now a Christian Church, its columns standing at the eastern end of what was once the Sacred Way.

In one corner of the excavation site was a large collection of column fragments and shaped stones in the process of being reconstructed. Directly in front of Eleanor and Ken was a cleared space with only a foundation and pedestals that had once held columns and statues. Signore Celino claimed this was where the ancient Temple of Vesta had stood, and Ken had agreed with him, based on its proximity to the Imperial Palace.

"Well, then. What do we know about the temple?" she asked, thinking they should take a methodical approach to the problem.

"I know what it looked like." He fished in his coat pocket and drew out a small pouch. "I have a coin with its image, and the Forma Urbis, though the additions are pure speculation, based on what I've read." He exhaled, sounding frustrated. "With so few visible landmarks, it's difficult even to orient myself."

Eleanor took the offered pouch, sliding the ancient coin out into her palm. She looked closer at the profile of Julius Caesar on one side and then turned it over, scrutinizing the image of the temple. Holding something so ancient in her hand felt sacred. "Such a treasure," she said quietly. "My father would have loved to see this." She touched her fingertips to the uneven surface of the metal, feeling the well-worn images, then returned it to its pouch.

"It was a gift from my grandfather," Ken said with a wistful smile. "He was a historian as well. The way he told stories made them come alive, especially to a young boy captivated by battles and heroic generals."

"I think his grandson possesses the same skill." Eleanor handed back the pouch.

Ken smiled gratefully, then turned his gaze to the pouch. "I imagine owning something from his own time was part of the reason Caesar became such a fascination of mine."

Eleanor understood exactly how he felt about his grandfather. Her father's love of history had been an immense influence on her own life and career choices. And in a way, she felt as though, in studying history, she carried on his legacy. That somewhere in the eternities, he was proud when she used the skills he'd taught her. She decided in that moment that nothing was more important than finding Caesar's temple with Ken.

If she had to dig up every inch of this . . . She stopped herself. A scholar's way was not to charge in and indiscriminately tear the heart of the empire apart. They needed to use the tools they possessed, the first of which was logical reasoning.

"Someone must have written about the location," she said, tapping her finger to her lip. She took out her notebook and scanned the pages, hoping something helpful might stand out.

Ken turned pages in his own book. "Of course there are records, but they speak only in vague terms. No paced off directions like Captain Flint's map."

"No pirate skeletons helpfully pointing the way?"

"What I wouldn't give for even a small *x* marking the spot," he said.

Eleanor turned a page and stopped. "Appian!" She turned the notebook toward him. "Appian of Alexandria wrote about the Forum less than a century after Caesar's death."

Ken nodded, taking the notebook from her and looking at the page. "Yes, I've read Appian's account—the Latin translation, I'm afraid. Ancient Greek is not my strong point. His writing is thorough, exhaustive even, but I don't believe in this he was more descriptive than any of his contemporaries."

"But at least Appian is a starting point," Eleanor pointed out. "Did you bring his writings?" As soon as she'd said it, she laughed, realizing how ridiculous the question was. Appian's *Roman History* covered twenty-four volumes.

Ken didn't laugh, however. He stared into the distance and shook his head slowly. "No, but I believe he's referred to by Herodotus—or was it Fabius?" His eyes grew suddenly bright, and he scratched his chin. "Hmm, if only someone nearby could translate ancient languages . . ."

Five hours later, a mound directly to the east of the Arch

of Septimus Severus buzzed with activity. Somehow Bodkin had convinced the local workers to move their operations to the site, and even the three young gentlemen shucked their coats and set to work. Ken was shoulder deep in a hole, sleeves rolled up, tossing out shovels full of dirt at a steady pace while Bodkin walked to and fro, supervising.

Eleanor sat on the picnic blanket between the Blakely sisters and a chaotic stack of books that she was trying to arrange into some semblance of order. Loose sheets poked from some of the volumes, and others were stacked open on top of each other. She carefully marked the important pages and made certain their notes were in order should any question arise as to how the results had been determined.

As soon as they'd fetched all of the volumes to the area, she and Ken had plunged into his research books, studying obscure texts, comparing maps and writings, and making notes of their own.

Ken was certain a particular grouping of broken columns belonged to the temple of the horsemen Castor and Pollux, and once a spring was located beside it, they were certain. The temple of Julius Caesar should be directly northeast. They went back through, checking and rechecking the readings and maps, and arrived at the same conclusion. Once the decision was made, Ken rushed away to start the excavation.

Eleanor had spent the last hours alternating between walking among the workers to offer water and refreshment procured by Signore Celino and moving back to their research to see if there was possibly something she'd missed. She felt too nervous to sit for long and found herself pacing or hovering over the diggers, which she didn't think they appreciated.

The hours wore on, and the work slowed as the initial fervor died down.

"Be careful not to break anything," Bodkin reminded the

diggers, picking his way through the piles of dirt. "You never know what might be historically significant."

"You'd think something as large as a temple would be easier to find," Mr. Curtis said, accepting a sandwich of salami on focaccia from Eleanor.

Rosalie joined them, twirling her parasol and smiling prettily, as if they were attending a garden party. "Perhaps you could try over there." She pointed to another section of the site.

"No, it must be here," Eleanor said. "Ken is sure of it."

Mr. Reid climbed from the hole he was digging and joined them, accepting a sandwich from Rosalie. "Evening is approaching," he said. "Do we have any idea how deep we need to dig?"

"Or what we're looking for?" Mr. Darrington said, rubbing his sore palms.

"Not precisely," Eleanor answered. She feared the three were losing their momentum. She prayed they'd continue. Ken wanted this so desperately. "It may be just a foundation or a few bricks. We've no idea what is left of the building, if anything."

Lillian came toward them, sketchpad in hand. "Then, if nothing is left, what are they digging for?"

"Well, hopefully *something* remains." Eleanor offered a cup to Bodkin. "Some evidence that this is the right location. Please, just a bit longer—"

"Eleanor!" Ken called from the other side of the mound. "Come quickly!"

The group looked at one another, then they all hurried across the hilltop.

The hole Ken had dug was the size of a large sofa and over five feet deep. He squatted down, tossed his shovel aside, and brushed loose dirt from a rock with his hand.

"Ken?" Eleanor peered over the side. "What is it? What did you find?"

He motioned her forward, grasping her waist and lowering her into the hole to join him. When he set her down, she held on to his arm to keep steady on the uneven ground. Beneath her fingers, she felt Ken shaking. "Just there." He pointed to the rock.

Eleanor bent closer, wondering exactly what she should be seeing. It appeared to be just a large, flat rock. She looked closer, then reached forward, running her fingers over the nearly invisible image carved into the block. A circle with eight rays shooting from it—a star. "Is that . . . ?"

"Caesar's comet," Ken whispered. The comet had appeared during a festival honoring the deceased emperor and became a sign of his divinity—the very symbol that would have been carved on his temple.

Eleanor's heartbeat quickened. She looked up, meeting Ken's expectant gaze.

His eyes shone.

"Ken, this is it. You found it."

He drew in a shaky breath, his smile wide. "I believe we did."

Two weeks later, Ken accepted the glass Bodkin offered and sat back into the soft chair, grateful for the small corner that offered some privacy at the crowded party. Harlan's aunt, Mrs. Daines, had arrived in Rome a week earlier and taken a very elegant suite on the Via Gregoriana. Tonight, she was hosting a gathering, and as she was a close friend of Bodkin's, Ken imagined some of the leading scholars in the city would be in attendance. A month ago, the prospect of socializing with such a group would have thrilled him, but tonight, there was only one person he looked forward to seeing. Harlan had requested that his friends, the Blakely sisters and their chaperone be invited, and Ken found himself anxiously watching the doorway as he had a few weeks earlier in the Aberlines' ballroom.

In the weeks since their day at the Forum, he'd only seen Eleanor twice. Once at church, and the other when he and his charges had paid a visit, though the young men and Bodkin had seen her and the Blakelys nearly every day. He'd been surprised at how his time had been monopolized, both at the Forum site and with callers who'd come to hear about his discovery. He missed her.

He raised the glass to Bodkin in thanks, feeling a lump in his jacket—Eleanor's notebook. In the commotion following the discovery of Caesar's temple, she'd left it behind with the other books. He'd not *meant* to read the entire thing, but he had glanced at it in curiosity and found it riveting. Eleanor had a scholar's mind. Her notes were organized. Questions she sought answers to led organically to further study, all of it meticulously documented. No wonder she'd so easily found the date of the Roman earthquake and her notes on Appian's histories.

But what had most fascinated him were her translations. Eleanor had a gift for languages that he'd rarely seen. He himself was considered an expert in Latin, but her grasp of the nuances of the language left his skills with much to be desired. He could only imagine her abilities in Greek were equally impressive.

A strange paradox had taken place inside him as he'd read her studies. He felt impressed beyond words, pleased at all she'd accomplished on her own with her limited opportunities for education. But Eleanor was quite possibly more intelligent than he, and a small thread of jealousy accompanied this thought.

Ken turned back to the conversation.

"Woodman asked me about you," Bodkin said.

"Not Professor Miles Woodman? From the Oxford Department of Antiquities?" His chest tingled with excitement.

"The very same." Bodkin raised his own glass, nodding toward a man that Ken recognized as the famous dean, and took a drink. "He's considering offering you a position."

In the weeks since the discovery at the Forum, Ken had received numerous speaking requests, as well as employment offers. But Oxford? His mouth went dry. "I'm flattered."

"I imagine you could go anywhere you choose now." Bodkin smiled a genuine smile. This was a man who truly wished the best for people and was pleased for their good fortune. No wonder he was so well-liked.

"I suppose—" Ken cut off his words when a man approached the seating area. He and Bodkin stood.

"Signore Romano," Bodkin said, holding his arms wide and smiling. "I am so pleased to see you."

Signore Romano gave a flourishing bow, complete with pointed toe. "Always a delight to see an old friend, Mr. Bodkin." He turned toward Ken. "And do I have the pleasure of meeting Professor Russell Kendrick?"

"None other, sir." Bodkin held a hand toward Ken. "Allow me to introduce Signore Matteo Romano from the University of Naples."

Ken's heartbeat quickened. "A pleasure." He bowed. "You work closely with Giuseppe Fiorelli at the excavation of Pompeii, I believe."

"Sì. That is correct." He motioned for the men to return to their seats and sat on a sofa across from them. "Professor, I will, as you English say, get right to the point, eh?" He leaned forward, resting his forearms on his knees. "After hearing of your extraordinary discovery, Signore Fiorelli sent me to meet you and ask if you'd be interested in working on our projects at Pompeii and Herculaneum. Of course, it is not your homeland of England, but the university adheres to the highest standards of education. And one cannot find a more beautiful setting than Campania and the Amalfi Coast."

"I am honored," Ken said. His mind was reeling. This was

the very opportunity he'd wished for. "I think very highly of Signore Fiorelli, and of course the excavations are fascinating. I—"

"No need to make a decision today," Signore Romano said, holding up a hand. "I am certain you have many other offers, but we hope you will consider ours."

"I will," Ken said.

Bodkin grinned. "Pompeii, eh? I've been to the site. An amazing discovery as ever there was."

Signore Romano leaned back into the sofa, crossing a leg over the other. "You are *corretta*, Mr. Bodkin. It is *magnifico*. Possibly the most important discovery of our time. And we are searching far and wide for the best minds to study it and bring the ancient world to life." He waved around his arms as he spoke. "Diggers we can train in a few hours, but scholars, they are more difficult to find."

Ken thought of Eleanor immediately. "I know a scholar," he said. "An expert in Latin and Roman history." He pulled Eleanor's notebook from his coat.

Bodkin's brows shot up, but he did not say anything.

Ken flipped through the pages until he found what he was searching for—an entry he'd marveled over: one page in Latin, and on the adjacent page, an unbelievably precise English translation. "See here. The understanding of the language goes beyond simple word-for-word recognition. The nuances and context—well, you can observe for yourself."

Signore Romano took the notebook, nodding as he read, impressed. He turned a page, then another. "Sì. This is exactly what we are looking for."

Ken felt a rush of energy. He leaned forward, gesturing to another entry. "And the organization, her meticulous notes and logical thought."

"Her?" Signore Romano looked up. He sighed and closed the book. "Professor, is this translator a woman?"

"Yes. A highly intelligent woman. She—"

Signore Romano held up a hand, shaking his head. "I don't doubt she is very clever, but we are attempting to entice sponsors. For that, we must have an impeccable reputation. We cannot decrease the credibility of the program on an indulgence."

Ken felt sick. "But you saw her work."

"Sì. And if it were up to me . . ." He sighed. "But it is not. I work to keep our benefactors happy, and this would cause too many problems. It would not be taken seriously." He rose, handing back the notebook.

Ken stood as well.

"Please consider our proposal, Professor. Signore Fiorelli will contact you."

"Yes, I will." Ken spoke automatically, his mind no longer on what he was saying. "And thank you."

"And it is always a pleasure to see you, Mr. Bodkin." Signore Romano bowed and departed.

Ken sank back into the chair, discouragement hanging like a wet rug on his shoulders. He'd thought it would be the perfect solution. And now what? He sighed, feeling sorry for himself. He was developing feelings for Eleanor. In fact, he thought he might be in love with her. But if he remained in Italy and she returned to London . . . The thought of not seeing her again was unbearable. She could possibly find a teaching appointment somewhere in Italy, but not of the same caliber as employment for a major university. And she'd worked too hard to be relegated to a lesser position. He'd hoped if he had something to offer her, she might . . .

A hand settled on his shoulder. "Don't be discouraged, Ken." Bodkin's face was filled with compassion. "The fact that you tried, when it could have cost you the very opportunity you've dreamed of . . . Well, that is exceptionally admirable in my opinion."

Ken blew out a breath. "I think I love her." Saying the words aloud made them real—and terrifying—but hearing them gave them authenticity. They were true.

"Of course you do. If you're just realizing that now, maybe you're not as brilliant as the rest of the world thinks." He grinned, but then his expression grew serious. "Love isn't easy, my friend, and it's seldom convenient."

Ken nodded, swallowing hard at the lump in his throat. He slipped the notebook back into his coat pocket.

"I'll speak to Romano," Bodkin said. "And Fiorelli. He may be more amenable to the idea than his associate thinks."

"Thank you."

Bodkin patted Ken's shoulder again, waggling his brows. "Chin up. You wouldn't want your lady friend to see you looking glum."

Ken looked toward the doorway. "Is she . . . ?"

Bodkin chuckled. He put a hand behind his ear and tilted his head. "Methinks I hear giggling."

Ken listened and, sure enough, he could hear that Rosalie had arrived. He stood. "You're a good friend, Bodkin."

Bodkin shrugged, color rising to his face. "You'd do the same for me."

As the two exited the room, Ken wondered if that was true. Was he as loyal a friend as Bodkin? He hoped very much that he was.

Ken saw Eleanor right away when he entered the room. She stood with the Blakely sisters near the entrance, greeting Mrs. Daines and looking beautiful in a lavender evening gown. Harlan was beside Rosalie, introducing her to his aunt, and the other two young men were talking with Lillian. The young lady had, of course, brought her sketchbook. and he imagined she would soon settle into a seat and begin to draw the least likely object in the room. Lillian's passion for her work was truly endearing.

Eleanor looked up, and when her gaze met his, Ken was rewarded with a bright smile. She excused herself and crossed the crowded room to join him. "Well, if it isn't the famous Professor Kendrick, discoverer of the Temple of Caesar? You know, the entire city is talking about you, sir."

Ken's neck heated. "I did not do it alone. In fact, I had a very capable partner."

She smiled, taking his offered arm as he led her to the side of the room. "Will you tell me how the excavation is progressing? What has been found so far?"

"So far, a few column fragments and part of one wall. I don't have high hopes for reconstructing the building." He had visited the site daily over the past weeks and never failed to feel an overwhelming sense of accomplishment, even though there was very little to show for it. "I shall take you to see it once it's further along. The site is rather dangerous at the moment."

They stopped at a large fireplace that was blessedly unlit this warm evening.

Eleanor released his arm and turned to face him. "I should like that. Ken, I am so happy for you." Her smile was tender and her eyes soft. "What you did is amazing."

He felt warm all over at her words. "Like I said, I didn't do it alone. Without your knowledge and research . . ."

She shook her head. "I only pointed out things you would eventually have seen on your own. You had it all there."

"You do not give yourself enough credit."

He leaned an arm on the mantel, looking at the hearth. This latest development should have him singing from the rooftops, but he felt heavy. Eleanor would leave Italy in just five weeks. How could he bear to say goodbye to her? His heart ached as he mulled over the dilemma. He couldn't ask her to give up what she worked for and stay with him, but could he give up Pompeii for *her*?

Eleanor stepped closer, studying his face. "Is everything all right? You seem . . ."

"Tired." He forced a smile. "I am tired."

"Yes, I can imagine. You must have a lot on your mind, and you've worked hard these last weeks."

"I fear I've neglected my friends."

"Not at all." Eleanor took his arm and led him toward the sofa in the far corner of the room. "Your friends understand. Here, sit. I'll fetch you a drink."

"No need. I—"

But she'd already left, making her way toward a refreshment table. He stretched his arm over the back of the sofa, idly watching the people in the room. He wished he didn't feel so despondent. He wished he didn't have to choose between the things he wanted most.

Eleanor was returning with two glasses when Bodkin stopped her. Ken watched as Eleanor was introduced to Signore Romano. She curtsied and smiled. The three spoke together for a moment, and Ken would have given nearly anything to hear what they were saying. He felt a tug of sadness knowing that no matter how she wanted it or how qualified she was, she'd not have the opportunities he had.

Bodkin said something that sounded very complimentary. Eleanor smiled, glancing toward Ken. Then a moment later, the Italian man spoke, and she laughed politely. After a short time, she excused herself and continued to where Ken sat.

Behind her, Bodkin whispered something to Signore Romano. The man nodded, his lips pursing pensively.

Eleanor handed Ken a drink and sat beside him. "That was interesting. Mr. Bodkin introduced me to an associate of Giuseppe Fiorelli's."

"Oh?" Ken tried to look innocent, as if he hadn't been spying and watching her every move over the back of the couch. "And what did he say?"

"Nothing significant," she replied, setting her glass onto a low table. "Just pleasantries. He does have a very high opinion of you, though." She smiled, her eyes sparkling. "Perhaps he thinks to offer you a position at Pompeii. Wouldn't that be grand?"

Ken looked away, his throat tight. His mouth tasted of the most bitter guilt. "I can't imagine he would," he managed to say.

"But if he did . . ." Her voice trailed off. She turned her head slightly, as if listening.

Ken glanced behind her and saw a group of matronly women gathered near the sofa. One woman was leaning in, speaking in a low voice. "Yes, I was correct. That is indeed Miss Rosalie Blakely." The woman spoke the name with a sneer. "I wonder if Mrs. Daines knows the young lady has been very exclusive with her nephew since she arrived in Rome—improperly so."

"A flirt," another of the ladies said, wrinkling her lip like it was the worst insult she could call another person.

The third lady leaned in, looking as if she had a treat to share with her friends. "I do believe there was some scandal surrounding Miss Blakely last Season." She paused for dramatic effect. "I heard she was involved with a sailor." The last word was whispered.

The first woman nodded sagely. "I remember hearing about it as well."

Another of the women looked shocked, holding a hand in front of her mouth. "Do you suppose it's true?"

"I wager that's the reason her parents rushed her away to the continent in the middle of her coming out Season."

The woman with the curled lip grunted. "And now here she is, at it again. Some people just cannot be depended upon to behave appropriately."

The first woman shook her head, clucking her tongue. "What a disgrace to a fine family name."

Ken looked at Eleanor, rolling his eyes at the gossiping old hags and ready with a retort about minding one's own business, but he stopped.

Eleanor sat frozen, her face white as a sheet.

He touched her hand. "Eleanor?"

Her eyes darted to him, then to the women and around the room. "I must go. I must take the girls and . . ."

And in that moment, he understood. No wonder Eleanor had been so worried about Harlan and Rosalie being seen together. The young lady had already been involved in one scandal. Her reputation hung by a thread. With the young lady's history, another disgrace, whether true or simply perceived, would devastate her family.

And Eleanor would be caught up in the outcome.

Ken's first reaction was anger. How could Rosalie's parents place such a responsibility on Eleanor? It wasn't fair for her to carry this burden. But anger wouldn't solve anything. She looked close to falling to pieces. Eleanor needed him.

"I'll get Lillian," he said. "We'll meet you at the entrance hall."

She nodded. "Yes. I'll find Rosalie."

He helped her to her feet, holding on to her arm until he was certain she was steady. He led her around the sofa, then nodded and started toward where he'd last seen Lillian. Eleanor grasped his arm.

When he turned, he saw tears in her eyes. "I can't allow Rosalie to see Mr. Reid anymore. If there is gossip about their association, it will only make things worse, for both of them."

"I know," Ken said.

"And that means I won't . . . *We* won't . . ."

"I understand."

Her chin quavered as she nodded.

And Ken knew he would give up Pompeii a hundred times to be with her.

The creak of the carriage and the sound of the horses' hooves on the paving stones were not enough to drown out Rosalie's weeping. Eleanor had apologized countless times since they left Mrs. Daines's residence, but her young charge wouldn't hear it.

Lillian sat beside her sister. She slid an arm around her shoulders and gave her a handkerchief. "Rosalie, it is just one party. The world isn't coming to an end."

Eleanor winced. If only that were the case, this would be so much easier. "Actually, I think it would be best if we didn't attend any more gatherings in Rome. In fact, tomorrow I will start making arrangements to leave the city." Her heart hurt as the words left her mouth. She'd loved Rome—loved the history and their new friends and all they'd experienced. She'd miss this city, but above everything else, she'd miss Ken.

"Leave the city?" Rosalie cried. "But what about my Mr. Reid?" Through the small window, streetlamps illuminated Rosalie's tear-streaked cheeks and red nose at regular intervals.

"Mr. Reid is precisely why we must go." Eleanor tried to make her voice gentle, while leaving no room for discussion. "I'm sorry, Rosalie. I promised your parents to do all within my power to protect your name."

"But I did nothing wrong. I followed all the rules. I was not alone with Mr. Reid, not once. I did what you asked."

Eleanor felt a wave a pity for the young lady, who had behaved as she should, yet it hadn't been enough to keep the gossips from speculating.

"I know you did. But the fact is that others perceive you're spending too much time with the gentleman. It only takes one person's speculation and a few whispers—"

"But Mr. Reid and I are in love," Rosalie burst out, her words hardly understandable between her sniffles and sobs. "Not seeing him will . . . it will break my heart."

"Rosalie," Lillian said. "It is not forever. Soon enough, you will both be back in London, and in the meantime, you can write letters—"

"But that is months away, maybe even a year," Rosalie said. "Miss Doyle, you can't do this to me. You don't understand how it feels to be in love. Leaving behind the man I care for . . . I just can't. You can't force me to leave."

"Perhaps if we were to . . . avoid certain company for a few weeks?" Lillian proposed. "Surely speculation would die down if Rosalie were not seen with Mr. Reid as often?"

Eleanor considered. They'd planned to spend at least two more months in Rome. In that time, surely the nosy Englishwomen would either move on with their tour or lose interest in Rosalie's affairs, especially if she were not seen with Mr. Reid. Besides, as she said, Rosalie was obeying the rules. It seemed cruel to punish her based on another person's assumptions.

And as Eleanor thought about it, a much more selfish

motive came into play that she couldn't ignore. She didn't want to leave. Once she left Rome, she would not see Ken again. Signore Romano told her he'd offered Ken a position in Naples, and of course he'd accept it. It was the very thing he'd wished for. He deserved it. She coughed, her throat constricting as tears pushed against the back of her eyes.

She turned to the side, discreetly wiping a tear from her cheek, grateful for the darkness. "I think that is a very reasonable compromise, Lillian," Eleanor said, once she had control of her voice. "Taking some time away from Mr. Reid—"

"This is too cruel," Rosalie sobbed. "We've just found one another, and to be separated . . ." She threw down the handkerchief, balling her fists. "You, neither of you, could possibly know how my heart is breaking."

A very miserable week passed, in which the women paid social calls, visited the Doria Palace Gallery, the Borghese Gardens, and St. Peters. Eleanor enjoyed the outings, and Lillian found content for her sketchbook, but Rosalie was miserable.

"How can I bear this tedium?" Rosalie slumped back into the sofa in the common room of their suite as another evening without an engagement dragged on. "We've refused so many invitations, and I am suffering for it. Why at this very moment, ladies could be flirting with my Mr. Reid at the Wheelers' ball." She sat upright. "Do you think he is dancing with one of them?" She hid her face in her hand and wept.

"I don't think he has had time for flirting," Lillian said, looking up from her sketchbook. She motioned toward the pile of letters on the table by the window. "Not with all the letters he's been writing."

A knock came at the door, and Signora Dellucci entered. "Another letter for you, Miss Blakely," she said, crossing the room and handing an envelope to Rosalie.

Rosalie tore it open and began reading.

"What did I tell you?" Lillian said.

"And a delivery for you as well, Miss Doyle."

Eleanor took the parcel from Signora Dellucci. "*Grazie*," she muttered as she unwrapped it. Inside, she found her notebook. She'd meant to ask Ken about it when she realized she'd left it among his books at the Forum excavation. An envelope poked out of the pages. She unfolded the paper, the racing of her heartbeat attesting to how few letters she'd received from gentlemen in her life.

Miss Eleanor Doyle,

I find myself as of late quite missing the company of my dear friend. As the necessity for our separation is essential for our young charges and does not issue from any desires of our own, I propose an excursion.

I do not wish for you to think my intentions are at all inappropriate, but if it is all the same to you, I'd prefer to keep the destination a secret. I shouldn't want to pass up the opportunity to see your eyes light up in surprise when you realize where we've gone.

If you do not send a message to the contrary, Bodkin and I will be waiting outside your pensione *at midnight, ready to whisk you off on an adventure. I hope that is sufficient time for your young ladies to be safely asleep. We will return well before they wake.*

Yours in anticipation,

Ken

P.S. For this particular adventure, I recommend a coat.

Eleanor stared at the letter, then reread it. She could feel that her cheeks were red and looked up to see if either of the Blakelys noticed. Both were occupied—Lillian with her drawing and Rosalie with her own letter. Neither paid attention to Eleanor's delivery.

Eleanor moved to the window, feeling overly warm. Should she accept? The invitation was rather presumptuous. A clandestine midnight meeting?

But it wouldn't be just the pair of them. Bodkin would be there. A third party kept the outing from being improper.

She tapped her fingers on the windowsill, excitement making her nerves tingle. She looked back at the letter. Ken had missed her, and he'd arranged . . . something. Where could he possibly take her that she'd need a coat?

"I am so tired," Rosalie said abruptly. She stood, letter in hand. "I think I shall go to sleep."

"So early?" Lillian asked. "Surely you can't be ready to sleep. The hour is not yet nine."

Rosalie's face shone. She dabbed her forehead with a handkerchief, looking toward the clock, then toward her bedchamber. "Yes, well, I've nothing else to do this evening." She gave a peculiar smile. "Well, then. Good night."

"How odd," Lillian said once her sister's door was closed.

"She may wish to read her letters in private," Eleanor reasoned. "Or perhaps she really is tired. The heat was quite oppressive today. I feel rather worn out myself."

"Yes, that must be it," Lillian said.

Three hours later, Eleanor stood at the same window, anticipation making her stomach fluttery. The *pensione* was in a relatively quiet area of the city; but even at this hour, a carriage wasn't unusual. Two conveyances had passed before one finally stopped and Ken stepped out.

He looked up and waved. The light of a gas lamp revealed a large smile.

Eleanor waved in return and crept down the stairs. She slipped out through the *pensione* door, closing it quietly behind her. She'd never done anything secretive in her entire life, and she was shaking, both from excitement and nervousness.

Ken took her hand, helping her inside the carriage.

"Delighted to see you, my dear." Bodkin sat on the seat across from her. He inclined his head and reached across the space to squeeze her hand.

"I'm so glad you came." Ken climbed inside and took the seat beside her. "And you brought your coat." He tapped the ceiling, and the carriage started off.

Eleanor folded the coat on her lap. "Are we going to the Alpine Mountains? I didn't realize we could make the journey there and back so quickly."

"Antarctica." Ken kept his face serious, though he couldn't prevent his eyes from sparkling.

"Ah," Eleanor said. "I should have known."

"It's been too long," Bodkin said. "I've missed you, Miss Doyle."

She smiled. "I've missed you as well, sir." Her eyes darted to Ken and away quickly. "Both of you."

Ken peered out the window, then pulled the curtains closed. He leaned across her to repeat the action on the other side, leaving the interior in darkness. "I hope you don't mind," he said. "I really do want to give you a surprise."

"You were able to get away, I see," Bodkin said.

Ken's knee bumped against hers.

"Yes, Rosalie went to sleep early, and Lillian not long after. A fortunate occurrence if ever there was one."

"Luck shines on our little venture," Bodkin said. Eleanor could hear the smile in his voice.

"I suppose even young people wear out eventually," Ken said. "My charges are even now attending a ball with Mrs. Daines."

"Oh yes, the Wheelers' ball. The Blakelys were quite sad to decline that invitation."

"I can believe it." Ken's voice sounded compassionate. "The villa is reputed to be one of the finest in Rome."

The ride lasted nearly twenty minutes in Eleanor's estimation. For the life of her, she couldn't think of where they might be going. But, even though she tried to keep track of the turns the carriage made, she was distracted by the proximity of Ken. Something about the darkness made her very aware of him. She could hear his breathing and feel the heat where his arm touched her shoulder.

The carriage drew to a stop, and Ken peeked through the curtains. "Are you ready?"

Eleanor nodded, though he couldn't see her. "I'm ready."

Ken opened the door and exited the carriage, holding her hand as she stepped out behind him. Bodkin followed.

She looked around, recognizing where they were immediately. Even in the dark, the shadow of the Colosseum was unmistakable. "Are we going to check on the progress of the Temple of Caesar?"

Ken smiled mischievously. His eyebrows bounced, but he didn't answer. He took her hand and walked up a hill in the other direction—away from the Forum. The *Basilica di San Clemente*? Baths of Titus? For the life of her, Eleanor couldn't figure out where Ken was leading her.

They stepped from the paving stones and onto the grass

of a park. Ahead, a grouping of lights shone, figures moving among them.

"*Buonasera*," Bodkin called.

The shadows waved in greeting. It appeared the people were expecting them. But why? And what were they doing here in the middle of the park?

"Miss Doyle, a pleasure to see you again." Eleanor recognized Signore Celino as they drew closer and he was no longer merely a shadow.

"Nice to see you as well, Signore Celino."

The guide bowed. "And Professor Kendrick. Come, the entrance is this way." He led them toward the lights, and after a moment, they were no longer walking on grass, but stone blocks covered with plants. The lights were clustered around a hole in the brick floor. And Eleanor knew precisely where they were—not a floor, but a ceiling.

"Domus Aurea," she breathed. Nero's Golden Palace. She clasped her hands together and turned toward Ken. "But the entrance is restricted."

He was grinning. "Restricted, yes, but not forbidden. Nothing is forbidden when your friend is Alastair Bodkin."

"Can we go inside?"

He nodded.

Eleanor was breathless. She couldn't keep her own grin from growing. "Oh, Ken. What a marvelous surprise!"

He watched her, his smile softening, then he tipped his head toward the entrance. "Shall we, then?"

They peered down into the hole. Lanterns were placed on the ground below, lighting up the interior of the vaulted underground space. A ladder of ropes with boards fastened between them hung downward.

"I'll descend first," Ken said. "I'll hold the ladder steady from beneath, so—"

"So if I fall, I'll squash you."

Bodkin laughed. "And then I'll fall and squash both of you."

Ken climbed onto the ladder, then called out when he reached the bottom.

Eleanor put on her coat, and Bodkin held her arm as she twisted around and moved backward to the opening. She held her skirts to the side, settling her boot onto the first board, the heel keeping her foot from slipping off. She started downward. The temperature dropped as she neared the floor. After only a few moments, she felt Ken's hand on her back and, with his help, stepped down the last few steps.

Ken held the ropes as Bodkin descended, and Eleanor stepped out of the way—even though he'd been joking, she didn't fancy being squashed by the round man—and looked around her in wonder. She stood in a domed room of brick and concrete with passages leading from it in various directions. Rubble covered the floors, and on the walls, between trailing vines and patches of decay, colorful frescoes, pictures of scenery, animals, and people were still visible.

Eleanor knew about the Domus Aurea from her readings, but she'd never imagined she'd actually be allowed inside.

In its time, Nero's Golden Palace had sprawled over an enormous portion of Rome. The extravagance of the palace was unequaled, and an embarrassment to later rulers, who stripped it of its finery and closed it up, constructing instead buildings for the people, such as the Baths of Caracalla and the Colosseum.

The palace was believed to have been lost until a young man in the fifteenth century fell into a hole on a hillside and found himself in a cave surrounded by vibrant mosaics.

Ken brought a lantern, holding it high so she could see the paintings on the domed ceiling. Most of the images were difficult to recognize with their missing pieces, but the colors were there—paint that had remained in place for nearly two millennia. He offered his arm. "Shall we?"

Eleanor nodded, utterly awestruck. Most of the exits were blocked, some completely collapsed, but Ken led them confidently forward toward a clear doorway. They followed a passageway and entered a wide room with high ceilings. The paintings on the walls were divided into irregular sections, and inside each was the image of a person. Men and women wearing robes, some with laurel-leaf crowns, looked into the room, as if peering through individual windows. Ken lifted the lantern, and by its glow, they studied the Roman faces.

"Seems like a friendly sort of chap," Bodkin said, holding his lantern near a painting of a man in a gold colored robe who held a glass of wine. "Someone you could have a drink with."

"I can't believe this," Eleanor said. She kept her voice low, but it still echoed through the chamber. "All these images, so perfectly preserved."

"Only a few of the rooms have been excavated, and we can only guess what treasures must be contained here, buried for so long. The emperor's decadence made this palace a marvel of architecture and artistic achievement." Ken's voice echoed through the chamber, the natural storyteller emerging.

"Imagine coming as a guest to Nero's Pleasure Palace," he said, leading them to another room. The walls in this chamber contained openings where statues must have once stood.

"I don't think Nero invited teachers to his parties," Eleanor pointed out.

"Probably right," Ken said. "We would not be part of his inner circle." He straightened his arm, releasing her hold on his elbow, then swept up her hand in his, leading her through another passageway. The action was so natural, yet it sent a thrill through her.

Ken continued as if nothing unusual had happened. "But pretend, for a moment, that you're a Roman citizen with an invitation to the Golden House. To arrive, you'd cross a man-made lake, which historians reported to be more like a sea, then climb the marble steps and cross between mighty pillars. You would pass through a courtyard displaying a colossal statue of the emperor—over one hundred and twenty feet high—then make your way through the three hundred rooms, each more spectacular than the last, with walls covered in rich paintings and intricate mosaics of ivory and gold inlaid with jewels. You'd enjoy lush gardens filled with statuary, waterfalls, fountains, and zoos with exotic animals. If you were hungry, you could feast in halls laden with table after table of delicacies. Perhaps you might stop for a time and watch a dramatic performance or a troupe of dancers or bathe in the enormous bath complex. You may choose to visit the marketplace. If you were one for art, you'd admire masterpieces and sculpture from Greece and Asia Minor in the galleries."

Ken pulled on her hand, leading her into the next room and held up the lantern to reveal a spacious round chamber. "Then, at last, you'd arrive at the emperor's main banquet hall."

Bodkin stepped in behind them, his lantern giving further light to the vast space.

Ken lifted his chin, pointing upward. "The ceiling of this room revolved slowly, day and night, in time with the sky. Panels could slide back to shower guests with flower petals, and hidden sprinklers would spray perfume."

"Unbelievable," Eleanor said. She looked around the room and tried to imagine the crumpled rocks and vines were gone, and instead it was filled with tables, music, and ancient Romans. "It must have been . . ." No words could convey her amazement at this place.

"Certainly knew how to throw a party, didn't he?" Bodkin said.

Ken showed them a large, brick-covered cylinder in the passageway beside the room. The massive construction extended from the floor to the ceiling. "This is believed to contain the device used to rotate the ceiling," he said. "But the place is still too fragile to break it open and see."

"Don't want the roof caving in on them, eh?" Bodkin said, peering up at the structure.

"There's something else you'll want to see," Ken said, squeezing her hand. "This way. I saved the best for last."

They walked back through the banquet hall and down the passageway to the window room, then took a different doorway.

"The access is not fully cleared," Ken said, leading her around a partially collapsed doorframe. A breeze blew in from above, indicating another opening to the outside nearby. They continued around piles of rocks and, at times, climbed over or ducked beneath when the passage became too small. "It's just ahead," Ken said.

They emerged into a large room, mosaics forming geometric shapes around the top of the wall near the ceiling. Here and there, tiles were missing, but the work was mostly intact. They studied the pattern for a moment, then Ken took her to the side of the chamber, lifting the lantern to reveal a smooth, white wall.

When she looked closer, she could see names—hundreds of them—had been carved into the plaster. "Oh, people shouldn't have . . ." she began, but stopped. "Does that say Raphael Sanzio?"

"It certainly does," Ken said. He pointed to another spot on the wall. "And here, Michelangelo Buonarroti signed his name as well. Artists and historians alike crawled in here throughout the centuries, studying the remains of the palace, especially the extraordinary paintings, then left evidence that they'd come." He showed her other names: Lord Byron, Cassanova, and the Marquis de Sade.

Eleanor thought the graffiti was almost as interesting as the palace. Some of the people had left dates beside their names, some carved images.

Ken handed her the lantern and pulled a small knife from his pocket. "What do you think? Should we add our names?"

"Oh, I don't—"

He didn't wait for her approval but set to work. After a few moments, he'd made a small E.D. & R.K directly beneath a painting of a flowering tree. A giggle bubbled up from inside, and Eleanor couldn't keep it from bursting out.

"What's so amusing?" Ken asked.

She shook her head, blushing. "Nothing."

He watched her for a moment, brows raised, waiting.

She pointed toward the letters. "It just seems adolescent—like something a starry-eyed youth would do."

Ken squinted, then turned back to carve a heart around the initials. Eleanor's eyes went wide, and her breath caught. The action was so silly, and yet its implications . . .

"Displays of affection aren't reserved for the young." Ken traced the heart with his finger. "Nor are the sentiments that inspire them."

His words sent a delicious shiver over her.

"Are you cold?" Ken slipped the knife back into his coat and moved closer, rubbing her arms up and down. "I should have brought you a scarf."

Bodkin had discreetly disappeared, and when she noticed

it, Eleanor blushed again. "It's not too cold." Feeling brave, she laid her cheek on his chest.

His arms went around her, pulling her against him.

"Tonight was more wonderful than I could have imagined," Eleanor said. "Thank you."

"I like surprising you. And your reaction didn't disappoint."

Ken stepped back but didn't release her. He crooked a finger beneath her chin, tipping her face up. The shadows from the lantern played over the planes of his face and shined in his eyes. "I'm glad you came to Rome, Miss Eleanor Doyle. More than I can say."

Eleanor's knees felt like pudding, and her heart fluttered. "As am I."

8

Ken held Eleanor's hand in the carriage, pleased that she leaned comfortably against him as they rode back to her *pensione*. They'd taken a different route home, delivering Bodkin to his apartments directly after leaving the Domus Aurea.

Bodkin had complained of a headache, but Ken thought his friend was just using the excuse to provide them with some time alone together.

The excursion had turned out even better than he'd hoped. Eleanor had been—Ken's heart warmed as he remembered the delight in her eyes when she realized their destination—Eleanor had been perfect.

The carriage stopped, and the two exited, stopping outside the *pensione* door.

She turned toward him, smoothing the coat over her arm. "Thank you again, Ken. Tonight was magical."

In the light of a streetlamp, he saw her cheeks redden. He lifted her hand, pressing a kiss on her gloved knuckles. "I wholeheartedly agree."

"I shall be sad when the time comes to bid farewell to Italy," Eleanor said. This last month . . ." She raised her gaze to his but then looked away quickly. "I have enjoyed it more than I can say."

Ken's chest felt light. "Then let's do it again. Find another night when the young people are—"

The door flew open. Lillian stood in her dressing gown, her eyes wide. "There you are, Miss Doyle." She looked past them toward the street. "And where is Rosalie?"

Eleanor stepped away from Ken. "What do you mean? She is in her bed."

Her voice trailed off as Lillian shook her head. "She isn't. I couldn't sleep, so I crept into her room to find the book she'd told me about." Lillian glanced at Ken, then pulled her robe tighter. "She's not there."

"Impossible." Eleanor rushed through the door and up the stairs, Lillian directly behind. His stomach sinking, Ken followed. Eleanor hurried through a doorway into what Ken assumed was Rosalie's bedchamber.

"Pardon my manners, Professor Kendrick," Lillian said. "I am a bit rattled tonight." She dipped in a curtsy.

"Think nothing of it." Ken didn't know what else to do, so he started lighting the gas lamps in the sitting room.

A moment later, Eleanor emerged from the bedchamber, a creased paper in her hand. "She's gone to the Wheelers' ball with Mr. Reid." Her voice wasn't panicked or angry, but the resignation in her flat tone was worse than either. Her shoulders were slumped and her eyes unfocused. She looked utterly devastated.

Ken jumped into action. He must make this right. "I'll fetch her."

"I'll go with you." Eleanor followed him toward the stairway.

He stopped, taking her by the arms. He wanted to pull her into an embrace, but he didn't think she'd appreciate it, not under these circumstances and in front of Lillian. "No." He spoke gently, tilting his head to catch her eye. "You need to stay here. She may return while I'm gone."

She shook her head, opening her mouth to answer, but he put an arm around her, leading her back to the sofa. "While I think you look fetching this evening, you aren't dressed for a ball. If you were to storm into the Wheelers' villa demanding to see Rosalie . . ." He eased her down to sit. "Well, I know you are hoping for discretion."

"You're right, of course," Eleanor said in the same flat voice.

"Perhaps some tea," Ken said to Lillian, motioning toward Eleanor. "I'll return within the hour."

Twenty minutes later, Ken entered the party. He knew his clothing wasn't suitable for the formal affair, but he was pleased to find his recent fame allowed others to forgive what they considered his eccentricities. Being dusty only contributed to the image, as did the fact that he didn't stop for small talk.

The villa was indeed marvelous, but he had no time to admire it. He scanned the ballroom and then, not seeing them, broadened his search. Eventually, he found Harlan on an outside balcony with Rosalie, Adrian, and his aunt, Mrs. Daines.

Rosalie's eyes widened when she saw him. She grasped Harlan's arm and looked like she was considering whether to run or hide.

"Ken, what . . . ?" Harlan said, looking pointedly at his dirty clothing.

"Good evening, Madam." Ken tipped his hat to a surprised Mrs. Daines, then turned to the young people. "I've just left two very worried women at Miss Blakely's *pensione*."

"But they were supposed to be asleep," Rosalie said, as if that excused her deception.

"Yes, well, they are not. Come along, Miss Blakely, and you as well, Harlan. The two of you have some explaining to do." He held out a hand toward the doorway. "And I think both Miss Doyle and Miss Blakely are owed an apology."

"Miss Doyle will be so angry with me." Rosalie pressed her fingers against her lips, then spoke through them, her forehead wrinkling. "Was she angry?"

"I'm afraid she was."

"Harlan, what is this?" Mrs. Daines asked. "You didn't tell Rosalie's companions that she was accompanying you tonight?"

"She wouldn't allow me to come," Rosalie said softly.

Adrian winced, his knowledge of the deception apparent in his guilty expression.

Harlan rubbed his eyes. "Ken, I assure you, we've not been improper. My aunt has remained with us, acting as chaperone the entire evening, and my intentions toward Miss Blakely are entirely honorable." He put an arm around Rosalie's waist.

Ken nodded, feeling suddenly tired. "You'll need to explain that to her sister and Miss Doyle, not to me. Come along. And try not to attract attention."

The carriage ride was silent. Rosalie wept quietly, and Harlan held her hand. The young man looked miserable, and Ken felt angry at their carelessness and sorry for both of them, but neither emotion accounted for the heaviness pressing down on his shoulders.

Eleanor would blame herself for Rosalie's misconduct, and she may decide to take the girls from Rome once and for all. The thought struck him hard, making his gut ache. He'd known, of course, that eventually they'd part ways and continue on their tours, but he'd not allowed himself to fully consider how it would be to bid Eleanor farewell. The ache inside him grew until it felt like a ball of lead, and he couldn't help but compare this carriage ride to the one along these very roads only an hour earlier. How completely things could change.

When Ken, Harlan, and Rosalie entered the sitting room, Eleanor and Lillian rose from the sofa. Lillian hurried forward to embraced Rosalie. "I was so worried about you."

"I'm sorry for leaving," Rosalie said, not looking sorry in the least. "I simply couldn't miss another party. And Harlan—I mean Mr. Reid—offered to take me."

"You shouldn't have stolen away," Eleanor said. Her jaw and shoulders were tight. "It was very wrong of you." She directed her gaze to Harlan. "Of both of you."

Harlan crossed the room toward her. "Miss Doyle, I take full blame. I didn't think through the consequences of my actions. I did not intend Miss Blakely any harm; I just wished to see her. Please accept my apology. All of you."

Ken felt proud of the young man for owning his responsibility in the situation, but it didn't excuse his erroneous actions.

"The fault was both of ours." Rosalie held up her chin. "Though if you hadn't been so strict, Miss Doyle, this entire thing would have been avoided."

Lillian frowned, the worry she'd felt for her sister replaced by disapproval.

"That's enough, Rosalie," Eleanor said. Her voice wasn't loud, but her tone left no room for argument. "We will discuss this in private in the morning."

The finality in her tone brought worry to the young lady's face. "But Miss Doyle—"

Eleanor shook her head. "Enough." She turned to Harlan, clasping her hands and inclining her head. "Thank you, Mr. Reid, for your apology. Now it is time for all of us to get some sleep."

The men said their farewells and left.

Eleanor followed them outside and closed the door behind her. "Ken? Might I speak with you for a moment?"

Harlan climbed into the carriage, giving them privacy.

Ken took her hands in his. "Eleanor, I'm so sorry."

"This is my fault," she said.

"No, of course it's not. You can't blame yourself for Rosalie's decision. Or Harlan's. The fault is not yours in the least."

Eleanor shook her head. "If I hadn't left tonight . . ." She closed her eyes, drawing a deep breath and letting it out. "I should have taken her away after Mrs. Daines's party, but I didn't . . . because I was selfish. I stayed because I . . ." She looked up at him. Her eyes were tight, as if the confession pained her.

He should have felt elated at what she implied, but the anguish in her expression dampened any pleasure he might have had. Eleanor looked at him expectantly, waiting for him to say something, but he didn't know what.

"I'm glad you stayed," he said finally, squeezing her hands

Eleanor sighed and extracted her hands from his. "Ken, we can't do this again." She took a step back. Reflexively, he reached for her, but she avoided his touch. "I did the very thing I asked Rosalie not to, and it could have cost us everything." She looked over his shoulder, not meeting his gaze as she spoke. "I was so selfish. I lost sight of my responsibility—all because I let myself get swept up in this." She motioned back and forth between them.

"I know," he said. "But—"

"I can't see you again."

Ken felt cold. "Eleanor?"

Her eyes filled with tears, and he reached for her again, but she leaned away. "The girls and I will leave Rome tomorrow." She clasped her fingers together, turning her gaze down. "This must be farewell."

He swallowed, making a decision. He couldn't lose Eleanor, though it meant rejecting Signore Romano's offer. "Perhaps not."

Her gaze rose, and she looked at him with wide, hopeful eyes.

"This will be only a short farewell. I've been offered a position at Oxford. We'll be together in London, and we—"

"No." Her voice lashed out, startling him. "Do not do that, Ken. Do not come to London because of me."

He gaped, unable to understand what she meant. A moment ago, it seemed as if she wished for them to be together. Had he misunderstood her? Were his feelings unreciprocated? "But, Eleanor, I don't . . ."

"Goodbye, Ken." Her tears spilled over, and she rushed inside.

Ken stared at the closed door. What had happened? How had this gone so completely wrong? He clenched his eyes shut and pushed his fist against his chest, willing the pain to lessen. Something inside seemed to be damaged. He turned away, leaving a piece of himself behind as he walked toward the carriage.

As Eleanor made her way back up the stairs, the sound of weeping grew louder, but when she arrived in the sitting room, she was surprised to see it was not Rosalie, but Lillian in tears. The young woman sat on the couch, her face in her hands and her shoulders shaking.

Rosalie stood in the doorway to her bedchamber looking as bewildered as Eleanor felt.

"Lillian," Eleanor crossed the room and sat beside her. "Whatever is the matter?"

"She thinks only of herself," Lillian said through her sobs. She lifted her head and glared at her younger sister. "Your heart isn't the only one broken, Rosalie. Because you were selfish, I shall not see Mr. Curtis again."

Eleanor took Lillian's hand. Dear shy Lillian. "I had no idea." She offered a handkerchief. "You care for Mr. Curtis?"

Lillian nodded and sniffed. "I couldn't . . . " She turned back to her sister. "I've guarded my feelings, as you are apparently unable to. Someone must care for our reputation."

Rosalie glared back at her sister. "Well, you've guarded them so well that Mr. Curtis hasn't the foggiest notion and will move on." She whirled and slammed the door.

A moment later, Lillian's door was slammed in return.

Eleanor did not bother to sleep through what remained of the night. She sorted through her clothing, determining how best to pack their trunks. Keeping herself busy prevented her from breaking down, but she knew it was only a matter of time before she couldn't find anything else to occupy her mind and the tears would come. They were there, waiting, prickling against her eyes, tightening her throat.

As soon as it was morning, she penned a note to the travel agency, requesting accommodation on the afternoon train to Genoa, then passage on the first steamship to London. That should give them time to pack their things. Anything else could be sent on after.

As soon as the messenger left, she sank into the sofa, her head in her hands. Had she done the right thing? She couldn't allow Ken to sacrifice the position in Naples. He would always wonder how it would have been; perhaps he would even grow to resent her. And she cared about him too much to allow him to give up his dream.

She wished she hadn't had to be cruel to do it. But if she'd acted at all as if it was a possibility, he'd have done it without a second thought. That's the type of man Ken was. Selfless, giving. That's why she loved him.

The thought carried a wave of pain, and Eleanor gasped, pressing her hand to her mouth. But she was unable to stop the torrent of tears.

A knock sounded, followed by footsteps on the stairs. Signora Dellucci entered the room. "Pardon me, miss, but I didn't know if you were taking visitors so early."

Bodkin stepped in behind her. "I hoped to catch you before—" He broke off, hurrying toward Eleanor. "But, Miss Doyle, what is the matter?"

Eleanor shook her head. "I'm sorry." Her words came out in gasps.

Bodkin sat on the sofa. He offered a handkerchief and patted her hand. "No need to apologize, my dear. Are you unwell? What can I do?" He looked toward the doorway. "*Pronto, signora*, please fetch Miss Doyle some tea."

Eleanor shook her head, willing herself, unsuccessfully, to get ahold of her emotions. "I'm sorry," she said again. "I am not ill." Her chin trembled, and she squeezed her eyes shut. "My heart aches." She felt immediately vulnerable at revealing something so personal, but she was exhausted, and her defenses had crumpled.

"There, there. You are sad to leave Rome."

"Ken." She drew in a shaky breath. "I am in love with him, you see."

"Of course you are, my dear. I hope you didn't think you were doing a good job of concealing it." His voice carried equal amounts of compassion and humor, which, surprisingly, helped calm her. "Leaving behind one's beloved is always painful."

She wiped the handkerchief beneath her eyes, her breathing still uneven. "He offered to come to London and take a position at Oxford to be near me, but I refused. I told him not to come."

"Oxford isn't a bad arrangement," Bodkin said. "Don't you wish to be together?"

"You saw him at the Forum site. He loves this, being part of the discovery, instead of just teaching about it. The position in Naples is what he wants. I can't ask him to turn it down."

Bodkin studied her for a moment. "Would you?"

"Would I what?" she asked.

"Would you turn down the position at the Royal Holloway College to stay here with Ken?"

"I would. In a heartbeat." She looked down at the handkerchief in her lap. "But he didn't ask me."

Bodkin leaned back. He nodded, scratching his cheek. "I see. You're both so concerned for the other's happiness that you're unwilling to accept a sacrifice on either side to be together, is that it?"

When he put it that way, it did sound rather simple.

"I suppose you're right," she said.

The tea was delivered, and Eleanor poured each of them a cup.

"I can't say I blame you for your sorrow," Bodkin said, taking the offered tea. "Men like Russell Kendrick are few and far between. Unfortunately, not many of my gender would tolerate a woman of your intellect. Most would be intimidated or disturbed by it, but not Ken. He boasts of your abilities to anyone who will listen. It's true." Bodkin gave a fond smile. "Did you know he showed your writing notebook to Signore Romano at Mrs. Daines's party?"

Eleanor's throat tightened, forcing more tears free, but she didn't bother to wipe them away. She stared at Bodkin. "He did? Why would he do that?"

He smiled, shrugged, and set his cup onto the low table in front of them. "He's a good man, Miss Doyle."

She nodded. "I wish I could change all this, that I knew what to do." She let out a sigh. "But it seems impossible."

"Difficult, yes. But not impossible." He shifted, knitting his fingers together over his belly. "Love is not easy, Miss Doyle. In the real world, love stories are not tidily wrapped up like they are in novels or fairy tales. Things don't work out perfectly, feelings are damaged, practical matters must be considered, and sometimes, instead of a fairy godmother bringing glass slippers, a balding man brings a letter." He slipped an envelope from inside his jacket, holding it toward her.

"What is this?"

He gave a knowing smile, nodding toward it. "I suggest you read it."

Eleanor opened the envelope and began to read. Her heart pounded in her ears. The letter was from Giuseppe Fiorelli of the University of Naples. "He writes to offer me a position at Pompeii," she whispered. "As a translator."

Bodkin grinned, clapping his hands together. "I must say I'm pleased as could be. Signore Romano had some concerns that a woman would weaken the program's credibility, but I told him that was nonsense. You are the most intelligent woman I've ever known." He held up a finger and winked. "Though if my wife should ask, I'll deny I ever made that statement."

"They want me at Pompeii. I can't believe it."

Eleanor read the letter again, unable to accept it as truth. This would fix everything. She and Ken could be together, each working in the post they'd dreamed of. But . . . "I don't know what to say to Ken," she admitted. "I rejected him—rather rudely. What if he's made up his mind against me?" She could hardly tell Ken that because circumstances had turned in her favor, she'd changed her mind about him, about *them*. That he would be insulted was an understatement.

Bodkin set down his tea and stood. "There, I cannot help you, my dear. Like I said, you're intelligent. You'll think of what to say. Personally, I recommend honesty—even though it is usually uncomfortable, and of course it is difficult to make oneself vulnerable." He took her hand as she rose, placing his other atop it. "If Ken truly cares for you as we hope, he'll understand."

Eleanor threw her arms around the man, feeling him chuckle as he patted her back. "Thank you, Bodkin."

Rosalie wept throughout the entire carriage ride. "It is all too cruel," she said.

Lillian fixed her sister with a flat stare. "I think Miss Doyle is being very kind—giving us a chance to say goodbye."

"But what will I do without my beloved Harlan?" Rosalie wailed.

Lillian turned to look out the window.

Once the carriage stopped, Eleanor left the girls in the shade and walked toward the fountain, just as she'd done a month earlier. Though, this time, her feelings were quite different. Anxiety made her stomach roil, and she clenched her hands to keep from fidgeting.

She stopped beside the fountain pool in the very same place where she'd spoken to Ken for the first time, staring at the sculptures and praying she would know what to say. And that Ken would understand.

She heard a carriage enter the piazza and turned, watching with a pounding heart as Mr. Darrington, Mr. Curtis, and Mr. Reid exited.

Rosalie ran directly to Harlan, throwing herself into his arms. Eleanor found herself envious of the girl's abandon. Rosalie was irresponsible and silly, but she didn't hide her feelings. Eleanor sighed. How had her own relationship become so complicated?

Mr. Curtis joined Lillian, offering his arm so the pair could stroll.

Ken stepped from the carriage and greeted the young

ladies. He turned toward the fountain and hesitated before starting toward Eleanor. His face was unreadable beneath the shade of his hat brim. Her shaking increased.

When he arrived, he inclined his head and clasped his hands behind his back. "Miss Doyle." His tone was polite and his expression guarded.

Eleanor was in danger of losing her breakfast. "Thank you for coming."

Ken raised his brows, waiting.

She opened her hand, revealing a coin in her palm. "I wanted you to be here when I tossed my second coin into the fountain," she said.

Ken didn't answer.

She threw the coin, hearing its plop as it hit the water, hoping the gesture would soften his heart toward her.

Ken remained silent, and Eleanor's stomach grew sicker. The demonstration hadn't had the effect she'd hoped for.

She drew a shaky breath. "Ken, I lied to you. I told you not to come to Oxford because I couldn't bear for you to sacrifice the opportunity in Naples." His face was impassive, but at least he was listening, so she continued. "Signore Romano told me about it at Mrs. Daines's party, and I knew it was the perfect thing for you. I—"

"Perhaps I might decide what is the perfect thing for me." His words were soft, but she felt the reprimand. "Eleanor, Oxford is an excellent prospect as well. And you would be there, working at a position you've aspired to. In my mind, *that* is the perfect thing for me."

She closed her eyes and drew a breath, then pushed out the words before she changed her mind. "Ken, ask me to stay in Italy."

"I can't expect you to sacrifice your position in London . . ."

"Please." She lowered her voice nearly to a whisper. "Ask me to stay. " Heat flooded her cheeks at the boldness of the request, but there was no turning back now. "You said you wanted to be with me, so ask me." She waited for his response, feeling completely exposed. What if he rejected her?

He squinted, studying her for a long moment. Her hopes dwindled. Her brashness had ruined everything.

Finally, Ken reached for her hand. "Eleanor Doyle, will you stay with me in Italy?"

She let out a shaky breath and collapsed into his arms. "Yes." Every bit of her was trembling. "Thank you," she whispered.

Ken's arms tightened around her, and her tension left in a shuddering exhalation.

He pulled back, slipping a hand beneath her ear to cup the back of her neck. His gaze held hers as he leaned forward. He spoke her name in a deep, breathy voice against her lips. "Eleanor."

She closed the space, heat filling all her empty places as his lips moved against hers. When she pulled away, she rested her hands on his chest lapels, her mind reeling. His eyes were dark, a fire burning inside them she never would have imagined the mild-mannered teacher possessed. The sight stole her breath, but she forced herself to focus. She grasped the remaining bit of her courage and plunged onward. "Ken, there is something else I need to tell you."

"Could it wait?" He leaned forward again, but she touched his lips, stopping him.

She shook her head and took the letter from her reticule.

Ken read it, the line between his brows deepening. He lowered the letter slowly. "You . . . you already intended to stay?"

"If you'd asked, I would have remained with or without

Signore Fiorelli's offer." She examined his face, willing him to understand. "I just needed to know you wanted me," she finished in a soft voice.

A smile pulled at the corners of Ken's mouth. He cupped her cheeks, his face inches from hers. "There is nothing I want more. *Nothing.* Not Pompeii or Caesar's Temple or any of it. I want you, Eleanor Doyle. And I'd gladly have taken the position at Oxford without a second thought."

"I know, but . . ."

His hands slipped down to her shoulders. "But what, my darling?"

"But this is where we belong. This is where I fell in love with you and—"

Ken's mouth closed over hers, stopping her words and leaving no doubt that he wholeheartedly agreed.

Epilogue

Ken stepped carefully along the edge of the mosaic floor as he led Bodkin through the newly excavated structure. He was pleased his friend had joined him and Eleanor on the return journey to Italy after attending the Blakely sisters' double wedding. "The latest work is taking place in this section of the city," he said.

"Fascinating." Bodkin slowed in the courtyard, admiring the detailed carving of the fountain. "Everywhere I turn, mosaics, perfectly preserved frescoes, intricate sculpture. Pompeii is truly a marvel."

"It is," Ken said, feeling an immense surge of pride at the work being done. "Signore Fiorelli has made vast improvements to the excavation procedures. He's arranged the site into grids, keeping detailed records of where objects, human remains, and artwork are found. He's also opted to keep works of art in their original locations instead of removing them to the museum, but in order to do so, engineers must make certain the walls are structurally sound." Ken spoke as they walked up a flight of stairs and crossed a house's upper story.

They reached the group of workers, and Bodkin leaned closer to watch as ash was carefully brushed from a wall beside a recently unearthed entrance. The portico above the doorway was supported by Doric columns, Ken noticed. The style would help in dating the building.

"What have you found, Piero?" he asked, studying the foreman's ledger. He was pleased to see columns were noted and categorized correctly.

"The outer wall is nearly clear, Professor. And we discovered more graffiti."

"Graffiti?" Bodkin asked. "Like in Nero's palace?"

The workers smiled, sharing looks. Once they were translated, the messages had been a source of entertainment for the personnel.

"The site is covered in it," Ken told his friend. "The citizens of Pompeii loved writing notes on walls. Some are simply greetings or names, but we've found others to be more . . . ah . . . well, let's just say our translator blushes often."

Bodkin laughed. "People haven't changed so very much in two thousand years, have they?" He followed Piero's direction and peered at the writing scratched on the wall beside the doorway. "Well? What does it say?"

Ken looked at it for a moment. The lettering was uneven, and most likely words were spelled incorrectly. He knew better than to even attempt to decipher it. "We should send for the expert."

"I will fetch Signora Kendrick," Piero said.

"She is working at the amphitheater, I think," Ken told him.

The foreman nodded, hurrying away. A few moments later, he returned with Eleanor. She wore a practical dress, the skirts covered in dust, and heavy boots for climbing over rocks. Tendrils of hair had come loose, hanging in wisps around her face, and in spite of her wide-brimmed hat, her nose was freckled from the sun. She was beautiful. Even though they encountered one another often during the day, Ken's heart still skipped when he saw her.

"More graffiti?" she asked, slipping her hand into Ken's.

Piero pointed to the wall.

"I do hope it's scandalous," Bodkin teased.

Eleanor bent closer. She squinted, her lips pursed in concentration. Ken thought she looked adorable when she was working.

"Oh, well, look at this," she muttered. "It's a love note."

"Excellent," Bodkin said, rubbing his hands together.

She studied it a moment longer, then pointed at the words as she read: "Secundus says hello to Prima, wherever she is." Eleanor said. "Then below, 'I ask, my lady, that you love me.'" She looked up. "It is so tender."

Ken slid his arm around her waist, pulling her close beneath his shoulder. "I suppose Secundus just wants what every man wants."

"Oh no, not again." Bodkin groaned good-naturedly.

Ken ignored his friend and leaned close to her ear. "I ask, my lady, that you love me."

"I will, always," Eleanor whispered.

Jennifer Moore is a passionate reader and writer of all things romance due to the need to balance the rest of her world that includes a perpetually traveling husband and four active sons, who create heaps of laundry that is anything but romantic. She suffers from an unhealthy addiction to 18th- and 19th- century military history and literature. Jennifer has a B.A. in linguistics from the University of Utah and is a Guitar Hero champion. She lives in northern Utah with her family, but most of the time wishes she was on board a frigate during the Age of Sail.

You can learn more about her at: AuthorJMoore.com

A Secret Arrangement

-Heather B. Moore-

England, 1855

Evelyn Cleopatra Tucker knew her last day at Mrs. Paddock's Finishing School for Young Ladies would be the worst day of her life. Therefore, when that day arrived, Evelyn refused to get out of bed. At least, for all of five minutes past the breakfast bell, since Evelyn's best friend Beatrice came to fetch her.

"Evelyn," Beatrice said the moment she opened the bedroom door and discovered Evelyn buried beneath her covers. Never mind that Evelyn's trunks had been packed for two days and her certificate of completion had been framed by Mrs. Paddock. It now sat atop the smallest of Evelyn's trunks.

"I'm not here," Evelyn said, her voice muffled through the blankets. She was grateful for her best friend, but Beatrice never missed a thing—which in this case meant that she'd noticed Evelyn's absence at breakfast.

The edge of her bed creaked as Beatrice sat next to Evelyn.

"You've got to remember our plan, all right?" Beatrice continued as if they were standing out in the open and Evelyn weren't buried beneath a mound of bedding. "We're to get married to London men so we might live in the same city. We'll raise our babies as best friends, meet at the park on Saturdays, and go out for ice cream on Sundays."

"What about Mondays through Fridays?" Evelyn mumbled.

Beatrice laughed. Her laugh was bright and cheerful and always warmed Evelyn's heart. Everything about Beatrice was bright, from her blonde hair, to her fair skin, to her sea-blue eyes. Evelyn was the complete opposite. In fact, when she told Beatrice that her middle name was Cleo, Beatrice insisted that she looked like Cleopatra—the *seventh*—because apparently there were quite a few, and Cleopatra VII was *the* Cleopatra.

Thus, Evelyn took it upon herself to give her middle name a bit of an embellishment, and she became Evelyn Cleopatra. She signed all her essays and artwork this way. Mrs. Paddock had not found this amusing.

Fortunately, Evelyn would not have to worry about Mrs. Paddock's disapprovals or approvals any longer. Unfortunately, Evelyn would be forced to say goodbye to her best friend, and really, *only* friend, this afternoon when Evelyn's aunt came to fetch her.

This thought caused Evelyn to sigh deep in her chest.

"There you are!" Beatrice pronounced, whipping the blankets off Evelyn in a sudden movement.

The change in air temperature startled Evelyn, and she gasped.

Beatrice laughed. "You look like you've just risen from a sarcophagus."

"Really?" Evelyn sat up, touching the mess that her dark hair had become. Her friend knew Evelyn couldn't resist comparisons to the ancient Egyptians. Ever since Beatrice had pronounced the name of Cleopatra upon Evelyn, she'd become very interested in Egyptian history. Beatrice teased that it had become an obsession, but Evelyn had full control over how much she read, wrote, and pondered about the Egyptian dynasties.

Besides, she was about to relegate herself to a lifetime of living in her aunt's dusty house.

"Now, get ready before Mrs. Paddock comes in here herself." Beatrice grasped Evelyn's hand and tugged her to the edge of the bed.

Evelyn shuddered at the thought. Mrs. Paddock's tiny beady eyes missed nothing, and she could smell any scent miles and miles away. If she came into Evelyn's room, Mrs. Paddock would be able to detect the incense that Evelyn had burned last night while she practiced her hieroglyphics.

Evelyn could hear Mrs. Paddock's censure now: "No young lady of mine will study the incestuous horrors of the Egyptians."

After today, Evelyn would never have to fear Mrs. Paddock's preachments.

"What are you smiling about?" Beatrice asked, nudging her.

Evelyn looked over at her friend. "I was just thinking that I'll never have to worry about Mrs. Paddock again. If you want, I can hide you in one of my trunks and get you out of here too."

"Oh, Evelyn," Beatrice gushed, throwing her arms about Evelyn's neck and pulling her into a fierce embrace. "I'm going to miss you so much. I don't know how I'll survive my final year without you. You must write to me every day!"

Evelyn hugged her friend back, and tears pricked her eyes. "I'll write you *twice* a day."

Beatrice laughed, and Evelyn laughed too, although the ache in her heart had doubled its strength.

"Remember," Beatrice continued, "don't let your aunt buy you any more gray dresses. Your best colors are burgundy red and emerald green."

"I'll try." Evelyn gave Beatrice a final squeeze before letting her go.

The next hours sped by, and Evelyn found that she couldn't concentrate at all in music class. She'd already received her passing marks, yet the only other option was to take on an extra round of kitchen chores. So Evelyn sat through music instruction and kept stealing glances at Beatrice, knowing it could be a full year before she saw her friend again.

Mrs. Paddock believed in turning out well-rounded Young Ladies. They were taught English grammar, needlework, writing and arithmetic, geography, history, botany, French, drawing, and music. History had been Evelyn's favorite, whereas Beatrice favored music.

All too soon, the afternoon passed, and as tea finished up, Mrs. Paddock bustled into the dining room. Every girl hushed at the headmistress's appearance. They all knew it was for one reason.

Her shoes clacked against the stone floor that had never given off an ounce of warmth. "Miss Tucker," Mrs. Paddock said as she came to stand at the end of the long table. Her tone was stiff and formal, complementing her straight back and lifted chin. "Your aunt's carriage has arrived."

Every pair of eyes turned to Evelyn. "Thank you," she said. Then she looked at Beatrice, who sat on her left. The girl was already tearing up.

"I'll help you take your things down," Beatrice said.

"Your things have already been brought down to the front foyer," Mrs. Paddock announced.

Evelyn could only nod because she didn't trust her own voice. She rose and cleared her tea things, setting the dish and cup and saucer on the dumbwaiter at the far side of the room. Mrs. Paddock watched Evelyn's every movement.

This was all happening too fast—way too fast.

"Thank you," Evelyn managed to say, even though her throat felt swollen. Several girls rushed forward to give her goodbye hugs.

Beatrice stayed stoically by her side, but Evelyn didn't look at her. Seeing her friend cry would only make Evelyn lose her composure.

It wasn't that she loved the boarding school, but Beatrice was dear to her, and the alternative—living with her aunt until Evelyn could marry and have her own household—was not something she was looking forward to.

The last time Evelyn had seen her aunt Margaret was at her uncle's funeral several months ago. Uncle James Tucker had passed away right before Christmastide. The day of the funeral had been gloomy and full of rain. Her aunt had been in complete hysterics during most of the visit. Evelyn had returned to the boarding school feeling even more dismal about her future. She hadn't even gone back to her relatives' place for the Christmas holiday.

Although Evelyn and Beatrice had plotted and planned, in truth Evelyn had no idea what her future would look like. While Aunt Margaret wore the latest fashions, Evelyn was treated as the poor relation—which of course she was. Everything that Aunt Margaret had suggested to purchase for Evelyn, Uncle James had immediately dismissed.

Evelyn's parents had both died in a train wreck when she

was ten years old. Evelyn had been left home with her tutor when her parents had taken a trip on a new railway line—thus her life had been spared. As a result, she'd been left completely alone, and living on another's charity had always made her feel a nuisance. It wasn't until her friendship with Beatrice started that Evelyn found love and hope in her life.

Finally, with all the goodbyes said and hugs given, Evelyn walked out of the dining hall, Beatrice clinging to her arm. Or was it the other way around? Whatever the case, Evelyn had a flash of clarity as she passed through the portrait hall for what she knew would be the last time. And it would be the last time she passed the headmistress's office, where she'd spent her share of time listening to reprimands and accepting discipline. Regardless, Evelyn somehow felt like she was walking to her doom.

Was this how the French aristocrats felt when they were being led to the guillotine?

Evelyn raised her chin a notch as her eyes burned with tears. It wasn't like she was going to *die,* exactly, just consign herself to the unknown.

Just before they reached the entrance to the front foyer, Beatrice pulled her to a stop.

"I will say my goodbyes here," she whispered.

Evelyn could barely swallow over the swollen lump in her throat. She tried to memorize everything about her friend, from her blonde curls, to her blue eyes, to the rose tinge on her cheeks.

"We'll be together before you know it," Beatrice said, her voice trembling with emotion. "Don't go having too much fun without me. And for heaven's sake, do not fall in love and get married. Promise me! We must attend parties and balls together and make sure the men are from London. I can't bear it if I'm stuck in here for another year while you're out there enjoying yourself too much."

"I promise," Evelyn said. She felt like laughing at Beatrice's oh-so-serious theatrics, but she wanted to cry as well. And she suspected that she hadn't yet felt the full impact of the pain of separation from her best friend. "I'll write to you about everything in such detail you'll feel like you are with me, in my room, staring out at the clouds while I count down the days."

Beatrice shook her head, her smile amused. "You, Evelyn Cleopatra Tucker, are not a daydreamer. That's my department."

Then Evelyn hugged her friend. Quickly and fiercely. Anything more would have brought her to tears. It was time to go. Delaying would only make her more upset.

After a deep breath and a nod to Beatrice, Evelyn turned and strode toward the door.

The Egyptian sun had baked Henry Gaiman's shirt right onto his back. He'd need a chisel to scrape the blasted linen off.

"Care for a warm lemonade, sir?" Percy Smith said, coming to stand by Henry as he surveyed the archaeological dig on the outskirts of Giza. Percy held two glasses in his hands, full of what they both knew was tepid refreshment.

Henry scoffed, but he took the glass anyway. "Is anything cold in Egypt?"

"Mrs. Lillian Worthen is cold," Percy said.

Henry took a long swallow of the tart, warm drink. The lemonade didn't feel refreshing, but he knew he had to keep drinking. He supposed he'd have to wait until they returned to Cairo and try their luck there for a cold drink. "Lillian Worthen is a forty-year-old woman—much too old for you, my friend."

Percy sighed, then took a sip of his own warm drink. "Age doesn't matter when the heart is involved."

Henry turned to look at his friend. They'd been best

friends for five years, having first met at university while involved in the archaeology program. Henry's dream project of excavating in Giza near the pyramids had been funded by benefactress Lillian Worthen soon after his graduation. A year later, Henry had brought in Percy as an assistant when the site near Giza had turned up a tomb dating back to the Nineteenth Dynasty.

Percy's dark, thick hair blew in the wind, and his skin had tanned over the past six months until he looked like a native. Henry knew he appeared much the same—his skin was nearly as tanned as Percy's, although his hair had become blonder with the constant exposure to sun. "If Lillian Worthen wasn't a wealthy widow and our benefactress, would you still be interested?"

"You wound me." Percy placed one hand over his heart. "How can you accuse me of being a fortune hunter?"

Henry laughed. Percy always made him laugh. Mrs. Worthen was not a woman to be trifled with. Having gone through two husbands already, both of whom had died and left their fortunes to her, Mrs. Worthen had more money than any single person Henry had ever been acquainted with.

Mrs. Worthen was a woman who might be beautiful, but there was something calculating about her, something off-putting. She reminded Henry of a cat—watching her prey, ready to pounce at any moment. Pounce on what, exactly, he didn't know. But he didn't have the heart to tell Percy that the woman had been making him uncomfortable lately. In fact, she'd tried to kiss him.

It was quite disconcerting.

The age difference was, of course, something that didn't appeal to Henry, but the way she watched him had begun to raise his hackles. And it didn't help that there were some distasteful rumors surrounding the deaths of her husbands.

She was referred to as the "black widow" by other university students.

Henry had kept his distance, but it seemed that Percy was curious.

"I hope you're not seriously considering pursuing Mrs. Worthen," Henry told Percy after another sip of the lemonade. "Money would never be worth risking your life."

It was Percy's turn to scoff now. "You can't honestly believe she had anything to do with either of her husbands' deaths."

"I don't give credit to rumors, but she's very . . . intimidating," Henry said. Not to mention she had been too aggressive for his taste.

"I think she's just lonely," Percy said.

Henry couldn't stop the groan coming from his lips.

"Look," Percy said, his voice tight. "The women don't fall at my feet like they do yours. I've got to consider an older woman—one who might be widowed. At least I don't have to raise another man's children with Lillian."

Henry raised his brows. "All right, *now* I'm calling you shallow." He drained the last of the lemonade and grimaced. It was beyond tart at the bottom. "I might have an easier time talking to women than you do, but no woman wants a husband who is dependent on grants and benefactors, or a *benefactress* in my case, in order to provide a living." He waved at their bleak surroundings that included miles and miles of sand, dozens of sweaty Egyptian laborers digging in the dirt, a group of makeshift tents that flapped in the constant wind . . . and that was just the beginning. There were the flies, mosquitoes, and scorpions to be considered.

"Women are romantics," Percy declared. "And you . . . you might be poor, but you're charismatic around the ladies.

Only I know that you're flirting; the women take it quite seriously."

If Henry had been still drinking his lemonade, he would have spit it out. "Flirting? Huh. As if that's a talent to be valued in the sweltering heat." Just then, a fly decided to land on Henry's neck. He swatted at it.

Percy waved away another fly. "Perhaps you're right about my interest in our benefactress," he said. "I've had too much sun, making even Lillian Worthen look appealing. The Egyptian desert isn't teeming with English ladies, that's for sure. Have you thought about returning home with me for my sister's wedding? You might enjoy the break. There will be several women of marriageable age who still have stars in their eyes."

"One of us has to be here," Henry said, although it was nice to have an invitation. He had spent a few holidays at the Smith estate just outside of London. Percy came from a rather large family, and as the third son, was down the line of inheritance.

Strange that Henry envied his friend's family life. Henry's own mother was alive and well, and still a busybody if anything was to be deduced from her many letters to him. Her frequent correspondence made no qualms about admonishing him to come home to take up a respectable teaching position, settle down and marry, then produce a handful of grandchildren that his mother could spoil the remainder of her days.

Somehow, Henry could never envision him taking after his father—living in a stuffy townhome, content to tutor university students in a library surrounded by books of history, geography, and science. From a young age, Henry had always wanted to go to the places he'd read about. Feel the air, touch the soil, breathe in the scents.

He hadn't exactly expected the temperatures to be boiling, the soil to be so dry, and the scents quite so feral. Ah well, it was part of the adventure. And despite the physical inconveniences, the thrill of the unknown treasures that were unearthed on a daily basis held his heart.

So here he was, living all that he'd dreamed of. His home country seemed a distant memory, even though he'd been gone only a year. The longer he remained abroad, the less he missed England. There was just so much space here. So much unexplored. So much potential for making the discovery of a lifetime.

Perhaps Henry was the romantic.

"Speaking of the she-devil herself," Percy said, nudging Henry.

His heart almost stopped at Percy's words. Henry turned away from the dig and looked past the billowing tents. A convoy of horses was approaching, and Mrs. Lillian Worthen sat atop the lead horse. Her white dress flowed about her, and she wore a wide-brimmed hat, which, in a miraculous feat, stayed on her head. Sand curled about the horses' hooves as the group approached the excavation site.

Mrs. Worthen wasn't supposed to visit the dig for at least another fortnight, and Henry had been enjoying the reprieve. The awkwardness of their last encounter was still fresh in his mind. She'd approached him in the evening, following the dinner hour. After talking about the newest finding of an ancient oil lamp, she'd grasped his arm and leaned toward him.

Her lips had been merely an inch away before he stupidly clued in to what was happening. Lillian was remarkably tall—nearly the same height as Henry. This, he convinced himself, was why he didn't understand her intentions.

When he realized she was about to kiss him, he'd leaned away.

She'd dropped her hand and huffed. "You're playing games, Henry," she'd said. "And I don't take kindly to that."

He had been too astounded to answer right away, and by the time he thought he might be able to come up with a reply, she'd walked away.

Her convoy had left at dawn the following morning, before Henry had a chance to speak to her and find out what she meant about him playing games.

Perhaps Percy was right. Perhaps the charisma he'd been gifted, or condemned with, however one might look at it, had been misconstrued as flirting in Mrs. Worthen's eyes. He would have to set her straight—apologize first—then set her straight.

And that occasion would be happening sooner than later, he quickly realized, as Mrs. Worthen dismounted her horse and began striding straight toward him.

Percy stepped away from Henry, as if he had no problem letting Henry take the brunt of whatever had Mrs. Worthen so stirred up.

"Mr. Gaiman," she said, her tone brisk. She was back to calling him Mr. Gaiman, which Henry was grateful for.

In her hand, she held a letter which she now extended to him. "It has come to my attention that you are heir to a London estate." Her blue eyes felt like hot daggers against his already-perspiring skin. "You've deceived me, and I won't stand for it." She waved the letter. "Go on, take the thing. And don't pretend that you're some poor university graduate in need of money to fund your projects. According to this letter, you can fund them yourself."

Henry took the letter, having no idea what the woman was talking about. Seeing that the seal was broken and the letter clearly read at least once, he said, "You opened it?" No matter who she was, she didn't have the right to read his personal correspondence.

"The letter was marked *Urgent*," she replied, no remorse in her voice as she folded her arms. "I needed to make sure it wasn't about your mother's demise or some other such emergency."

Henry didn't like any of this, not one bit. He tugged the letter out of the envelope, finding that the collection of papers was actually more than one letter. One was from his mother. He recognized her scrawled cursive immediately. He skipped over it for now.

The second letter was from a solicitor informing him that he had inherited the London estate of Mr. James Tucker.

"Who's James Tucker?" Percy asked, reading over Henry's shoulder.

Is nothing private in Lower Egypt?

"He's . . ." Henry had to search his memory. "He's my father's cousin, second cousin actually. Maybe once removed. I'm not entirely sure." His mother had prided herself in her family genealogy charts. When his father had died five years previously, she'd explained the chart in great detail so that he'd have a reference at his father's funeral.

Had James Tucker attended the funeral?

Now it seemed that James Tucker had had a funeral of his own—way back in December. It being June now, and Henry having been at this dig site for over a year, he was quite out of touch with events back home. He was surprised his mother hadn't written of it. Or perhaps she had.

He now turned to his mother's letter. *Ah.* There it was. He skimmed his mother's gushing prose about the inheritance and how he must return to London immediately. She also repeated some of the details found in the solicitor's letter: that his father's second cousin, James Tucker, had left his London estate to Henry. There was a tidy sum that had been left to care for Tucker's widow. She also inherited any furniture that had been purchased during their marriage. But all the original estate furniture would remain the property of the estate and transfer to the heir.

By the time Henry finished reading the entirety of his mother's letter, his head was swimming, and a distinct ache had started in his forehead.

"You are . . . you are a wealthy man," Percy said in a tone of amazement, clapping Henry enthusiastically on the back.

Henry nearly stumbled.

"Condolences for your father's cousin, though," Percy continued. "Were you close?"

"No," Henry mumbled. "We weren't close. I don't understand how this happened."

"Well, your uncle died, that's how it happened," Mrs. Worthen cut in. "In December." Her eyes narrowed. "I'll have my man of business tally up all the expenses starting from the time of your uncle's death . . ." She snatched the papers from Henry. "Since December fifteenth."

Henry let her hold the blasted papers as he strode away from the nosy group. He couldn't return to England now. Inside the supply tent were two long tables filled with artifacts pulled from the tomb. Oil lamps, pottery pieces, gold statues of Isis . . .

Egypt was in his blood. He couldn't leave the dig site now, not when Percy was leaving for his sister's wedding.

"Darling," Margaret Tucker said as Evelyn entered the lobby.

Evelyn nearly missed her step. Her aunt had never used any term of endearment toward her. Aunt Margaret was dressed in her finest, as usual. Her light-brown hair was swept in an elegant twist that contradicted her full figure. Her dress was a bright purple with silver-trimmed buttons going all the way from her neckline to her waist. The bustle that extended behind the dress only made Margaret look larger than life. Yet there wasn't a trace of the hysterical woman that Evelyn had last seen at her uncle's funeral.

This woman was composed and . . . smiling. At Evelyn.

"Aunt Margaret," Evelyn managed to say, her voice sounding a bit breathless—astonished really. "How kind of you to come pick me up."

Margaret's smile widened. "What a polite young woman you are. I approve wholeheartedly of Mrs. Paddock's work." She rifled through a small satchel she held in her hands. "In fact, I have brought a small token of appreciation for your headmistress."

"My goodness," Mrs. Paddock said, bustling in as if she'd been eavesdropping in the corridor. "You are too generous." In moments, Mrs. Paddock had taken the bills and kissed Margaret on both cheeks.

"Evelyn was a dear," Mrs. Paddock gushed. "She will be missed by everyone." She turned to Evelyn and embraced her.

Evelyn was so shocked she didn't react for a moment, then she reached to embrace Mrs. Paddock, but the woman had already moved away.

"Come along, then," Margaret said. "Jones has already loaded your trunks."

"Jones?" Evelyn asked, trailing after her aunt. Who was Jones?

A man who looked to be in his forties stood at the ready in front a sleek black carriage Evelyn hadn't seen before. Jones wore a long navy coat and a black top hat. Not only were Evelyn's trunks loaded on the back of the carriage, but three others as well. Evelyn didn't have time to question her aunt about the extra trunks before Jones opened the carriage door and motioned for them to climb inside. Evelyn followed Margaret as she was handed up into the carriage.

"This is nice," Evelyn said, running her hands along the velvet-covered cushions when she was seated.

"It's new," Margaret said with a sweet smile. "Well, new since January. Jones is new too. I hired him in January as well."

There was something Evelyn wasn't quite sure of behind that smile. Sitting this close to her aunt showed that Margaret's remarkable affability had an edge to it.

"How are you feeling, dear?" Margaret asked.

Again with the term of endearment. "I am well," Evelyn said.

"I am so pleased," Margaret continued, reaching over and patting Evelyn's knee. "Your health is very important to me."

"Thank you," Evelyn said, because she had to say something and this was the strangest conversation she'd ever had with her aunt. She wondered if Margaret had fallen and injured her head.

Margaret was frowning now. "Is that your traveling dress?"

Evelyn looked down at her pale-gray dress with dingy white cuffs on the sleeves. It was about a year old, but she'd kept it in good condition. "I don't have a dress specified for traveling."

Margaret's brows arched. "I suppose that's my fault. I let my James make all the decisions for me, even in regards to you. Well, things are different now. What else is in your trunks?"

"Only the clothing that you and Uncle gave me," she said.

"The clothing that was altered from my sister?" Margaret's voice went up an octave.

"I believe so," Evelyn said.

"Do you not have gloves?" Margaret asked.

"My last pair have quite worn through."

"Oh laws, you can't wear that sort of clothing where we're going." Margaret tapped on the ceiling of the carriage.

"Where *are* we going?"

Margaret didn't answer her but merely pursed her lips as the carriage slowed. Moments later, Jones opened the door.

"Take us to Janene's Millinery first."

"Yes, ma'am," Jones said, then snapped the carriage door shut.

"Where are we going?" Evelyn asked again.

Margaret straightened her gloves. "You'll see soon

enough. I feel like I have a lot of apologizing I need to do. Being a widow has shown me the error of many of my ways."

The "soon enough" turned out to be the train station.

Evelyn stared out the carriage window as they came to a stop near the ticket office. Her heart nearly stopped when she realized that her aunt planned to travel by train somewhere. That's why she'd brought along trunks, and that's why she'd insisted that Evelyn purchase new gloves, a parasol, two hats, and two shawls. She'd never been witness to so much money being spent at once.

Evelyn was still staring out the window when Margaret tapped her arm. "Come along, dear; don't dally. We've got a train to catch."

Slowly, Evelyn turned to look at her aunt. "A . . . train to catch?"

"Have they turned you into a parrot at the finishing school?" Margaret asked. "We've no time to waste." She swept out of the carriage, then turned back, looking expectantly at Evelyn.

Margaret was like a stranger. Changed from the uppity, formal aunt who abided by every strict rule of her husband's to a woman who was ordering everyone about, spending money on Evelyn like she was her own daughter, and using terms of endearment.

"My parents died on a train," she said in a trembling voice. "I haven't even . . . been to a train station."

"Many people die each day," Margaret pronounced. "Some on trains, some in carriages, others catch pneumonia from swimming. You can't live your life confined to a boarding house."

Evelyn's eyes burned with tears, and she tried to stop them before they fell. It proved impossible.

Margaret's eyes narrowed. "Now, now, none of that. I'll

explain everything on the train." She turned to look toward the back of the carriage where Jones was unloading the trunks. "Jones, please help Evelyn down from the carriage. She's having a bit of trouble."

"I'll manage," Evelyn said, sniffling and trying not to let the tears multiply. Dozens of people were at the station, and once she stepped out, she was sure that everyone would stare at her.

Evelyn took a deep breath and exited the carriage. The sound of a train whistle chose that moment to pierce the air. Evelyn snapped her head to look in the direction of the noise. The train engine sounded and felt like an approaching thunderstorm.

Evelyn couldn't move for a moment as she stared. People hurried to the platform, carrying baggage, ushering children, and calling out to one another. As the commotion buzzed around her, Evelyn tried to focus on calming her racing pulse.

"This is Mrs. Jones," Margaret said, grasping Evelyn's arm.

Evelyn pulled her gaze away from the steam engine and found herself looking at a stout woman with a tuft of white hair at her forehead, blending with a head full of black-as-night hair. Evelyn guessed her to be about forty.

"Pleased to meet you, miss," Mrs. Jones said with a brief curtsy. "When my husband said we were hired to accompany you on your grand tour, I thought I'd died and gone to heaven, I did."

Evelyn blinked. *Grand tour?* A man in the crowd jostled against her, nearly knocking her down.

"Excuse me, miss," he said, then was quickly distracted by the two young boys tugging on his hands.

Evelyn looked to her aunt for an explanation, but she was ordering Mr. Jones about as he unloaded the trunks. A train porter was also in the mix, apparently commissioned to load their trunks onto the train.

"Where does this train go?" Evelyn asked.

She wasn't entirely sure she'd spoken aloud until Mrs. Jones said, "Why, we're taking the train all the way to—"

"Evelyn," her aunt cut in. "We must secure our compartment now. The train is booked solid, and I don't want anyone thinking they can share our compartment." Her arm linked through Evelyn's, and with quite a bit of force, Margaret propelled her toward the train platform.

Evelyn was still in shock as she walked with her aunt across the platform, moving through the crowd until they boarded the train itself.

The interior was nicer and homier than Evelyn expected. Yet her heart felt like it was about to hammer right out of her chest.

"Where are we going?" she said to her aunt as the woman led her along a corridor. Mrs. Jones followed close behind, and Evelyn assumed that Mr. Jones was still dealing with all of their luggage.

"Ah, here we are," Margaret said in a triumphant tone. "Compartment fifteen." She opened a door and ushered Evelyn inside.

Plush velvet seats lined two of the walls, and heavy curtains half concealed a large window that looked out over the milling crowd outside.

"Well, what do you think?" Margaret said, clapping her hands together.

When Evelyn didn't reply, couldn't reply, Mrs. Jones said, "It's lovely, ma'am. Shall I order tea?"

"That would be excellent," Margaret said, then drew back the curtain. "I've been looking forward to this for ages."

Mrs. Jones bustled out of the compartment with a soft laugh, sliding the door shut behind her.

"Aunt Margaret," Evelyn said, her voice shaking with trepidation, not only from being on the train but from the fact that they were apparently traveling someplace far away.

Her aunt released a sigh. "All right, dear, I'll explain everything now that we're aboard. You should sit down first."

Evelyn sat.

"Your uncle left the estate to his cousin's son," Margaret said. She peeled off her gloves, then settled across from Evelyn. "The new owner of the estate hasn't signed any papers yet, so I can still access all the money. That is, until he returns to England to sign everything. I've decided that while I still have access to my husband's money, my money, too, that I'm going to spend it."

Evelyn had been shocked into silence. She stared at her aunt, trying to comprehend what she'd just been told.

Margaret smoothed her skirts and smiled as if they were talking about a new recipe for tea cakes. "Can you believe that my home is going to belong to someone else? James and I were married for thirty years. Thirty!" She shook her head as if she couldn't believe it herself. "I've been waiting for this day for a long time—until you finished your schooling—and now, we are to go on a grand adventure. Paris . . . here we come."

As if on cue, the train belted out a long, shrill whistle.

"Paris?" Evelyn said in disbelief as Mrs. Jones opened the door, followed by Mr. Jones pushing a tea cart.

"Venice, Rome," her aunt said. "If you can dream of it, we're going there."

"What about Cairo?" Mrs. Jones said, her eyes shining as if she were joining in a child's game.

"Cairo too!" Margaret said with a laugh. "In a few weeks'

time, we'll be floating down the Nile with the crocodiles. It will be marvelous!"

Evelyn looked from one woman to the other. Both of their faces were flushed pink, their eyes were shining, and they were grinning. Had they gone mad?

The train heaved forward, and Evelyn placed a hand over her stomach as it lurched along with the train.

Mr. Jones barely grabbed the tea tray to keep it from rolling across the compartment.

Margaret trilled a laugh at all the commotion.

Evelyn could only stare at them in disbelief as they discussed the various places they wanted to go—one more outlandish than the next. Then her gaze was pulled toward the window and the sites of London passing by.

As the train gained momentum, the noise grew louder, and the scenery sped by faster. Despite the anxiety rolling in her stomach, Evelyn found herself fascinated with the motion of the train. She felt like she was running faster than she'd ever thought possible. But there was no wind.

"Would you care for a cup of tea, miss?" Mrs. Jones asked.

"No, thank you," Evelyn said, her eyes drawn to the window once again. It seemed that Mrs. Jones was moving about quite safely, so Evelyn rose from her seat and walked to the window to look out.

The movement of the train was a bit unsettling, but Evelyn held onto the windowsill to keep her full balance. She'd never seen London like this—all in one fell swoop. It was like looking at a painting or a picture. She focused on one person, only to have their image whisked away and replaced by another image. Buildings, carts, carriages, women, men, children, dogs . . . all passed in a colorful blur.

The door to the compartment banged open, and Margaret gasped just as Evelyn turned to see who'd entered.

A tall man stood in the doorway, holding his hat in his hands. His blond hair was a disheveled mess, and his eyes were the deepest green Evelyn had ever seen—reminding her of a painting she'd seen of the Nile River—and his skin . . . was either very tanned or dark. Was he Italian or Spanish? Were Italians ever blond?

The man was out of breath as if he'd run to catch the train. His gray suit coat was unbuttoned, and he wore no vest. His cream linen shirt was unbuttoned at the neck, and there was no sign of a tie. He scanned the compartment, his gaze temporarily landing on Evelyn before he focused on Margaret. Evelyn didn't know what to think about the intrusion. The blond man had a positive wildness about him—perhaps a desperation.

Aunt Margaret rose to her feet. She lifted a trembling hand and pointed to the stranger. "You . . . *you*, sir, have ruined my life."

"Did you find them?" Percy asked, coming up behind Henry. "Oh . . ."

Percy joined Henry in the doorway. "Well, here we are. Hello, everyone."

Henry wanted to clamp his hand over his friend's mouth and tell him to stop talking immediately. Mrs. Tucker was staring Henry down like a fierce lion stuck in a trap. She was caught, and she knew it.

After a second letter from the solicitor, Henry had finally consented to return to England. His trip coincided with Percy's return for his sister's wedding. It was just as well. The archaeological dig was on hold while Mrs. Lillian Worthen decided if she wanted to bring a legal complaint against Henry for not disclosing that he had funds.

Fortunately, Percy had done the sweet-talking with Mrs. Worthen, and she'd relented somewhat and promised she wouldn't do anything drastic until they returned to Giza.

As if that were comforting.

Still, Henry was impatient to return to Egypt. The England summer was sticky, and the crowded streets and shops reminded him of why he'd enjoyed the open spaces of the desert. Not to mention the quiet stillness and the nights where the sky seemed to include the entire heavens. His determination to locate Mrs. Tucker had finally paid off after over a week of searching.

The day after the wedding, Henry had paid a visit to the Tucker estate, only to be told that Mrs. Tucker was not in. He returned the next day, and the next. Henry eventually realized that he was being stood up.

He'd explained things to his mother, and she didn't understand why he insisted on speaking with Mrs. Tucker before signing the inheritance papers.

Henry couldn't give his mother a solid reason, just that it felt like it was the right thing to do. The past few days had been a wild chase about London as he was told he'd "just missed" her when he arrived at the estate, then tried to catch her at various shops, and finally, this morning, he'd been told by the Tucker's housekeeper that Mrs. Tucker was catching a train out of London.

Apparently, he had to buy a train ticket just to speak with Mrs. Tucker. Now, she was staring at him with venom in her eyes.

"Mrs. Tucker," Henry said, collecting his wits. "I don't think we've formally met. I'm Henry Gaiman, a relative of your husband's." He stuck out his hand.

She ignored the gesture. "I know who you are, Mr. Gaiman. What you and your mother have done is despicable. Get out of this compartment before I call the constable."

"My *mother*?" What was this woman about? Yes, his mother could be a bit difficult at times, but to imply that she somehow orchestrated this inheritance was ridiculous. He took a step inside the compartment, although he remained close to the doorway where Percy was standing.

"My mother has nothing to do with the entailment of your late husband's estate," Henry continued. "I'm not sure where you've come up with your accusations, but I assure you, my mother and I were both surprised." Henry wasn't going to turn back now. He glanced about the room. Every single person was staring at him. From a young woman at the window to an older couple. He turned back to Mrs. Tucker. "Is there some place we could speak more privately?"

Mrs. Tucker lifted her chin, a double chin that looked quite regal nonetheless. "I have nothing to say to you, sir. Besides, I refuse to be alone with you."

Percy moved to stand behind him, and Henry knew he had to be firm. He didn't want to scare the woman, but he'd gone through too much to back down now. "Can we sit and talk this through?"

Mrs. Tucker didn't respond, but her eyes seemed to be watering.

Was the woman going to cry? Henry felt like she'd used a weapon against him.

Without having to be asked, Percy pulled the compartment door shut, at least giving them privacy from anyone who might happen to pass along the corridor.

Henry moved to the seat closest to the door. "May I?"

Mrs. Tucker gave the barest of nods.

Henry sat, and he nodded to Percy, who sat opposite him. The older couple was sitting next to Henry, while Mrs. Tucker was on Percy's side. The young woman chose to sit on the other side of Mrs. Tucker. Henry didn't know who the young woman was, but she was striking with her dark hair and her dark eyes—quite a contrast to Mrs. Tucker. Yet the young woman had an aura of innocence, and she was staring, quite unabashedly, at Henry.

When his gaze caught hers, instead of looking away, she just continued to stare as if she were watching a zoo exhibit.

Henry supposed this event was close to a zoo exhibit. He also supposed he should begin. He cleared his throat. "Well, I've been trying to meet with you for over a week now," he started. "I've come to your home every day and found you quite elusive."

Mrs. Tucker kept her chin elevated, her blue gaze steady on him. Henry had to be impressed. Percy nodded his encouragement. Good old Percy.

"My mother is widowed too," Henry continued. "So I understand quite well the concerns that you must have at this time. I want to be clear when I say that I don't want to turn you out of your home."

Mrs. Tucker's eyebrows lifted. Clearly, she didn't believe him.

"Let me explain," he said. "I live in Cairo, and I have no intention of taking up residence in England any time soon. Therefore, you will continue to have a place to live and full use of the estate. I will also offer you a yearly income for your personal use. All estate expenses will, of course, be covered by me."

Mrs. Tucker brought her hand to her mouth. Her eyes were watering, but then she lowered her hand and said, "What about when you return to England? What about when you marry?" Her voice had risen an octave.

"That won't happen in the foreseeable future," Henry said. "I have no intentions to marry for now, and my work in Egypt will take several years. When the time comes, and if it comes, for me to change my residence, I am sure we can work out something that will benefit both of us."

Mrs. Tucker took a shuddering breath. "Oh my heavens," she said. "I . . . I don't know what to say." She turned to the young lady at her side and grasped her hands. "Did you hear that? We still have a home!"

We? What did Mrs. Tucker mean by *we*? Henry knew that Mrs. Tucker had a niece under her care, but he'd thought she'd be much younger than the woman beside her.

Mrs. Tucker dabbed her eyes with a handkerchief that she'd withdrawn from somewhere within the depths of her voluminous skirts.

"That is good news," the young woman said in a quiet voice.

"My goodness," Mrs. Tucker blurted out. "We must make introductions. Now that my home isn't being ripped away from me, I find that I'm am feeling much more affable." She sent a watery smile toward Henry, then looked pointedly at Percy.

"This is Percy Smith, my colleague and first assistant on my archaeological dig," Henry said.

"Pleased to meet you all," Percy said, looking at each person in turn.

Mrs. Tucker patted his hand. "You look like a fine young man."

The tips of Percy's ears pinked, and Henry might have teased him about it if they weren't amid such mixed, and volatile, company.

"I'd like you to meet Mr. and Mrs. Jones," Mrs. Tucker said, motioning to the couple sitting on the same side as Henry. Both greeted Henry and Percy. "And this is my niece, Evelyn Tucker, fresh from Mrs. Paddock's Finishing School for Young Ladies." Her voice was filled with pride as if Mrs. Tucker had graduated herself.

Henry's gaze couldn't move from the young woman's.

Evelyn was her name. He must have heard his mother mention this niece's name, since it now seemed familiar to him. He guessed her to be nineteen or twenty. He also guessed that the dim lighting inside the train compartment made her eyes look black, when in fact they were most likely brown.

"Evelyn's my elder sister's daughter, God rest her soul," Mrs. Tucker continued. "We've given her our last name to ward off the questions. When she was ten, her parents were killed in a train crash."

Henry blinked. A train crash? Both parents? He didn't remember his mother telling him of that.

"It was all long ago," Mrs. Tucker continued, and Henry wondered if Evelyn was bothered by her aunt giving such a deluge of information. "Now Evelyn is all grown up and quite a fine young woman. I suppose when we return from our grand tour we'll have to find her a husband." She trilled a laugh.

Evelyn's smile was tight. This told Henry that she was feeling as uncomfortable as he was.

"A grand tour, eh?" Percy broke in. "That sounds like quite the adventure."

Until Percy mentioned it, Henry realized he had been watching Evelyn more than he was listening to her aunt.

"Oh, it will be an adventure," Mrs. Tucker said, turning her smile upon Percy. Her gaze scanned him from head to foot. "Tell us about yourself, Mr. Smith."

No, Mrs. Tucker wasn't going to get away without explaining. "Let's hear about your grand tour first," Henry pressed.

Mrs. Tucker's cheeks reddened. *Interesting.*

"Well," she said, smiling brightly. "I thought that since my niece has successfully completed finishing school, it was time she saw the world for herself. At least, part of it." Her cheeks were still red. "I knew that once you took possession of the house, my funds would be greatly reduced."

Henry could feel Percy staring at him—was he thinking what Henry was thinking? Was Mrs. Tucker making a run to spend the money before he received it? "How . . . how long is your tour for?"

"I hadn't really planned the exact timing of it."

She is just trying to avoid me and spend as much of my inheritance as possible, Henry thought. Just a few weeks ago, he didn't even know he had such an inheritance. Yet Mrs. Tucker's boldness was unsettling.

Mrs. Tucker's chin lifted again. "My niece is an excellent student of history, and she'll be able to enlighten us all on our travels."

Henry couldn't decipher the surprised look that Evelyn gave her aunt.

Mrs. Tucker kept talking, oblivious to how her niece was reacting. "Of course, we'd love to have two young, intelligent gentlemen such as yourselves accompany us."

Henry's eyes nearly popped out. Percy brought his hand to his mouth and coughed.

"Thank you for the invitation," Henry finally managed to say. "We've got to return to Giza to continue our excavation. Things have been . . . complicated by the event of this inheritance."

"Nonsense," Mrs. Tucker said. "There's nothing in Egypt that can't wait for a few more months."

"What are you excavating?" Evelyn cut in before he could reply to her aunt's rather caustic remark.

He didn't miss the bright interest in her eyes or the way she leaned forward, her gaze intent on him. Also, this was the first direct thing Evelyn had said to him.

"We've, ah, uncovered a t-tomb that dates back to the

Nineteenth Dynasty." Henry had never stuttered a day in his life, yet here he was, stumbling over every word. He supposed that the charm Percy claimed Henry had with the ladies had just flown out the train window.

Percy coughed into his hand. Henry knew he was being warned not to speak too much of the excavation. Such things were kept private until an article could be published on the findings. If other archaeologists got wind that they were on the brink of an important find, they would descend upon the site in droves. The Egyptian government would provide digging grants to the highest bidder.

"The Nineteenth Dynasty?" Evelyn said, her voice rising with interest. "So, the era of Ramses the first and Ramses the second? Early or late period?"

Percy coughed again. Henry ignored him. This young woman seemed to know her history—her aunt had been right.

"We haven't pinned down the exact decade yet," Henry said, keeping his gaze on Evelyn alone, even though out of the corner of his eye he could see Percy's eyebrows aiming for the ceiling. "But we are confident that the tomb belongs to a priest, or at least someone very important to the royal family."

"Astounding," Evelyn said. "What sort of items have you excavated? Any mummies?"

"Evelyn Cleo Tucker," Mrs. Tucker cut in. "Let's not discuss something so morbid."

Evelyn didn't seem put off by her aunt's reprimand.

"Cleo is your middle name?" Percy said. "As in *Cleopatra*?"

Mrs. Tucker laughed. "Of course not; Cleo is a family name. Who would use a name so ostentatious as Cleopatra? Didn't she marry her brother or some such thing? There's a scandal if I ever heard one."

Evelyn's lips twitched, and she looked over at Percy.

This afforded Henry a view of her profile, and for a moment he could see that perhaps Cleopatra was a fitting name for Evelyn. The midnight color of her hair, her dark lashes that framed her dark eyes, and her warm honey complexion. He could almost feel the heat of the Egyptian sun and the hot breeze. What would Evelyn look like in one of those linen dresses with her hair unbound and hanging down her back in small braids like an Egyptian princess?

"Let's serve up that tea, Mrs. Jones," Mrs. Tucker said, cutting into the mirage that Henry had fallen into.

There was no sand beneath his feet, no pyramids within a stone's throw. Suddenly, the delay in his plans to return to Egypt didn't seem such a bother after all. He might be on a train racing through England's countryside to who knew where, but he found he didn't mind so much. Evelyn Cleo Tucker was proving to be a very intriguing person.

Life is quite inane, really, Evelyn thought. Life didn't really go like this. Being whisked away onto a train, heading to Paris for the first stop of their "grand tour," where two handsome men burst into their compartment, one of them declaring that Aunt Margaret would be provided for the rest of her life, and now said men taking tea while Aunt Margaret spoke to them of Evelyn's marriage prospects . . .

Evelyn hadn't had much opportunity to blush throughout her life, having attended a finishing school for young ladies since the age of ten, but it seemed that she was about to make up for that oversight.

If only she could tell Beatrice what was going on now. Beatrice would absolutely thrill at the idea of a grand tour.

"You must know how relieved I am feeling now," Margaret said to Mr. Henry Gaiman, the man who'd just risen to hero status in her eyes. "Now we'll not need to force ourselves upon unsuspecting men on our grand tour in order to secure dear Evelyn a husband."

Evelyn nearly gasped. Her aunt was so bold and plain

speaking. Not exactly what Evelyn learned at finishing school. Men appreciated direct interest, but only on topics that they, too, were fascinated about.

"Now that we have a permanent home, we'll be able to seek out potential suitors right in London," Margaret said.

Evelyn took a sip at her tea and barely swallowed it down. She didn't dare look at either of their guests. Mr. Percy Smith seemed a nice enough fellow, but Mr. Henry Gaiman had gained her full attention. Not because he was an heir, of course; that was too shallow for Evelyn. But because he was an archaeologist. His looks were, well, arresting, but more fascinating was his work.

She scrambled for a way to redirect the conversation from her aunt's comments about marriage.

"Mr. Smith," her aunt was saying. "Tell us about yourself and your station in life."

Evelyn wanted to disappear. The question was quite blatant considering the topic of marriage. When Mr. Smith mentioned that he was the third son and worked for Mr. Gaiman, Margaret's attention seemed to refocus on Mr. Gaiman—the man with healthier finances.

Evelyn was already having trouble keeping her curious gaze off Henry Gaiman. She didn't want him to think she was interested in him that way.

Taking a deep breath, Evelyn set her cup down. "Have you done a lot of traveling?" she asked Mr. Gaiman, but included his friend in her question.

Mr. Gaiman's eyes connected with hers, and Evelyn felt quite intrigued by their dark-green depths.

"Henry would be content to live in a dusty tent the rest of his life," Mr. Smith jumped in to answer. "He'd still be there now, if it weren't for the solicitor's letter, his mother's letter, and my persuasion to travel with me."

One side of Mr. Gaiman's mouth lifted, and Evelyn could see he was amused with his friend's statement. "Percy's right," he said. "We're in the middle of what might be a major archaeological find, and I would have been quite content to remain in Giza."

"Do you really live in a tent?" Evelyn asked, unable to contain her interest.

"Of course he doesn't," Margaret said. "Young men like to exaggerate their circumstances."

"I do live in a tent," Mr. Gaiman said, his gaze holding Evelyn's. "I have an apartment in Cairo but rarely visit there, since the excavation work requires constant supervision and security."

"My heavens," Margaret said, bringing a hand to her chest. "How barbaric."

Evelyn wanted to say "my heavens," too, but not for the same reasons. Mr. Gaiman certainly lived a different life—about as different from London as anyone could get.

"Henry is singularly devoted to his profession," Percy announced, then leaned closer to Margaret. "You'll probably have the London estate to yourself for decades."

Margaret found that funny, but Evelyn was still watching Mr. Gaiman. He seemed to take the teasing in stride. She wanted to explain that she didn't share her aunt's views on most things, so he shouldn't think that she agreed with Margaret. But Evelyn doubted she'd get the chance.

She assumed that Mr. Gaiman and his friend would get off at the next stop. As it was, Mr. Gaiman didn't look like he was used to taking English tea. The teacup looked like a doll's toy in his hand and biscuits a far cry from a satisfying refreshment. This all made it difficult to ignore his hands and how they were tanned and sturdy.

"Would you mind if we discussed a couple of repairs my

dear husband and I had talked about before he died but never got around to doing?" Margaret said.

"Certainly," Mr. Gaiman said, although his brows had lifted. His attention was fully on Evelyn's aunt, which gave her another opportunity to notice how his gray suit coat strained at the shoulder seams, which might mean that the coat wasn't his or that it no longer fit.

The breadth of his shoulders was not to be missed, and Evelyn guessed that he did plenty of labor at his excavation site. And he probably didn't wear a suit coat when he was beneath the hot sun.

While Margaret droned on about an archway that had started to crumble and how the garden paths needed a new layer of gravel, Evelyn's mind strayed much farther than it should have.

She imagined herself visiting Giza with Mr. Gaiman as her guide. Living in a tent would just be part of the experience. Perhaps she could help excavate or catalog or something. But then she thought of Beatrice and their pact. If Evelyn were in Egypt, she'd be able to stay only a year. Without even discussing it with her aunt, she knew the answer would be no.

So Evelyn let her fantasy die right there on the spot.

"What about you, Miss Tucker?" Mr. Gaiman suddenly said.

At least Evelyn thought it was sudden because she hadn't been paying attention to the conversation because of said daydreaming. Her blank look must have given her away.

"What do you think of the British Museum?"

"She's never been," her aunt piped in.

"I've read about it," Evelyn admitted. "I would love to see the displays. I read an article about some of the excavations they've funded."

Mr. Gaiman and Mr. Smith both looked at her with surprise.

Her aunt shook her head and said, “Evelyn, you’ve become quite obsessed over your interest in history.”

Evelyn ignored her aunt’s caustic remark and was grateful when Mr. Gaiman said, “I met with the director this past week, and they are considering putting funds into my excavation since I may not have a benefactor any longer.”

“Benefactress,” Mr. Smith cut in. “Mrs. Lillian Worthen had been funding the excavation—but she may be pulling out.”

Mr. Gaiman looked a bit uncomfortable now. “When she found out about my inheritance, she thought I’d been a charlatan.”

“Oh, that’s nonsense,” Mrs. Tucker said. “I could be your witness. James took us all by surprise, that dear, infuriating man.”

“What happens if the British Museum doesn’t support your project?” Evelyn asked, too curious to let the opportunity pass.

“We’ll be packing up when we return to Egypt, that’s what,” Mr. Smith said.

Mr. Gaiman glanced at his friend. “I’ll be on my own, that’s what. I won’t be able to afford an assistant, and I’ll have to cut the crew in half.”

Mr. Smith shook his head. “If Henry is anything, it’s determined. He could be flat broke, yet he’d still rise each morning and dig in the dirt, hoping to find the eighth wonder of the world.”

Mrs. Tucker laughed. “The two of you are certainly entertaining.”

Evelyn didn’t laugh. Although Mr. Gaiman was smiling along with everyone else, she could see that his passion about his archaeology project was deep seated. She wished she could speak with him about it without so many others chiming in.

Evelyn tried to diffuse the teasing. "The article I read was about Charles Fellows's expedition in Asia Minor and the tombs of the rulers of ancient Lycia."

"How extraordinary that you've read that article," Mr. Gaiman said.

A warm thrill ran through Evelyn as Mr. Gaiman's eyes lit up.

"We didn't have much entertainment at the boarding house," Evelyn said, trying to sound nonchalant when inside she was overjoyed to have such a conversation with someone like Mr. Gaiman. "I find excavation work fascinating."

"Perhaps you found yourself a new assistant, Henry," Mr. Smith piped in with a chuckle.

Before Evelyn could respond, her aunt said, "No woman would put up with that much sand. Our delicate sensibilities need regular beds and carpets beneath our feet."

Evelyn didn't know if she was blushing because Mr. Smith had guessed her thoughts or because her aunt was once again overriding her every opinion.

"Do you mind sand and broiling hot temperatures, Miss Tucker?" Mr. Smith asked with a chortle.

Evelyn gave a small smile when she looked at Mr. Gaiman, who was decidedly watching her. "I suppose an Englishwoman might be able to enjoy Egypt as much as an Egyptian woman."

Mr. Smith laughed. But best of all, Mr. Gaiman was smiling—directly at Evelyn.

"Enough of that," her aunt said. "Visiting Egypt will be enough of an adventure for me. What do you recommend we see while we're there, Mr. Gaiman?"

"You're going to Egypt too?" he asked, his eyes alighting on Evelyn once again before returning to her aunt.

"Oh yes," her aunt said. "Although I'm not too keen to travel for a full year now that we have our future secured and a home to live in when we return." She flashed a wide smile. "Thanks to you, dear Mr. Gaiman."

He tilted his head. "Perhaps when you come to Egypt, we can give you a tour."

"Are you sure you'll be able to pull yourself away from the expedition?" Mr. Smith said.

"For Mrs. Tucker and Miss Tucker, I'll make sure of it," Mr. Gaiman said.

Tea was over all too soon, and Mr. Gaiman and Mr. Smith left the compartment. They would be getting off at the very next stop and heading back to London so that they could retrieve their belongings, secure a follow-up meeting with the British Museum committee, and say goodbye to their families.

Evelyn's aunt wasted no time on commenting when the compartment door shut between them.

"What fine young men," she said, patting Evelyn's hand. "Either of them would make a good match, but I'd prefer Mr. Henry Gaiman over Mr. Smith, wouldn't you?"

"I hardly know them," Evelyn said, wondering if she'd been too forward or if her aunt had been off-putting. She'd seen the interest in Mr. Gaiman's eyes when they'd discussed his profession, but she knew that interest didn't extend to her personally.

Mrs. Jones cleared away the tea things, and Mr. Jones wheeled the tray out of the compartment. It was time to look forward to whatever adventures lay before her and not dwell on the impossible.

Three weeks later

"She's coming," Percy said as Henry finished up his meal.

They'd been expecting Mrs. Lillian Worthen for the past couple of days, after sending a letter that they were back on the dig in Giza. He didn't blame her for the delay. The pyramids at Giza were a beautiful thing to behold in the early dawn hours or during the sunsets that splashed palettes of color across the sky. But the rest of the hours in the day, the pyramids were a dirty brown, the wind sharp and hot, and the sand a constant irritant. Still, Henry loved it all.

He gazed across the expanse of desert to see that, indeed, a party was making its way toward the excavation. There looked to be about six riders.

Since their return to Giza, only about one-third of the crew could be rounded up and rehired. Now, the crew was on a short break to eat, and then they'd return to work for a couple more hours before the sun completely set and stole all the light.

Henry and Percy had been doing just as much labor in the sweltering heat as the crew and then staying up well into the night working by light of oil lamps to clean and identify the artifacts they'd been pulling out of the main tomb.

They'd been fortunate that no one had overtaken the excavation site while they were in England and that the two security guards they'd hired had done their job well.

Now it was a question of whether this excavation could continue until completion—which might take years—or if he'd be forced to wrap up in a few months. Even with the recent inheritance, he wouldn't be able to finance such a project long-term. His disposable income would increase, yes, but not enough to support the excavation properly. The only other option would be to sell the London property, but he refused to as long as Mrs. Tucker was alive.

He'd made a promise, and he intended to keep it. The fact that Evelyn was dependent upon her aunt, at least until she married, had only solidified his decision. He couldn't very well turn out a widow and her niece. And even though Evelyn wasn't technically related to him, he felt responsible for her too. Besides, if Percy's glowing praise about Evelyn was any indication, Henry was sure the woman wouldn't be on the marriage market for long.

She was a striking young lady, with intelligence to impress even the most avid scholar—all things that Percy had commented on more than once. This made Henry question Percy's former interest in Mrs. Lillian Worthen. It seemed his friend was quick to fall in love with an idea more than an actual woman.

After leaving Mrs. Tucker and Miss Tucker at the next train stop, he and Percy had returned to London. The second meeting with the British Museum had gone well, but the curator had requested a few of the artifacts to be sent back so he could decide if they were willing to help fund the project. All of this would take several weeks.

"She's almost here," Percy said, bringing Henry back to the present.

Henry rose to his feet, brushed off his hands, and stepped out of the open-sided tent to join Percy as he watched the arriving entourage. As usual, Mrs. Worthen rode at the front of the group, her white dress blowing in the wind, her wide-brimmed hat secured firmly on her head.

"Welcome back!" she said as she approached. "I see you've resurrected the excavation."

For an older woman, and for one whom Henry wasn't attracted to in the least, she looked quite queenly.

Henry grasped the reins of her horse to steady the beast as she climbed down. "We've done our best with a smaller crew."

"Ah, of course," Mrs. Worthen said, pulling off her riding gloves. "Is there someplace we can talk privately?" Her gaze flickered to Percy, then to the other men she'd ridden with.

"We have a small sitting area in our tent," Henry said, motioning toward the sleeping tent he shared with Percy. They had a couple of wooden chairs that weren't much in the way of comfort, but they were serviceable.

Mrs. Worthen wrinkled her nose. "Some place less . . . confined."

"We can walk over to the dig site," Henry said. "The crew does not speak English anyway."

Mrs. Worthen nodded. "Very well. Lead the way."

Henry tried to lead the way, but in fact, Mrs. Worthen linked her arm through his. Henry didn't mind entirely since the ground was quite uneven with all the blowing sand. But he hoped she wasn't taking it as encouragement.

They'd walked several paces from where Percy was

offering the other riders to share in their meal, when Mrs. Worthen said, "I don't have time to wait upon convention. I'm in need of a husband, Henry. And I've decided you'll fit the position."

Henry's mind went completely blank, and he hoped he hadn't heard her correctly.

"Apparently, some of the details of my estate have been called into question by a distant relative," she continued, moving a tad closer to him. "Having just undergone an inheritance issue yourself, I'm sure you understand."

"I . . ." Henry understood nothing.

"To be quite frank, I need an heir," Mrs. Worthen said. "I've been to the European physician in Cairo, and he assured me that a woman of my age can still conceive. He said that there's no reason I cannot have a healthy son."

"A son?" Henry finally stopped, pulled away from her, and looked her in the eyes.

Her thin lips curled into a bare semblance of a smile. "Yes. A son. I need a son to inherit. Before that happens, I need to a marry a virile man."

Henry's throat felt as if he'd swallowed a bucket full of sand.

"You're a healthy man," she said, resting her hand atop his folded arms. "There's a small Christian church in Cairo, and I've already spoken to the reverend. We would then need to return to England as husband and wife, for only a year or so. Produce our heir, and after a few years, I'll send the child to a boarding school. You could return to Egypt and continue your projects while our son is educated with other English boys. I'll keep my money, and you'll keep your excavations."

She watched him expectantly, as if she thought he'd embrace her in joy.

Why me? Why not Percy? Henry wanted to blurt out.

Yet, despite Percy's earlier insinuation about Mrs. Worthen, Henry wouldn't offer up his friend as the sacrifice.

His mind spun. Mrs. Worthen had buried two husbands, but that wasn't the only reason Henry wanted to refuse. And it wasn't because he had the misconception that he'd find the love of his life someday and marry her instead. It was because he couldn't picture himself with this woman in the way that she was implying. Returning to England for a year? The very thought made his heart sink. And then what? Return to Egypt and share the narrow cot in his tent?

Or would she expect him to share her Cairo apartment?

Every future image Henry had of his life, of becoming a well-known and highly respected archaeologist, seemed to fade before his eyes. He'd just worked out the inheritance of James Tucker's property, and now . . .

"I am very flattered by your offer," he said, feeling absolutely nauseated and completely desperate. "But when I returned to England, I became . . . engaged . . . to a young woman there."

Mrs. Worthen's eyes snapped wide. "Engaged? To whom?"

Henry had never told such a bare-faced lie, but he was frantic. "She's, uh, she's a relative of my extended family. I don't think you know her."

"What's her name?" Mrs. Worthen asked, her eyes narrowing.

Did she not believe him? Was he such a terrible liar after all? Henry didn't want to name anyone specific, but he knew if he didn't give Mrs. Worthen a real name, she'd find him out. He looked toward the tents and hoped that Percy would cover for him.

Not to mention the woman he was about to name—should she ever cross paths with Mrs. Worthen.

"She goes by Evelyn Tucker," he said. "Although she's not a Tucker by birth, she's taken on the name of her aunt and uncle."

Mrs. Worthen held very still for a moment, and it seemed the wind stopped blowing for a moment, as if at her command. "She's coming *here* to live?"

Henry exhaled. "We haven't made final plans yet. She's traveling to Egypt with her aunt, and we will decide from there."

Mrs. Worthen looked him up and down, and the wind started to blow again. "Interesting," she said in a tone that said she didn't find it interesting at all. "I didn't know you had it in you, Henry. You seemed so focused on your work."

"The, uh, opportunity presented itself," Henry said lamely.

"Well then, I suppose I'll have to look elsewhere." She smoothed some blowing hair from her face. "Too bad Percy isn't as hardy as you," she continued as if she were talking about an animal at a fair. "He has a pleasant personality, but I don't really see him as someone I wish to share nights with."

Henry's neck felt like it had caught on fire. He was utterly speechless. Finally, he came up with something. "Would you like to tour the dig site?"

"Perhaps another time," Mrs. Worthen said. "When is your fiancée arriving?"

Henry blew out a breath. They were back to his fabricated story. "A couple of weeks, perhaps longer. They are making a few stops along the way." Truthfully, he had no idea. He'd left the invitation open with Mrs. Tucker, and she'd said they would write of their possible visit. But there had been no mail from her.

"I'll be interested to meet my competition," Mrs. Worthen said, her brows lifting as she leaned toward him and gave him a suggestive smile. "Perhaps you'll change your mind."

Henry didn't miss the fact that she'd leaned close enough that her dress brushed against his arm. He had to force himself not to pull away. He didn't want to be rude, but he also didn't want to give her the idea that there was any sort of competition going on.

If he had to match Evelyn against Mrs. Worthen, there would be no competition.

"I'll go and check on the men you brought along to see if they've had enough supper," Henry said, trying not to confound his words. He really wanted to speak to Percy before Mrs. Worthen brought up the subject of Evelyn Tucker.

"I'll join you later," Mrs. Worthen said. "I thought we might enjoy the sunset together this evening, but it seems that might be inappropriate now."

Henry took another step back. "You're a lovely woman," he started. Another lie. "And I'm sure you will be able to accomplish all that you desire very soon."

When Mrs. Worthen gave him a regal nod, he took it as permission to take his leave. He strode toward the collection of tents, trying not to break into an all-out run.

Another three weeks later

Evelyn craned her neck as she gazed at the ceiling of the catacombs that she and her aunt stood in, along with another group of English tourists. They'd arrived in Alexandria the night before, and at dinner in the hotel, she and her aunt had been approached by a group of English who were all traveling together. They were all from England and were in Alexandria for a few days, then planned to cruise the Nile River all the way to Luxor.

One of the gentlemen, a Mr. Purdie, who was there with his wife, announced that his cousin, Mrs. Lillian Worthen, was an expert Egyptologist and would be meeting them in Cairo. It hadn't taken much persuasion to get her aunt to agree to join the party with the Purdies.

This morning, their excursion was to the catacombs of Kom el Shoqafa. The place was fascinating, and Evelyn had read a book once that included details about this medieval wonder.

Their guide, Mr. Dawson, a former professor, continued in his lengthy narration. Even Evelyn had tuned out from time to time. She just wanted to absorb the ancient walls and gaze at the ornate etchings and sculptures.

"Here we have the Hall of Caracalla," Mr. Dawson continued. "This is a gruesome feature of the catacombs, since it was once a mass burial chamber for the humans and animals massacred by Emperor Caracalla in AD 215."

Some of the ladies in the party gasped, but Evelyn was only intrigued. The narrative was no longer monotonous. They continued through the catacombs until it was time to return to the hotel.

At the hotel, Evelyn's aunt announced that she would rest the remainder of the afternoon and join everyone else for dinner. Evelyn took the opportunity to read through the brochure the guide had handed her when she asked if there was anything more she could read about the catacombs.

When they reached their room, her aunt said, "Why, look, there's a letter for you."

Evelyn had yet to receive letters on their tour. She hadn't even heard from Beatrice because she had told her friend to send her correspondence to the London house. Their travel plans were too unpredictable.

So a letter was definitely a surprise. She took it from her aunt and looked at the script. It wasn't in Beatrice's handwriting.

"Who could it be from?" her aunt asked. "Did Beatrice write to you at last?"

"I don't think so." Evelyn opened the seal and started to read. She couldn't help the gasp that came from her throat.

"What is it? Did something terrible happen?" her aunt fussed.

There was no way Evelyn could hide the news, so she handed the letter over to her aunt to read.

"How dare he!" Margaret said after she finished reading. "This is infuriating. Does Henry Gaiman not know that he is compromising your reputation? Besides, how can he think you would go along with this charade without even asking you first? From this letter, it's all said and done. This Lillian Worthen thinks you're engaged, so who knows how far the news will spread now?"

Evelyn didn't respond to her aunt's tirade because all the awful things she was saying were the same things Evelyn was thinking herself. She paced the room and finally sat down on a chair. Then she rose to her feet again.

Margaret paused in her verbal attack on Mr. Gaiman. "What if this letter hadn't reached us before we met up with Mr. Gaiman and Mrs. Worthen in Cairo? What a mess that would have been!"

Evelyn nodded. "I suppose that Mr. Gaiman would have been found out, and he would be made to look the fool."

"He is a fool!" her aunt spat out. "Look at what he says here: *I cannot bring myself to accept a proposal from Mrs. Worthen, no matter the circumstance.*" She looked over at Evelyn. "Yet he expects *you* to accept this situation! He's a hypocrite!"

Evelyn blew out a breath as her stomach tightened into a knot. She moved to the window of the hotel room and looked out over the tree-lined street below. The stately palm trees blew gently in the wind as if there were no cares in the world. How frightening was Mrs. Worthen? She must be wealthy if she was the benefactress on the archaeology project. Evelyn could readily admit that Mr. Gaiman was a striking and handsome man. All things that would equally draw another woman, such as this widow who had proposed to him.

Evelyn turned to face her aunt. "We must play along with the ruse, no matter how distasteful it might seem. Mr. Gaiman is legally the owner of your estate now, and I don't want to displease him or give him cause to turn you out."

Her aunt's face paled. "So we are to be coerced and threatened into this?"

Evelyn closed her eyes for a moment to regain her composure. "We will go along with this for now, until we see for ourselves what type of woman Mrs. Worthen is. If you think about it, what if he does marry her, and then she proves to be a tyrant and has us thrown out of our home?"

Margaret brought a hand to her mouth. "You're right. We could very well lose our home if Mr. Gaiman marries this woman, or any woman, so soon." She set the letter on the side table and crossed the room to take Evelyn's hands in hers. "You are a wise young woman. We will play his game for now, but if I think your reputation cannot be repaired, I will make him confess the whole of it."

Evelyn nodded, although she still felt like she couldn't quite wrap her mind around this turn of events.

Her aunt continued, "When we see him, we must maintain the sham while we are with him and that . . . woman. We'll pretend that we know him much better than we actually do."

"Yes," Evelyn agreed.

Her aunt released her hands and looked out the window as well. "We're going to have to stick together on this. We are dependent on Mr. Gaiman, you know."

"We will stick together," Evelyn said, feeling her throat grow tight. She hadn't seen her aunt admit to such vulnerability.

Her aunt gave a regal nod. "That's settled, then. I'll inform Mr. and Mrs. Jones as well so they can be a part of our planning." She looked Evelyn directly in the eyes. "Keep your chin up, dear. You are an engaged woman now."

Evelyn swallowed as nerves swept through her body. The thought of being engaged to a man like Mr. Gaiman made her feel out of sorts, but not in the way that her aunt might be thinking.

"We will not announce your engagement in any formal way," her aunt continued. "If someone in our party happens to ask, then we can share the news with them."

"Yes, that sounds fair," Evelyn said.

"I'll leave you now," her aunt said, patting her arm. "I need my rest, although I'm not sure if I'll actually be able to sleep now. The dinner hour will be here all too soon."

"Yes," Evelyn murmured. It seemed she was quite at a loss for words. When her aunt went into the bedroom, Evelyn remained in the sitting room.

She picked up the letter from the side table and sat down to read it again. Sure enough, the words were still there in the exact order and formation as the first two times she'd read them. Mr. Gaiman wanted her to pretend they were engaged for an undetermined amount of time.

Evelyn fanned herself with the letter, stirring up a small breeze. How could one letter change everything in her life so drastically? She didn't know what she truly thought, only that she'd never expected this type of adventure to ever befall her.

She didn't know if she was appalled or excited. Was she up to the task of acting out such a ruse, or would everyone, including Mrs. Worthen, see right through her? Evelyn ached to be able to discuss all of this with Beatrice. Her friend would laugh and urge her on. But Evelyn was afraid that her heart might actually become involved with this charade. What then?

Henry paced along the road in front of the café where Percy sat enjoying cold tea and pastries. But Henry couldn't sit still. He'd sent two letters, and there had been no reply. He didn't know what to make of it. Had Evelyn received the letters explaining his blunder? Or had she not received the letters and was about to step off the ferry to be met by an English entourage led by Mrs. Worthen? Henry had sent the letters to the hotel in Alexandria that they should have been staying at the past several days, according to the itinerary Mrs. Worthen had informed him about.

Mrs. Worthen had ridden out to their excavation site a few days before, announcing that she'd had a letter from a cousin who was asking to see her in Cairo. The cousin, Mr. Purdie, had mentioned the members of the group he was traveling in and how they all wanted to take a ferry along the Nile, from Alexandria to Cairo.

Mrs. Worthen had been delighted to point out that her cousin had listed Mrs. Tucker and her niece, Miss Tucker, and their traveling companions, Mr. and Mrs. Jones. "What a coincidence!" Mrs. Worthen had needlessly pointed out. "I will, of course, offer to travel with them along the Nile. After Cairo, we can show them Memphis, Karak, and Luxor. When they arrive in Cairo, they will surely want a close-up view of the pyramids and the sphinx. You and Percy should accompany us. I might even be able to convince everyone into taking an excursion to the Valley of the Kings."

So, here Henry was, taking more time away from the work on his excavation. He expected to receive a final decision from the British Museum any day now, and that had been the only benefit of traveling to Cairo and visiting his apartment.

It had also been nice to sleep in a real bed.

Henry knew that when the English were traveling abroad, they tended to congregate together, joining one another for meals, taking day trips, and sometimes combining their excursions. It was said that you were more likely to run into a distant relative on a grand tour than you were right in London.

Henry only wondered if he'd have a chance to speak with Mrs. Tucker and her niece before Mrs. Worthen introduced herself and offered congratulations.

He was perspiring. He really should get out of the hot sun. So he forced himself to walk back toward Percy.

"Henry! Come have a drink," Percy called out as soon as he spotted him. "Mrs. Worthen has just arrived."

Henry turned to see that Mrs. Worthen had indeed arrived, accompanied by two other men—one was her man of business, and another was a bodyguard.

When Henry had told Percy what he'd told Mrs. Worthen about being engaged, Percy had burst out laughing. In fact, that first night, in their shared tent, Henry had been awakened more than once to Percy's bouts of laughter.

The joke was very, very old now. All that replaced the

mirth was anxiety. Percy hadn't even been offended that Mrs. Worthen had so readily dismissed him as a man virile enough to meet her expectations for a third husband. In fact, Percy had offered to be a distraction to Mrs. Worthen as Henry tried to cut off Mrs. Tucker and Miss Tucker before introductions.

There was no doubt that Percy found this all quite amusing.

The steam-powered ferry would be stopping in Cairo overnight, and the passengers would all be staying at Shepheard's Hotel. A dinner was planned, as well as music and dancing. There would be plenty of time for Mrs. Worthen to speak to Miss Tucker before the travelers continued on their journey.

As Henry reached the café, Percy pointed past him. "There are the runners."

Henry turned to see a mob of young boys and girls running alongside the bank. As they grew closer, Henry could hear their shouts and laughter.

"What are they doing?" Mrs. Worthen asked.

"They've spotted the ferry and are eager to get into position to sell their trinkets."

Sure enough, the children were carrying things to sell.

Henry turned from the café and strode to the river's bank. He didn't want to appear too eager, but he couldn't stop himself either.

"There he goes," Percy commented after him. "He's looking forward to welcoming his fiancée to Cairo."

Henry's neck prickled with the continued deception.

The steamboat came into view, and Henry's heart thumped in anticipation. So be it if Mrs. Worthen thought he was eager to see his fiancée. Eager he would be.

Henry waved the children away who wanted to sell trinkets to him. If he bought one thing, he'd be swarmed.

A couple of Egyptians hurried past him and shouted at the children in Arabic, telling them to move away and not mob the new arrivals. Henry waited while the Egyptians did their work, then he had to chuckle when he recognized one of the men as a local shop owner himself.

Everyone would be competing for the attention of the travelers, including Henry.

Henry kept his gaze firmly on the approaching steamboat. The passengers were at the rail, pointing and talking to one another. Some of them waved. There were several dozen of them, but they were too far away to make out their faces.

He didn't have long to wait because he picked out Mrs. Tucker soon after. She wore a yellow-and-blue dress that looked quite garish compared to the white dresses of the other women. And, not surprisingly, next to her stood the young woman that Henry had been thinking a lot about.

Miss Tucker wore a traditional white dress. Her straw hat was narrow brimmed but adequately shaded her face from the sun. She seemed to be searching for someone, or something, while her aunt was talking nonstop. Miss Tucker nodded but didn't seem to be part of her aunt's one-sided conversation.

Then he realized she was looking right at him. He stood apart from the crowd gathering at the small dock. The children had congregated again, and Percy, true to his word, had engaged Mrs. Worthen in some animated discussion near the road. As of now, Henry was much closer to where the boat passengers would alight.

The steamboat grew closer and closer, and Henry held Miss Tucker's gaze. He couldn't read her expression yet, and he doubted he'd be able to truly read her eyes unless she was standing right before him. She looked healthy and fresh and not travel worn as he'd expected.

When the boat docked, the jostling of the passengers

started. The family groups were coming off together, and Miss Tucker and her aunt were somewhere in the middle of the throng.

Henry waited until there was a break in the commotion, then he made his way through the passengers until he'd reached the dock.

Mrs. Tucker walked regally, as if she were the queen of the ferry boat. Her large straw hat seemed to be sprouting yellow and white feathers. Whereas Mrs. Tucker's clothing drew attention, Miss Tucker's white dress was simple, yet elegant. Up close, he realized the dress was a blue-and-white pinstripe. And although it was modest to the extreme, the fit showed off her slenderness and rather perfect curves.

He should stop staring.

"Mrs. Tucker," Henry began, focusing on the older woman and extending his hand to shake hers.

She slowed her step—although she wasn't moving all that fast. "Well, Mr. Gaiman, I certainly hope you can answer for yourself."

Henry went cold. He hadn't exactly considered the censure coming first from Mrs. Tucker.

Mrs. Tucker linked her arm with Miss Tucker's. "My niece is more understanding than I am, so you will have to sort it out with her."

Henry looked at Miss Tucker now. Her chin was tilted down so that her straw hat hid her eyes. But she was carrying two letters—the ones that he had written to her. She *had* received them. He was so relieved, he wanted to shout.

"I must apologize for the nature of the letters," he began in a low voice. "As I explained, I was put into a difficult position and spoke without considering the consequences."

"Not here," Mrs. Tucker said in a fierce whisper. "Not now." She looked around the milling crowd. "I'm assuming your benefactress is here someplace?"

"Yes, she's speaking with Percy."

Mrs. Tucker seemed to have spotted the woman, because next Mrs. Tucker's narrowed gaze was on Henry. "I hope you know what you are doing, sir. Keep in mind that you have a young lady's reputation to consider."

Henry nodded and stole a glance at Miss Tucker. Her dark eyes met his, and his nerves went on alert.

"Well, Mr. Gaiman," Miss Tucker said. "I suppose you should show us your city."

Then she did the most extraordinary thing. She linked her arm with his, as if they were truly an engaged couple. He placed his hand over hers, thinking that was only natural. "Are you all right?"

"I am," she said, looking up at him. "I don't mind an adventure."

Mrs. Tucker harrumphed, but then she linked her arm with his other arm. Henry escorted the two women off the dock. He hadn't had time to decipher Miss Tucker's expression. Was she angry? Disappointed? Or was this really an adventure to her? They followed the other passengers as they made their way to the road through the congregating children eager to sell trinkets.

Henry using the bits of Arabic he'd picked up to shoo off the children.

"Oh, we can buy one small thing, can't we, Aunt Margaret?" Miss Tucker said.

"I don't think you want to do that—" Henry started. It was to no avail because Mrs. Tucker had already agreed and had pulled out a few coins from her satchel.

The children swarmed them, each of them holding up trinkets of fake gold sphinxes, wooden beaded necklaces, wilted flowers, and painted clay scarabs.

Henry was about to command the children to stay away,

but then Miss Tucker laughed as a young girl held up a bunch of wilting flowers. "Oh, they are sweet. Here, let's buy one thing from each child."

"What an excellent plan," Mrs. Tucker said, handing over a dozen or so coins to Miss Tucker.

Frankly, Henry was surprised at the women's generosity and patience. He'd have thought they'd want to get to the hotel as quickly as possible. Instead, he stood by as the women carefully selected a trinket from each child, then handed over a coin. The children were delighted, and when they pressed for more, Henry repeated his instructions in Arabic. Eventually the children moved on to the next set of passengers coming off the dock.

"May I carry your purchases for you?" Henry asked the women.

The women handed over some of the trinkets to him, and he had a couple of awkward moments trying to hold and balance everything.

"Thank you," Miss Tucker said.

"You are quite generous with the children," Henry said to Miss Tucker.

"They are poor, starving things," Mrs. Tucker said. "Why wouldn't we be generous when we have so much compared to them? Besides, it's *your* money we are spending until everything transfers to you."

Henry blinked. She was right. He looked over at Miss Tucker. She had raised her brows at her aunt's audacious comments. But when she met Henry's gaze, her mouth curved into an amused smile.

"I suppose you're right," Henry replied to Mrs. Tucker, although his gaze was still on Miss Tucker. "We should be generous when we can. Shall we get you to the hotel, Miss Tucker?" He extended his arm.

Miss Tucker took his arm again. "I suppose if we are to continue the charade of being engaged, you ought to call me Evelyn."

"Evelyn," he said in a low voice, unsure why his pulse was racing. "Then you must call me Henry."

She nodded but kept her gaze lowered.

Her aunt took her place on his other side, and he continued to escort them toward the road that led to the hotel. *Evelyn.* He hadn't exactly dared think of her in such intimate terms, but of course she was right. If they were truly engaged, she'd call him Henry, and he'd call her Evelyn. And it seemed that Henry's funds were indeed paying for Mrs. and Miss Tucker and all of their incidentals. It was a bit like being truly engaged, and Henry found he didn't entirely mind.

9

Evelyn leaned on the balcony rail and breathed in the hot, dusty air. It was finally starting to cool off with the sun moving behind the western horizon. Below her, a group of children waited near the hotel entrance, likely hoping for a tourist to exit. The streets had started to come alive in the past half hour with the drop in temperature, and she found herself fascinated by the men driving carts full of hay or sacks of grain, and the woman ushering small children about as if they were goats.

Evelyn had been ready for the dinner party for over an hour. After arriving at their luxurious hotel, they were served tea in the opulent lobby, which was complete with stained glass windows, Persian carpets, and granite pillars. Evelyn had never tasted tea so strong, and she supposed that was the reason she'd been unable to rest. Her aunt had had no trouble falling asleep for a couple of hours, and now Mrs. Jones was attending to her to help her get ready for dinner.

Smoothing down her pale-green skirt, Evelyn found she was looking forward to seeing Mr. Gaiman—Henry—again this evening. He'd been nothing but polite, helpful, and respectful. She'd also seen remorse in his gaze, and she knew that he was truly sorry for putting her into this situation. She and her aunt had yet to meet Mrs. Lillian Worthen, but Evelyn was more than curious about the benefactress who'd proposed to Henry.

Such a proposal was practically unheard of. Evelyn had wished she could write to Beatrice all about the intrigue, but she was afraid that the letter might fall into the wrong hands. What if Mrs. Paddock heard that she had entered into a sham of an engagement? It was best to wait, however torturous it might be, to tell Beatrice in person.

Evelyn admitted that the past six weeks had sped by, and never had she enjoyed herself so much. This added adventure had been unexpected, but it was also thrilling in a small way.

"Are you ready, dear?" her aunt's voice cut into her thoughts.

Evelyn turned to see Margaret coming toward the balcony. She wore a deep-blue evening gown and looked quite splendid. Her headpiece was adorned with elaborate feathers, and her gloves were snowy white.

"I'm ready," Evelyn said.

"You look lovely," Margaret said. "Mr. Gaiman will want to propose for real."

Evelyn laughed, but inside her pulse was racing. She'd perhaps been fantasizing a bit too much after receiving Henry's second letter. It had repeated much of the same information as the first letter, but the tone had been more imploring. Evelyn didn't mind the feeling that she was helping out Henry when he most needed it. But she had dressed in her best gown they'd purchased in Paris. The soft green brought out her eye color, that she knew, and the off-shoulder cut was more daring than anything she'd ever worn.

"Let's not make everyone wait," her aunt continued. "We're already a few minutes late. And remember to say as little as possible to Mrs. Worthen, in case she turns out to be a nosy old biddy."

Evelyn smiled and shook her head. Her widowed aunt was nothing like her married aunt. Evelyn took her aunt's arm, and the two women left their rooms and made their way down the staircase. The lobby was filled with their traveling companions from the Nile cruise. They joined Percy Smith, who stood with a woman who looked to be about forty; it was plain she was Mrs. Worthen, since Mr. and Mrs. Purdie, their friends from Alexandria, were also with her.

"I've been looking for you two," Mr. Smith said, bowing over each of their hands.

Margaret laughed. "We were whisked away by Henry as soon as we landed."

Evelyn kept her gaze on Mr. Smith, trying to keep her expression relaxed and affable, all the while knowing that the woman at his side was studying her.

"Of course you are acquainted with Mr. and Mrs. Purdie, so I'd like to introduce Mrs. Lillian Worthen," Mr. Smith said with a smile. "She's been integral to our dig at Giza."

Evelyn finally met the woman's gaze and was taken off guard at the iciness of her blue eyes. "Lovely to meet you at last," she said, hoping it sounded like she and Henry had had more than one conversation about the benefactress. The woman was dressed in gold and white, and she seemed to have bronzed her skin. Perhaps she was trying to look like an Egyptian princess herself?

"Enchanted," Mrs. Worthen said, nodding her head, then looking at Margaret. "And you are . . . ?"

Mrs. Worthen knew very well who her aunt was. "This is my aunt, Mrs. Margaret Tucker," Evelyn said anyway.

"We're so pleased to meet you at last," Margaret said. "Henry and Percy have told us so much about you and your generosity."

Evelyn held back a smile. Mr. Smith had gone quite pale. Perhaps their plan to give credence to the engagement was being taken too far, because Mrs. Worthen's brows had lifted sky-high.

"Oh?" she said. "What have they said of me?"

Margaret had no trouble elaborating, her eyes sparkling as she did so.

Evelyn hadn't known that her aunt was such an accomplished actress.

"They will be forever grateful that you provided the seed money to start the excavation, and one that has caught the attention of the British Museum." Margaret was unstoppable now. "Because of you, history will be uncovered and made known to the rest of the world."

Evelyn didn't know whether to cringe or to applaud her aunt.

"There you both are," a voice spoke behind him.

Henry had arrived. Everyone turned to look at him.

He was dressed finer than Evelyn had ever seen him. His tailored suit emphasized his broad shoulders and tapered waist. Somehow he seemed taller than Evelyn remembered. His sun-blond hair was combed, and he smelled . . . divine. He had shaved the scruff of whiskers that she had noticed at the boat launch. She hadn't minded the scruff, and she supposed it was difficult to shave each day when one was on an excavation. But now, he looked almost regal.

"Aunt Margaret," Henry said, grasping her hand and kissing the back of it.

Next, his green eyes alighted on Evelyn. His voice was lower, richer, when he said, "You look lovely as always, Evelyn." He bent over her hand and kissed it.

Through her gloves, she felt the warmth and softness of his mouth. No wonder Lillian Worthen had set her sights on Henry.

Thank goodness he wasn't engaged to the woman. This thought sent a jolt through Evelyn. *He's engaged to me.* Fictitiously, of course, but the way her heart was now racing, made her feel like their understanding was genuine.

"I see you've met Mrs. Worthen, and you already know her relatives, the Purdies."

Evelyn merely nodded. She couldn't quite look away from Henry. She was imagining a dinner sitting next to Henry while he told her endearing memories of his childhood, and then he'd ask her to dance, more than once. She'd twirl in his arms the rest of the night while an orchestra played in the background.

"And how do you like Cairo?" her aunt asked the general party at large.

Evelyn was more than aware of Henry standing by her side, not touching her at all, while the conversation floated about her. Lillian Worthen might not have been outright staring at Evelyn, but she felt the woman's scrutiny all the same.

A dinner gong sounded, and the murmured conve-rsations around them suddenly quieted.

"This way," someone said in an accented voice.

"That's our call," Henry said, extending his arm toward Evelyn. "Shall we?"

"I thought you were going to escort me in," Lillian Worthen said.

Evelyn's face heated with embarrassment. "Please, allow me the pleasure, Mrs. Worthen," Percy said, coming to the rescue.

Evelyn wanted to kiss the man right there and then—on the cheek, of course.

Percy then motioned to her aunt. "I'd be honored to escort two lovely ladies into dinner." Her aunt beamed and took his other arm.

Mr. and Mrs. Purdie led their small group, following the other guests into the dining room.

So it was that Evelyn found herself walking arm in arm with Henry.

"You really do look lovely, Evelyn," Henry said close to her ear in a low voice. "I know that our engagement isn't real, but not everything else about me is a fraud."

Evelyn glanced up at him and nearly became lost in his dark-green eyes. She found she believed in his sincerity, which only made her feel like she was standing on the edge of a cliff.

They took their seats at a large round table. Throughout the dining room, the tables were arranged close together. Evelyn didn't know how any dancing might be accomplished.

Henry sat on her left, and her aunt sat on her right. Directly across from her, Mrs. Worthen took her seat. Although Evelyn had just met the woman, she found her scrutiny off-putting, even rude.

"Well, the cat is certainly watching her prey," her aunt whispered to Evelyn.

"Yes," Evelyn agreed, although she felt uncomfortable whispering about Mrs. Worthen when she was such a short distance away.

Evelyn took a sip of the cold, sweet drink before her. She nearly spat it out. It was much too sweet and had probably resembled tea at some point.

Her aunt had the same reaction. "What is this?" she said, holding up her glass.

Percy grinned. "Awful, isn't it? It's the Egyptian version of English tea. Their own stuff is much more herbal tasting, but strong, so it takes some getting used to."

Henry tried his drink and grimaced. "I don't care for either type of tea."

"You must miss England very much," Mrs. Worthen said, her gaze directed at Evelyn.

Evelyn set her glass down after her second, smaller swallow. If she weren't so thirsty, she would have left it alone. "I miss only my friend Beatrice," she said honestly. "Otherwise, I'm having a grand time."

"Who's Beatrice, pray tell?" Mrs. Worthen asked.

Her aunt took the opportunity to join into the conversation. "They've been best friends for years at their boarding school."

Mrs. Worthen's brows shot up. "Boarding school? How long have you been out?"

Oh no, Evelyn thought. *Too many questions already.*

"Not long," her aunt said. "She extended her stay while I was getting my house in order after my husband's death."

"I'm sorry about your loss," Mrs. Worthen said dutifully.

"Thank you," her aunt said. "I don't know if I'll ever get used to the idea of being a widow."

Evelyn secretly thought her aunt had adjusted quite well.

"I am sure you're grateful to have your niece with you as a comfort," Mrs. Worthen said, offering a flat smile.

"Of course, she is a dear," her aunt said, returning a more genuine smile.

Evelyn desperately tried to think of a way to change the subject, but nothing at all came to mind. Which, of course, gave Mrs. Worthen an opening to continue.

"I was so surprised when Henry returned from England after such a short trip only to announce that he was engaged," Mrs. Worthen said.

Evelyn wanted to groan. Henry said nothing, just took a sip of the nasty tea.

"Young people these days can be full of surprises," her aunt replied, clearly implying that Lillian Worthen didn't fit into the category of young people.

Henry nearly choked on the sweet tea a second time. Mrs. Lillian Worthen hadn't wasted a single moment to start in with the questions. His neck heated at the awkwardness of it all. Why had he not prepared for this? He was astounded at the audacity of his benefactress.

Mrs. Tucker was doing a good job at keeping the conversation deflected, and Percy talked to the accountant. Apparently they had some friends in common.

Henry had to do something, say something—but what would silence Mrs. Worthen yet not be incredibly rude?

"When Henry told me his dig would take years—like most of them do—I didn't think he'd be pursuing a wife anytime soon," Mrs. Worthen continued.

Evelyn's hand closest to Henry was resting on the table, and her other hand gripped her glass of tea. Henry rested his hand over her free hand, and even though he knew it was a bold move, he needed to get the point across to Mrs. Worthen that he was indeed engaged. And he hoped she'd believe it was a love match.

His mind finally settled on what needed to be said. "Evelyn and I have known of each other for some time, so it was fortuitous that our paths crossed once again in London." He smiled at her and was rewarded with a return smile—of relief. "Evelyn is a student of history, and she is also fascinated by archaeology."

Evelyn nodded. "Indeed, Henry's profession is quite wonderful."

Henry. He liked hearing her say his given name. He also liked that she was complimenting him—even if it was forced.

And, she hadn't pulled her hand away.

The color was high on Mrs. Worthen's face. "Pray tell, where will you have your wife live?" she said in an arched voice.

Would the woman not give up?

"We have yet to discuss details," Evelyn said in a bright voice.

Bless her.

"I am sure the young people will inform us of their plans as soon as they are made," Mrs. Tucker added.

Bless Mrs. Tucker.

Just then three waiters arrived, bearing trays laden with platters of food. The timing was perfect. Mrs. Worthen turned her attention to nitpicking and complaining about some of the particular dishes. Henry had grown accustomed and even enjoyed Egyptian food now.

He saw Evelyn hesitate as she looked at the various dishes. They were to help themselves, and although Henry could identify every dish, he realized that some of it might be new to Evelyn, despite the fact that she'd spent several days in Alexandria.

"These are stuffed grape leaves," he said, picking up a platter. "If you've had Greek food, they will taste familiar.

They have a strong flavor, but you might enjoy them." In truth, he had no idea what she might enjoy.

"All right, I'll try them," she said.

He set three of them on her plate, then picked up a large bowl. "And this is tabbouleh, a sort of salad with chopped vegetables, plenty of parsley, and bulgur." With her nod, he scooped a spoonful onto her plate. "Things are less formal in Egypt, if you haven't noticed."

The edges of her mouth lifted. "I haven't really noticed."

Was she teasing him? He found he liked it very much. "Some things are less formal, but . . ." He leaned closer so that only she would hear. "Things like courting and marriage are much more formal."

"How so?" she asked, looking genuinely curious.

"Most marriages are arranged in this country," he said. "A man and woman might meet for the first time on their wedding day."

"That's remarkable." Her gaze held his.

He'd never seen such depth in someone's eyes, and he felt he could gaze into them for quite some time.

"What do you think that would be like?" she asked. "I mean, the first days together, the first week. Do they ask each other what their favorite colors are? Their favorite composers? Their favorite artists?"

Good questions, he thought. "Perhaps some of that is known in advance—you know—because the parents, or at least the fathers, have met or corresponded and discussed each of their children."

"Yes, to determine if they're a good fit." She looked thoughtful as she cut into the stuffed grape leaf. "At least one would hope." She took a bite and chewed.

"What do you think?" Henry asked after a moment, when he was sure she'd swallowed.

"Unexpected," she said. "I think I like it—although it's quite different than anything I've ever tasted. Who would have thought of eating a grape leaf?" She spooned up a bit of the tabbouleh and took a bite of that. "Oh," she said a second later. "Not too appealing."

Henry found that watching her try the new foods was quite fascinating. "Egyptian food is definitely an acquired taste. I didn't like tabbouleh the first time I tasted it. You just need to keep eating it."

"I don't think I'll grow fond of tabbouleh" she said. "The aftertaste is too strong." She ate another bite of the stuffed grape leaf. "Much better."

Henry chuckled.

"What are you two in cahoots about?" Mrs. Tucker said.

"Henry's trying to convince me that Egyptian food will become more palatable with frequent eating," Evelyn said.

Henry sensed that Mrs. Worthen was paying them more attention than she was to her own cousin, Mr. Purdie.

"The meat kabobs are wonderful," Mrs. Tucker said.

"I'm enjoying it well enough," Evelyn continued. "What's this?" she asked, pointing at a bowl.

Henry scooped a dollop on her plate, then handed over the platter of warm pita bread. "It's a tahini dip that's very good. You dip the pita bread into it."

Evelyn tried it, and Henry realized he was holding his breath, waiting for her to make her pronouncement.

She gave him a brief smile, then dipped another piece of pita into the tahini and ate it. "This is delicious. What's it made of?"

"Sesame seeds mostly," Henry said, grinning.

"Mmm," Evelyn said, dipping more pita into the sauce. "I think I've fallen in love."

Her words buzzed through Henry, making him feel very,

very pleased and sort of light-headed if truth be told. He scooped tahini onto his own plate and joined Evelyn in eating. He was certain Mrs. Worthen had noted the entire exchange as well as overhead parts of their conversation. Hopefully it would be enough to convince her that he was completely off the market. Not that Henry was flattering himself about Mrs. Worthen's attentions toward him, but he didn't want her to think he was available now, or in the future.

He didn't know how exactly to handle the future—would his pretend engagement have to stay in place until Mrs. Worthen found another man to marry? Most likely. This thought only made him feel more guilty.

Yet ... he'd discovered that he was enjoying every moment with Evelyn. He'd never considered introducing a woman to his love of Egypt. He'd always thought that perhaps a decade or two down the road, he'd return to England, marry, then take shorter trips abroad.

Now, smiling over the food choices with Evelyn and discussing the oddities of arranged marriages in other cultures, he realized that he was more than enjoying himself. It was as if he, too, were falling in love with Egypt all over again.

The four-person orchestra was a poor substitute for any social event in England, but Evelyn didn't mind. She was quickly growing to appreciate the culture surrounding her. The young, respectful men serving as waiters, wearing long white robes that Henry had told her were called *galibayas*. The very sweet, cold tea. The stuffed grape leaves. Best of all, the pastries that had been served for dessert were creations unlike anything she'd ever seen.

And now, Henry rose to his feet and extended his hand toward her. "Would you care to dance, Evelyn?"

She felt all eyes around the table on her, and she was fairly certain her aunt was swooning. Although, Margaret should know better—this was all a charade. But as long as Evelyn was playing a part, she might as well enjoy it to the fullest. She'd never danced in a real assembly with an actual dancing partner. She'd danced with the school dancing instructor and then partnered with Beatrice and a few of the other girls as they traded off who was acting in the "male" role.

So, by the time she'd placed her hand in Henry's and

allowed him to pull her to her feet, her heart was hammering madly. He led her to the dance floor, where the four musicians were warming up.

"I'm sorry the music isn't more polished," Henry said, a hint of a smile on his face.

"I don't think it would make me a better dancer if it were," Evelyn told him. "I've never been to a ball or assembly."

His brows pulled together. "I had no idea."

The confusion on his face was a bit endearing. "I've been in a boarding school all this time, with only young ladies in attendance," she said. "We did have a dancing instructor, though, so I'm not completely inept."

"Of course not," Henry was quick to say. "I am just astounded that you never attended society functions with your aunt and uncle."

They reached the center of the floor where other couples had gathered.

"I visited them only during the Christmas holiday for a couple of days at a time," Evelyn confided. "My aunt now isn't the same woman as when her husband was alive. It's as if she's shed shackles of doom." As soon as the words were out, she regretted them. She didn't want to come across as critical of her aunt or ungrateful in any way.

But Henry only looked at her with amusement. "Then I am a fortunate man indeed." He clasped her right hand in his left and raised them together. Then he settled his other hand at her waist. She lifted her left arm and placed her hand on his shoulder just as the cobbled orchestra began a slightly offbeat rendition of a waltz.

Evelyn didn't mind. The music was but a backdrop to the rhythmic steps that Henry led her through. She focused on the steps and keeping her posture erect while also trying to follow Henry's lead.

"You're doing fine," Henry said in a low voice after a few moments.

She looked up.

Gazing at him this close wasn't something she'd thought might affect her. But it did. She could smell his masculine scent of spice, and she became very aware of the feel of their linked hands and the way his other one spanned across her back. His shoulder was solid and muscled. She had a sudden image of him working at a dig site, doing manual labor alongside the hired workers. She wouldn't be surprised if he pitched in. It would explain the strength of his broad shoulders.

She also wouldn't be surprised if there was a blazing fire in the hearth at one end of the dining hall. But in actuality, there was no hearth, and no fire. She was overheating, and she didn't know if it was from her nervousness at dancing her first real dance or because of the man's arms she was currently in.

"Truly, you're dancing well," Henry continued. "Try to relax and enjoy yourself. No one here is watching us—not like London society."

"Except Mrs. Worthen," Evelyn said.

Henry glanced past her. "Well, perhaps her."

"And my aunt is surely watching," she said.

"You're likely right about that," he conceded.

"Percy might be watching as well."

Henry laughed.

She loved the way he laughed because it seemed he reserved it for when he was truly amused.

"You've outfoxed me," he said. "We *are* being watched, but you are still a natural dancer."

"Thank you," she said. "You're making it easier than I thought it would be."

His eyes seemed to change then, going from amused to contemplative as he gazed at her.

If possible, her heartrate quickened from its already thumping state.

"Your aunt has been very helpful tonight, especially with Mrs. Worthen," Henry said.

Evelyn couldn't agree more. "Aunt Margaret has surprised me. Once she got over the shock of your first letter, that is. I think she's quite enjoying her part in this drama."

Henry chuckled. "She's a bright woman, although I feel bad about putting the two of you in this position. I hope to find a way to make it up to you, once this can be put behind us."

Disappointment swept through Evelyn, and she silently chastised herself. Why should she be disappointed to bring the charade to an end and move on with her life? "How long do you think it will take for Mrs. Worthen to find a husband?"

Henry glanced past her again. Evelyn looked over as well to see Mrs. Worthen dancing with one of the older men who'd been on the tour. Mr. Beaumont, if Evelyn remembered right. He was traveling with a few other men who were archaeology enthusiasts.

"I can't say," Henry said. "I do know that it will be an interesting week."

Interesting, indeed, Evelyn thought. The dance came to a close, and Evelyn knew she couldn't very well dance two in a row with Henry, even though they were supposedly engaged.

Henry escorted Evelyn back toward the table, where they were intercepted by Mr. Percy Smith. "May I have this dance?" Mr. Smith asked Evelyn.

She was grateful to now have a bit of experience. Although as she began to dance with Mr. Smith, she noticed that Mrs. Worthen had snared Henry into a dance. There was no reason to be envious. Henry had made it quite plain he didn't care for Mrs. Worthen in a romantic way—he'd turned down her proposal—but Evelyn's spirits plunged regardless.

She tried to focus on what Mr. Smith was telling her about the archaeology site they'd be visiting tomorrow. Evelyn was quite looking forward to it, and she was grateful that Mr. Smith wasn't entering into any gossip about Henry and Mrs. Worthen, although Mr. Smith looked their way more than once.

"As usual, Henry is the brains behind this operation," Mr. Smith said. "At the university, that was often the case. He'd come up with brilliant plans, and unlike other men who'd let their dreams fade away, Henry would find a way to make it happen. As you can see, he's quite good at getting his way."

Evelyn blinked at that comment. Was Henry simply using his handsomeness and charm as a means to an end? She'd enjoyed her dance with him and their dinner conversation. In fact, he was starting to feel like a friend. "I guess it takes that type of personality to be a philanthropist," she observed. "I certainly couldn't manage it."

"Nor I," Mr. Smith said with a chuckle. "You've been a good sport through all of this. I believe you both have Mrs. Worthen well convinced."

"I certainly hope so," she said, although doubt was starting to creep in. Mrs. Worthen laughed, loud enough for Evelyn to hear.

"I have a confession to make," Mr. Smith said.

Evelyn refocused on him. "Oh?" She didn't really like this turn in conversation. She knew Mr. Smith less than she knew Henry.

"I would not mind being married to Mrs. Worthen myself," he said.

Evelyn couldn't have been more surprised.

His face flushed. "Don't look so shocked. She's older than me, yes, but she's an interesting woman. As the third son, you could very well understand that I don't have much to recommend me."

Evelyn's mind raced. She had no idea what to say to such a confession, but she did know that Mr. Smith was a pleasant, good-looking fellow. "It's my opinion, Mr. Smith, that you underestimate yourself. I don't know the reason Mrs. Worthen can't see that for herself. It seems she's set her eyes on the wrong man."

A slow smile spread across his face. He really was a nice-looking man, although there was nothing about him that sped up her pulse. "You're an extraordinary young woman," he said.

She wasn't completely immune to his compliment, though, and was sure that her own blush stained her face.

"Henry is one lucky devil, is all I can say," he continued. "I know your engagement is only an act, but he would be a fool to let someone like you go."

Her face was definitely red now, but he only continued smiling at her. "You are your own charmer, Mr. Smith."

He laughed, and that, of course, drew the attention of plenty of people around them. "This will be an interesting week," he said.

Henry had just told her that moments ago. She couldn't help but notice that Henry had looked over at her dancing with Mr. Smith plenty of times throughout the dance. When the dance ended, and Mr. Smith led her off the floor, Margaret met them at the table.

"I have a headache coming on," Margaret said.

"Oh," Evelyn said, momentarily stunned. Then, collecting her thoughts, she said, "We'll retire for the evening, then. Tomorrow we begin early."

"Yes," her aunt said and looked over at Mr. Smith. "I wish you a good night."

He gave a half bow just as Henry and Mrs. Worthen joined them.

"Leaving so soon?" Mrs. Worthen asked. She must have had hearing like a cat.

"My aunt is ready to retire," Evelyn said. "We will look forward to seeing everyone in the morning."

"I'll walk you to the stairs," Henry rushed to say.

So it was that the three of them walked to the stairs that led to the upper hallway of rooms.

"Thank you for the dance and introducing me to Cairo's cuisine," Evelyn said with a smile.

Henry grasped her hand, quite earnestly in fact. Then he bent over it and pressed a kiss on her gloved hand. "It's been an enchanting night."

Evelyn must have murmured another thank you, but she wasn't quite sure. Her aunt bid farewell, and then she linked arms with Evelyn. They started up the stairs together, and as they walked down the hallway, Evelyn said, "I hope your headache won't last long."

Her aunt gave a small laugh. "I don't have a headache, dear, but thank you for your concern. I saw what was happening between you and Henry, then Mr. Smith, and I thought it better that you take an early leave."

Evelyn slowed her step and looked at her aunt. "What do you mean?"

"I think you are in great danger of having two men fall in love with you."

Evelyn couldn't be more shocked. "Surely you're jesting."

"You are not aware of how lovely you look this evening," her aunt continued in a kind tone. "In a desert such as this, you're like a beautiful oasis."

"You don't understand," Evelyn said. She hadn't planned on divulging Mr. Smith's confidence, but she had no choice now. "Mr. Smith is pining for Mrs. Worthen."

Her aunt's brows flew up. "What? Are you certain?"

"He confessed it to me during our dance, but it seems that she has eyes for Henry. And thus the proposal."

"My goodness," her aunt said. "The plot has thickened. You, Mr. Smith, Mr. Gaiman, Mrs. Worthen. Oh my."

"We will enjoy the rest of our trip and then leave them all behind to sort it out," Evelyn said in a determined tone. "If the men are interested in me, it is as you said—they are devoid of eligible women here, so I am an anomaly."

"I don't know about that, dear." Her aunt patted her hand. "I saw the way you responded to Henry Gaiman. You are not as immune to him as you might claim."

"Perhaps it is because he was my first bona fide dance partner," Evelyn said.

Her aunt merely smiled, a knowing look in her eyes. It seemed that Evelyn was poor at convincing her aunt.

"I'm looking forward to an interesting week," her aunt said.

The horses galloped a steady, if moderate, pace across the desert toward the billowing white tents that marked the Giza dig site. It turned out that only about half of the travelers were proficient horsewomen or horsemen, and so the party took the journey slow. Henry kept his horse near Evelyn and her aunt. Their companions, Mr. and Mrs. Jones, rode ahead with the group. They seemed well situated on their saddles. And Mrs. Tucker was clearly an excellent horsewoman, too, whereas Evelyn looked about as skittish as a newborn colt when she first mounted the horse.

Last night, after Evelyn and her aunt had left, Henry took his leave soon after. He didn't want to dance with Mrs. Worthen again, and he told Percy to dance with her.

"Are you sure I'm virile enough?" Percy had joked, but Henry knew that his friend had some level of hurt over the woman's proposal to Henry.

Life never seemed to have any degree of predictability.

Henry had also spent part of the night unable to sleep because his thoughts were a mixture of guilt over lying to Mrs.

Worthen and forcing Evelyn and her aunt to take part in his deception; yet he had also felt elated be in Evelyn's company. She was truly an interesting person to speak to. And when they'd danced, he was impressed with her determination to dance well, and it didn't hurt that she seemed to fit perfectly in his arms.

In fact, there were quite a few perfect things about Evelyn Tucker. For instance, the way that her dark hair had come loose from its bun and now streamed behind her as they rode. She smiled at him each time their gazes connected.

"Are you all right?" he called out above the wind.

"Yes, I am fine—" she said, the wind cutting her words away.

The others in the party had sped up some time ago, so the others reached the tents first. Henry didn't mind keeping whatever pace Evelyn and her aunt felt comfortable with. As long as they didn't ride too fast, Evelyn seemed thrilled to be atop a desert horse.

Once they reached the row of tents, the others were already enjoying refreshments.

Henry dismounted, then helped down Mrs. Tucker.

"Thank you, young man," she said with a smile, although she was quite out of breath and her forehead was beaded with perspiration. They'd left Cairo just after sunrise, but the desert sun was quick to heat up.

"The refreshments are just over here," he said. "Let me help Evelyn down, and I'll take you inside."

"Don't worry about me," Mrs. Tucker said. "I can walk a few paces on my own, even in sand."

Henry nodded, then turned to assist Evelyn. She looked down at him, a grin on her face. "That was wonderful, Henry," she said.

"I'm glad you think so." He felt genuinely pleased at her

enthusiasm. He raised his hands to assist her, and she slid off the horse, right into Henry's arms.

He caught her at the waist, and her feet landed directly on his.

"My apologies," she said, moving back to give him room, although her smile gave her away.

He kept hold of her waist. "You have very light feet, Miss Tucker."

She tilted her head as she studied him. Her eyes were positively bright, even in their deep-brown color, and her dark hair tumbled about her shoulders like a garden fairy. He couldn't stop staring at her.

"I must look a fright," she said, touching the wild locks of her hair. "Oh, it's all come undone."

"Yes," he said, smoothing a rather rebellious lock back from the edge of her face. "It's all come undone."

Her breath seemed to hitch, and he wasn't even sure he was breathing. The sun was still a couple of hours from its zenith, yet he could have sworn the day had reached its hottest peak.

Evelyn's horse nickered behind them, and it was enough to break whatever spell Henry had been under. "I'll get the horses to the trough so they can drink. Then I'll show you where the others are taking their refreshments."

"I'll help you," Evelyn said, turning and grasping the reins of the horse she'd ridden.

"You don't have to," he said. "I'm sure you're quite thirsty."

"I want to help," she said, and began to walk toward the grove of palms where the horses were stationed.

He caught up soon enough, leading the other two horses. Soon, the horses stood happily in the shade, drinking from the trough of what was surely lukewarm water.

On the return to the tents, Henry was thrilled that Evelyn accepted the offer of his arm so naturally. Everything about her seemed to fit him, intellectually, and . . . physically.

Her pale-blue linen dress was an oasis in and of itself in this desert setting. The hubbub of conversation grew as they neared the tent where everyone had gathered. Beyond the tents was the dig site, and now the full view of the excavation appeared.

Evelyn slowed her pace. "I didn't realize there was work going on in your absence."

"As long as they are being paid, they will work," Henry said. "They'll take a break in a couple of hours while the heat of the day passes. Then they'll get another few hours in before dark."

"I can't wait to see what you've dug up so far," Evelyn said.

Henry grinned. "I can't wait to show you."

They rounded the corner of a large white tent and stepped through the opening. The interior was cooler than outside but still plenty warm. The guests were sitting on various cushions surrounding a large woven rug. In the center sat several platters of food, including fruits, cheeses, and breads. Alongside the food was cold tea. All very European.

They settled on the cushions between Percy and Mrs. Tucker. Henry felt Mrs. Worthen's gaze upon him, and he refused to look over at her. There were plenty of people in the tent to speak with—she didn't always have to single him out.

The woman didn't even compare to Evelyn in his mind. No other woman did. This thought brought him up short. Did he truly admire Evelyn to such an extent? Could he honestly say that he was so enamored of her?

Evelyn laughed at something Percy had said, and Henry looked over at them. He wanted to be the one she was laughing with. At this thought, Henry shook his head. He might as well admit it. He'd become attached to Evelyn Tucker.

"I was hoping we'd get some more of that tahini," she said, turning her attention once again in his direction.

"I'm sure we'll have some for dinner back at the hotel." He would make sure, in fact.

When the group had finished eating, most of them followed Henry and Percy out to the dig site. The laborers were only too happy to take a break from excavating, and Henry led Mrs. Tucker down a set of makeshift wooden steps to the first excavation level. Then he extended his hand to Evelyn.

As she walked around and asked him questions, he saw the excavation site with new eyes. It might look like only a large dug-out rectangle to the average person, but Evelyn was fascinated.

"I can take only a couple of people at a time into the tomb," Henry announced to the group at large. "Don't touch anything—not even the walls. And try not to scuff up the ground with your shoes. It will create a lot of dust in the air."

"Perhaps you should take the older guests down first, Mr. Gaiman," Mrs. Worthen said.

It might have sounded like a thoughtful remark, but everyone knew that she was directing her comment specifically to Mrs. Tucker, who was the oldest guest of the party.

"Normally, I'd love to go first, but I find that I can't abide close quarters with little light," Mrs. Tucker said, folding her hands in front of her.

"Very well," Henry said, not wanting to give any more attention to the fact that Mrs. Tucker might be uncomfortable. "Who would like to be in the first group?"

A couple of people raised their hands, then another group did. Henry made five or six trips into the tomb before it was Evelyn's turn. Even though he'd given his narration several times now, it was different when he helped Evelyn descend the narrow stairs into the gloomy interior. Mr. and Mrs. Jones made up the rest of their group.

The sun had nearly set, which made the place darker than previously, but there was still enough light to point out the hieroglyphics on the walls. On one side of the tomb was a stone sarcophagus. Not the elegant gold-leaf inlay that would house a pharaoh, but one made of simple stone.

"It feels different down here," Evelyn said in a hushed tone. "Like a cemetery." She held onto his arm as they stood in the middle of the chamber. Mr. and Mrs. Jones kept near the stairs as if they were hesitant to fully step into the tomb.

"I feel it too," Henry said. "I suppose because it is a burial place, and the Egyptians were religious in their burial rites, centering them around their traditions of the afterlife."

Evelyn nodded, and her hair brushed against his shoulder.

"How long has it been since you uncovered this tomb?" she asked.

"We broke into it last December," he said. "We were all stunned and couldn't believe our fortune. Of course we knew it was always a possibility, yet to be there the moment it happened was an incredible experience."

"Who broke through?" Mr. Jones asked from behind them. "One of the laborers?"

Henry looked over at Mr. Jones. "It was actually me," he said with a shrug. "But that's not the important thing."

"That's amazing," Evelyn said in a soft voice.

Everything about her was soft. Her voice, her hand on his arm, the way her unbound hair swept against him, the occasional brush of her dress against his arm. Even her scent was soft, reminding him of a desert wildflower.

"It doesn't make you a braggart to share the information," Mr. Jones said with a chuckle.

"Perhaps you're right," Henry said. "Although, as you can see, this excavation could never be handled by a single person. I would have never broken into this tomb if it hadn't been for the collective effort of all those involved." He pointed to the carved stone shelf that ran along the wall next to the sarcophagus. "We found priceless trinkets lining this shelf, including the canopic jars for the deceased person's organs."

"Their burial practices seem so barbaric," Mrs. Jones spoke up.

"To us, perhaps," Henry said.

"I find it fascinating," Evelyn said. "They were so advanced for their era, and yet so archaic. They might have removed the brain and other organs, but they always left the heart inside the body."

"The heart?" Mrs. Jones said.

"Yes." Henry couldn't help but look at Evelyn when he said, "The ancient Egyptians believed the heart contained the moral aspect of the soul of a person."

"Which I suppose is true," Evelyn said, meeting his gaze. "A very interesting concept."

Mrs. Jones stepped forward, coming into the chamber. She placed a hand on her heart. "That does make sense. Our heart is the center of our soul. It contains our love and hate—all of our emotions."

Mr. Jones moved next to Mrs. Jones and put his arm around her. "You are correct, my dear."

At that moment, Henry wished there weren't so much need for propriety between he and Evelyn, even though they were supposedly engaged. Linking arms as he escorted her somewhere was all the affection he was allowed.

The cool air started to settle around them, and he wasn't

surprised when Evelyn shivered. He wished he could pull Evelyn into his arms and warm her.

"Can you read the hieroglyphics?" Mrs. Jones asked.

"I've some knowledge," Henry said.

Evelyn moved closer to the wall of characters. "I, coming for the Amun, pure of heart within the pure body . . . I live through my words."

Henry was stunned. "How did you learn hieroglyphics?"

She glanced at him, a sheepish look on her face. "From a book. Although I learned only a handful of them."

"You know more than a handful," Henry said, impressed. He motioned for Mr. and Mrs. Jones to join them at the wall. "This is part of a prayer, which Evelyn just read. Amun is one of the primeval Egyptian gods. He is thought to be the creator."

Between Henry and Evelyn, they continued to read through the text of the ancient prayer. Henry had, of course, inscribed everything on the walls into his journal, and then into an official text that he hoped to have published in an article about the excavation one day. But hearing Evelyn repeat the prayer in her soft tones made the tomb feel different. Sacred.

He hadn't realized they'd spent extra time in the tomb until he heard Mrs. Worthen's voice call down to them. "We've only a bit of daylight left and one more group to come down."

Cringing at the way her voice grated through him, so unlike Evelyn's, he moved to the base of the steps. "We're coming up now." He let Mr. and Mrs. Jones precede them.

Evelyn was right behind him, and she linked her arm with his.

"Thank you," she said. "Seeing an Egyptian tomb has always been a dream of mine."

He couldn't help but smile at her, wanting to ask her what her other dreams were and if he by chance might be able to fulfill them. But Mrs. Worthen's voice sailed down the steps a second time as she greeted Mr. and Mrs. Jones, inquiring after their thoughts.

Before joining the others, the only thing he had time to say was, "You're most welcome, Evelyn."

13

The dark-green water parted before the steamboat as they left Cairo proper, and Evelyn leaned against the rail, keeping her gaze focused on the churning water. The entire party had boarded the steamboat a short time ago, including Mrs. Worthen, Mr. Smith, and Henry. The morning bloomed along the Nile with waving palm trees, sleek flowers, and chattering birds. Lively conversation sounded all around her, but Evelyn kept herself apart from everyone for a few moments.

Inside the tomb and on the ride back to Cairo, Evelyn had felt something shift between her and Henry Gaiman. She didn't know if it was his words—his compliments to be exact—or perhaps *her* heart. Maybe it was because they had been in close company for nearly two days, and she'd somehow grown attached.

Now, above the hum of conversation, she heard him speaking with Mr. Smith. Was it because she knew his voice so well? Henry laughed. She loved his laugh. Deliberately, she kept her gaze on the Nile. She needed to take a step back from all the socializing and understand what her true thoughts and feelings were. This wasn't something she could speak to her aunt about—Evelyn already knew that her aunt would encourage her affections toward Henry.

But Evelyn wanted to know what *she* wanted. What *she* was willing to risk. She also wanted to know what Henry was truly thinking. He'd been courteous, even flirtatious. Kind, respectful, interesting . . . fascinating. The longer she was around him, the more she wanted to know him. He lived such a foreign and exotic life out here in Egypt. His life might seem completely opposite of hers, yet they both loved history and Egyptology.

Surely that was some sort of sign?

Watching the river wasn't helping to clear her mind because the river only reminded her of the color of Henry's eyes.

When much of their party went inside the cabin area to settle into their rooms to escape the heat of the progressing morning, Evelyn reveled in the quiet.

She felt Henry's presence before he spoke. "Your aunt has gone to her quarters."

"All right," she said, glancing over at him, then redirecting her gaze to the water. He had shaved, and she noticed the smooth skin of his jaw and the fresh scent of soap.

He rested his hands on the rail, and the sleeve of his linen shirt brushed against her forearm as he leaned over to look at the water.

"We'll be passing through a herd of hippos in a few hours," he said.

"What they must think of this steamboat," Evelyn replied.

Henry chuckled. "What they must think of any of us. It

would be interesting to be inside an animal's mind for a few moments."

"Yes."

A few moments passed as they both watched the river in silence, and Evelyn wondered why Mrs. Worthen was leaving them alone so long. Perhaps she'd gone to her room as well. The sounds of a few people playing whist on one of the deck tables reached them.

"Evelyn," Henry said in a quiet voice.

The way he said her name made her heart thump.

"I know that I've apologized more than once for putting you in this situation," he began.

Evelyn looked up at him. "It won't last much longer," she said. "After I return to England with my aunt, you won't have to work so hard keeping up pretenses."

Henry turned, leaning a hip against the rail so that he was facing her. "That's just the thing," he said. "It might have all started out as a pretense, but I find that I like you. Very much. And I've decided to confess to Mrs. Worthen before dinner tonight."

She didn't know what to say. How did he expect her to answer? Regardless, her eyes started to sting, and she had to look down and rapidly blink. He was going to change everything between them, and she didn't know how she felt about that.

"Evelyn," Henry said in that low voice again. He touched her chin and raised it.

"I don't mean to be e-emotional," she stuttered. "I think I'm just tired. Or maybe it's the heat. But I don't think you should confess to Mrs. Worthen."

Henry didn't reply for a moment, only searched her gaze until she felt that she must be blushing furiously. "I know that Mrs. Worthen will be furious and most likely embarrassed.

There's a good chance that she'll withdraw her patronage, which means that my budget will be reduced drastically. I'll have to let go of my apartment and live at the excavation site permanently."

"Then don't tell her," Evelyn said, her voice pleading. Henry had told her he liked her. And he was touching her chin. And he was going to confess his deceit to Mrs. Worthen. Evelyn didn't want to face the woman's censure while stuck on a close-quartered steamboat. "Don't tell her, yet. At least wait until I am gone. I . . . I fear what Mrs. Worthen might say to me or my aunt."

He exhaled, dropping his hand. "You're right." Rubbing his hand over his jaw, he turned to face the water once again. "I suppose I can't expect you to return my regard since I literally have nothing to offer a wife. A tent hardly suffices as a home. The desert scorpions will make sure of that." His chuckle was dry and bitter.

The breath left Evelyn. Henry had brought up marriage, in a self-deprecating way—shooting it down before she could even answer.

He continued in a wry tone. "Sand, wind, and heat don't make an ideal backdrop for raising a family—"

"Henry," Evelyn cut in. She placed her hand over his.

He paused, and she knew he was startled. Neither of them were wearing gloves, and the skin-to-skin contact was unexpected even to her. But she braved through her racing pulse and wrapped her fingers around his.

"This has been the greatest adventure of my life," she said. "And I want to tell you that I like you too."

He stared at her, and she stared back. She could no longer hear the whist players or anyone else who might be on the deck. She didn't know if anyone else was observing them, and she found she didn't care. The wind was gentle and warm, contrasting with the coolness rising from the river.

Henry stepped closer, linking their fingers together. He opened his mouth to speak, then closed it. He looked past her for a moment, focusing on nothing. When he met her gaze again, his eyes were darker, unreadable.

"I honestly don't know what to do with you, Evelyn," he said at last. He squeezed her fingers, then released them. "I apologize. I must leave now."

Before she could reply, he'd moved past her and disappeared inside the side entrance to the cabins.

Evelyn remained by the rail for quite some time, gathering her thoughts. She couldn't very well show up inside her shared cabin with her aunt and burst into tears, but that was exactly what she felt like doing.

Dinner was hours away. That's when she'd likely see Henry next, but she didn't know if she could bear it.

Once this cruise was over, Mrs. Worthen would learn the whole of their deception. And Evelyn's adventures in Egypt would be only a distant memory. She felt the pang of longing grow within her breast. She was already missing this enchanting land. The fact of the matter was she'd confessed to Henry that she'd liked him, and he'd left.

Tears threatened again, and she knew she had to get away from public eyes. Thankfully, when she opened the door to her shared cabin, Margaret was asleep. Evelyn had a short cry, one that she hoped wouldn't make her face blotchy. When she felt composed once again, she joined Mrs. Jones on the deck. They sat in lounge chairs and watched the Nile banks pass by as they chatted now and then. All the while, Evelyn felt twinges of dread. Once Mrs. Worthen knew about the pretend engagement, would she manage to secure Henry as a husband after all? Would his guilt drive him to accept her proposal? Or perhaps his desperation to fund his excavation?

People married for financial security often. Evelyn had

just allowed herself to hope . . . and now that Henry had confessed he liked her, yet flatly discounted any notion of a future between them, Evelyn was feeling out of sorts. Quite melancholy, in fact.

She should have known better than to let herself think outside of her small life experience. She was a poor relation to her aunt, and she needed to be grateful she had a home to go back to.

"We should prepare for dinner," Mrs. Jones said, interrupting Evelyn's meandering thoughts.

It was then that Evelyn realized the entire day had passed without her seeing Henry. He must have kept to the other side of the boat. Had he seen where she was sitting?

She rose with Mrs. Jones, and they returned to their cabins. While Mrs. Jones helped Margaret change into a more formal dress for dinner, Evelyn barely listened to their conversation. She wore a lavender gown that had been one of the many generous purchases on the trip—courtesy of her aunt, or perhaps Henry, since it was his money after all.

Here he was, facing an uncertain financial future because of the potential wrath of Mrs. Worthen, and Evelyn was wearing an expensive gown. It couldn't be helped now, but she felt the guilt all the same. She pulled on her gloves just as her aunt announced she was ready.

"You've been very quiet," Margaret said as they walked along the corridor to the dining area. "Are you well?"

"I have a bit of a headache," Evelyn admitted, for it was true. "Perhaps a good supper will help."

"You do enjoy the Egyptian food more than I do," her aunt said with a laugh.

Evelyn smiled, although she didn't feel much like smiling. She felt as if a part of her had been carved out and she had been left hollow. Mrs. Worthen would eventually learn about the pretend engagement, and before the year was out, Henry might find himself a married man.

Upon their departure, Evelyn feared she'd be leaving behind more than memories. Her heart could very well become a casualty.

The dining area buzzed with activity. Mr. Smith was the first to greet them, his eyes shining with excitement. Evelyn didn't have time to wonder what he was all about before Mr. and Mrs. Jones joined them. They all sat together at a table for six. Evelyn hoped that Henry would join them, and when she saw him enter the dining room, her heart hammered as he strode directly toward their table.

After greeting everyone, he took his place next to Evelyn. It both exhilarated her and made her sad. She could no longer enjoy their ruse, their adventure, when she knew the ending would be sharp and final.

The conversation at the table centered around the upcoming sites, and Evelyn should have been fascinated to hear Henry's narrative, but she couldn't relax.

When the tinkling of a glass sounded, Evelyn was pulled from her ruminating.

Mr. Percy Smith, one table over, had risen to his feet and was tapping his glass with a spoon. "I'd like everyone's attention, if you please." His eyes were still bright with excitement, and he looked as if he had the most delicious news to share. "I have an important announcement to make."

All conversation in the room halted, and even the waiters, carrying platters of food, paused.

Mr. Smith's grin seemed a permanent thing on his face. He turned his gaze on Mrs. Worthen, who was at his same table. She was watching him with a smile.

"My important announcement is that Lillian Worthen has agreed to be my wife."

Several people in the room gasped, others clapped, but Evelyn didn't move. Henry seemed to sag next to Evelyn. "Percy can't do this," he whispered. "He can't sacrifice himself for me." He looked at Evelyn straight on. "I'm so sorry, but I can't let Percy do this. Please forgive me."

Before Evelyn could react, Henry bolted to his feet as if he'd been sitting on hot coals.

"You don't have to cover for me, Percy," Henry said.

Evelyn felt every bit of heat drain from her body.

Mr. Smith turned to face his friend, his brows drawing together. "Whatever are you saying, Henry? I believe congratulations are in order, my friend."

Henry pushed back his chair with such force that it clattered to the wooden floor. He moved around the table and faced Mr. Smith. "I cannot let you do this. I must own up to my own fallacies."

Mrs. Worthen stood now. "What is this about?" she asked, looking from Henry to Mr. Smith.

Evelyn wanted to disappear. To shrink away and hide under the table. To be anywhere but there. Because in the very next moments, Henry confessed it all. From his initial disinterest in marrying while excavating in Egypt, to his increased disinterest to take Mrs. Worthen to wife, to his bald lies, to his urgent letters to Evelyn, to Evelyn and her aunt's agreement to act their part.

Next to Evelyn, Margaret clenched her hands together in her lap until her knuckles turned white. Evelyn grasped her aunt's hands and clung to them as if they were the only life preserver in an ocean.

When Henry finished his impassioned explanations and multiple apologies, Evelyn couldn't take it anymore. She grabbed her aunt's arm, and the two of them rose and left the dining room without so much as a glance back.

As the steamboat neared the dock at the Dendera Temple complex the next morning, Henry stayed in his place by the rail. He would not be getting off here to tour the temple complex with the rest of the group. He was aware that Percy and Mrs. Worthen would be taking their leave here and abandoning the tour, traveling north again. And it was all Henry's fault. It was his fault that so many feelings were hurt last night and so many beliefs destroyed.

From his friend Percy, to their benefactress Mrs. Worthen, to Mrs. Tucker and Evelyn, along with all those associated with them. Henry was not naïve to the fact that his actions would have long and far-reaching consequences.

"Mr. Gaiman," a man said.

Startled that anyone cared to speak to him, he turned to see Mr. Jones.

"Mr. Percy Smith requests that you join him in his cabin." Mr. Jones turned and walked away before Henry could reply.

The steamboat felt empty, since the passengers had

already off-loaded, and Henry had assumed that Percy had been among them. Henry made his way to the cabins and knocked on the door that belonged to Percy.

It opened immediately, and Percy stood there. Beyond him was a packed valise on his single bed.

"Come in," Percy said in a tight voice. He promptly shut the door, then faced Henry and folded his arms.

"Percy, I am so sorry, and I—" Henry began.

Percy raised a hand to silence Henry. "It's your turn to hear me out. I'm not *you.* I don't want to spend my life living out of a tent. I want a family. I want a wife. I want to someday sit in my home library and remember excavations with a fondness, but they will never be what I eat, live, and breathe."

"Percy, I—"

"My marriage to Lillian is going to happen, with or without your approval," Percy continued. "We may not be a love match, but we respect each other. She needs me, and I . . . I don't have a lot of options. Neither of us are getting younger, and I want to make something of myself. I want to feel like I am making a difference in someone's life, and I can do that for Lillian."

"You don't have to—"

"It's not about *you,*" Percy said, his voice growing louder, his face flushing red. "This is about *me.* This is about *Lillian.* Your mistakes are your mistakes, and Lillian knows that you and she would have never suited. Especially after learning the lengths you went to in order to avoid her."

Henry winced at this.

Percy managed to lower his voice. "I don't know what will happen with the excavation or whether we will continue to finance it. Once this all blows over, I imagine that all of us will have matured and grown wiser for the experience. Perhaps our love for archaeology will supersede our emotions."

Henry exhaled. He felt awful but, strangely, better. He'd

never seen Percy so passionate about anything before. It reminded Henry of . . . himself.

"You are truly going to marry Mrs. Worthen?" he asked.

"Yes," Percy said, his jaw twitching. "And you will not disrespect my wife or do any foolish thing toward her again."

"I will not." Henry's heart and mind ached, but he could see the forgiveness in Percy's eyes. "Thank you. I will spend the rest of my days making this up to you."

Percy shook his head. "No. As far as I'm concerned, that is in the past, and I want it left there." He opened the door, signaling the end of their conversation. "But if you were to make it up to me, I know what you would need to do."

"What?" Henry asked. This was an unexpected olive branch.

"Go to the temple complex, and find that woman whom you are so enamored with," Percy said. "She deserves your apology the most out of everyone, and she also deserves a true marriage proposal."

Henry's mouth dropped open.

Percy raised his hand—he was becoming quite proficient at this—and said, "I've watched you mooning over her these past few days. And I know that you'll throw up a dozen arguments about having a wife and exposing her to Egypt. But Mrs. Worthen and I aren't going anywhere. We'll be living out of her apartments, and Miss Tucker will have opportunity for female companionship. Besides, her aunt is the spunkiest woman I know, and I wouldn't be surprised if she decided to stay in Cairo too."

Henry was speechless.

Percy chuckled, shaking his head. "Who would have thought that I'd be counseling you in matters of the heart? Go on now. Find Evelyn. Tell her how you feel, and do the right thing by her. Then let her decide where fate might take you both."

Percy turned to pick up his suitcase, and then he moved out into the corridor, passing by Henry. Without saying another word, he continued toward the deck.

There were still so many unanswered questions he had about Percy and Lillian Worthen's relationship, but as he replayed his friend's words in his mind, he knew that Percy was right. Henry had to speak with Evelyn. The only question now was whether she'd give him the chance.

By the time Henry reached the deck, all passengers had left the boat. He could see a group of them—the last group—up ahead, on horses and camels as they traveled toward the Dendera Temple complex. Just as in Cairo, a group of children had gathered at the launch area and were eagerly awaiting the straggling passengers—which happened to be Henry this time.

He was about to shoo them off, and then he saw a young girl holding up a bunch of red flowers. He hesitated only a moment, then handed her a couple of coins and bought all the flowers she held.

One of the merchants was happy to hire out his horse, and Henry mounted the beast and headed after the others. By the time he caught up with them, most of them had dismounted their horses and were walking through the temple complex.

He could clearly hear Mr. Purdie explaining some of the historical details to the group he was with, which included Mrs. Tucker and the Joneses. Henry scanned for Evelyn but didn't see her immediately.

He had been sure she would be at the ruins and wondered for a moment if she had in fact stayed on the boat. But he couldn't imagine her missing the site that contained one of the best-preserved temples in all of Egypt. One of the crowning features were the depictions of Cleopatra VI on the temple walls, in addition to a carving of Cleopatra VII and her son Ptolemy XV.

Henry followed his instinct and continued past the group who was listening to Mr. Purdie, keeping his eyes and ears open for any sign of Evelyn.

When he spotted her, he told himself he shouldn't have been surprised in the least. She was walking along the outside temple wall, where the position of the sun created a nice patch of shade. Her pale-yellow dress seemed to float about her, reminding Henry of a delicate butterfly. She carried her straw hat in one hand. Her hair was in a coiled braid, with several strands having escaped.

She looked a vision, and Henry knew when she left Egypt, he would feel her absence keenly. Evelyn was beautiful, witty, intelligent, and passionate about Egyptian history. He couldn't ask for a better woman, no matter how far and wide he searched. He could only hope that she would give him another chance.

As he approached, she didn't see him at first, so when she turned her head, her brows shot up in surprise.

"Henry," she said, then corrected to, "Mr. Gaiman."

He took the last few strides, the bunch of flowers clutched in his hand. His heart thundered, and his pulse raced. Her dark eyes were upon him, and he didn't like the wariness that he saw there. When he reached her, he gave a short bow.

She stepped back, as if she wanted to be anywhere but standing before him.

"Please," he said. "Hear me out."

She clasped her hands together, her hat dangling in front of her by the ribbons. Then she gave a small nod.

Henry felt as if he'd just been proclaimed a pharaoh. "It seems that from the first moment I met you, I've been apologizing." He looked down at the flowers in his hand that he was now practically crushing. "You have been patient, you have been understanding . . ." He looked up to meet her gaze. Her expression had softened, but the wariness remained. "You have been an angel, a goddess."

A small smile touched her lips, and Henry took it as encouragement to continue.

"I have a confession to make," he continued. "I told you that I like you, but I more than like you."

She simply stared at him.

"I've little to offer a wife, Evelyn—you know my situation better than anyone. Yet I can't imagine letting you return to England without at least considering my offer of marriage."

"Marriage?" Evelyn whispered. Her hands fell to her sides, and she released her hat.

"I know it might seem sudden, but I don't think it really is," he said. "I named you as my fiancée for a reason, although it wasn't known to me at the time."

Evelyn blinked a few times. "Are you asking me to *marry* you, Henry?"

He cleared his throat. "Yes. I know that I don't live the typical life and that I don't have the typical home to offer—at least not here in Egypt—"

"Henry," Evelyn cut in. "Why are you asking me to marry you? You told me last night that—"

He cut her off now by stepping forward and grasping her hand. "Last night I was a fool. I should have never called out Percy in front of everyone. I hurt you and your aunt by doing it, and your reputation could have been ruined. I can only ask for your forgiveness even though I'm still a fool. I don't want to lose you, Evelyn." He took a much-needed breath. "If I have to give up my excavation and return to England to become a respectable homeowner, then I'll do it. What do you say, Evelyn? Will you have me as your husband?"

Her expression was incredulous.

"Dear Evelyn," he said. "I've fallen in love with you, don't you see?"

Slowly, she smiled, and he thought it was the most beautiful thing he'd ever seen.

"Are those flowers for me?" she asked.

He'd nearly forgotten about them. "They are."

"You're crushing them."

He looked down. The flowers were crushed between their bodies, and he realized how close he was standing to Evelyn. Why, she was practically in his arms.

"Henry, I don't care where we live." She took the flowers from his hand and brought them to her nose to smell.

She did it so casually, like she hadn't just said something extraordinary.

"Does that mean you'll marry me?" he asked.

"I will insist on our own sleeping tent, Mr. Gaiman," she said, settling her hands on his shoulders while still holding the flowers in one hand.

He rested his hands on her hips and gazed into her brown eyes. "That won't be a problem, Miss Tucker." He lowered his head. She smelled of sunshine and wind and the flowers he'd purchased. When she didn't move away, he closed his eyes and kissed her.

Her arms wrapped around his neck as he pulled her closer. Her mouth yielded to his, and he deepened the kiss. They were engaged, truly engaged, and he wasn't going to play any more games with her.

She released the flowers as she moved her fingers along his neck and into his hair. The red petals floated to the ground, puddling at their feet, but Henry didn't care. He kissed her until they both had to catch their breath, and as she caught hers, he kissed her jaw, then her neck. He'd never felt skin so soft.

"I'll also need tahini each day with supper," she whispered.

He chuckled. "What else, my love?"

"Flowers," she murmured.

"Anything." Henry found her lips again and kissed her anew. She fit perfectly in his arms, and he hoped that she'd be content to marry in Egypt. He didn't have the patience to travel to another country. As of now, he didn't want to stop kissing her. The sooner they were married, the more proper their engagement could be.

Someone clapped, and Henry startled. He drew away from Evelyn. She turned as well, keeping one hand on his arm.

Percy and Lillian Worthen were walking toward them, both smiling broadly. Not too far behind came Mrs. Tucker and a few others, including Mr. Purdie and the Joneses.

"It's about time, my friend," Percy called out. "I take it she said 'yes' for real this time."

Henry couldn't form a response.

"When I told Lillian about our conversation on the boat, she insisted that we find out what transpired," Percy said, patting Lillian's hand that she'd hooked on his arm. "So, what's the news?"

Henry cleared his throat, sure that his face was a bright red. Hadn't he'd made a spectacle enough of his life, and now all of these people were here to witness him kissing Evelyn?

Before he could speak, Evelyn did it for him. "I've said yes."

"Wonderful!" her aunt said. "I was wondering how long it would take the two of you to figure things out."

"Aunt Margaret," Evelyn started, her tone disbelieving. "I thought—"

"Never mind what you thought, my dear." Her aunt moved toward Evelyn and kissed her cheek.

Evelyn released Henry and embraced her aunt.

Henry met Lillian Worthen's gaze and found only amusement in her eyes.

"You are certainly an interesting man, Henry Gaiman," she said, holding out her hand to him.

He took her hand and shook it. He was confused, but appreciative.

"Percy and I decided that if you were man enough to propose to Evelyn here, then I would continue as the benefactress to the excavation," Mrs. Worthen said. "I can't in good conscience have Evelyn living out of a tent, surrounded by men all the time. You'll be able to keep your apartment in Cairo, and the two of us will become great friends. Of course, her aunt is welcome to stay as long as she wants, too."

Henry was astounded.

"Oh, won't you stay, Aunt Margaret?" Evelyn gushed.

"For a while, my dear," she said, patting Evelyn's hand.

As the conversation buzzed around them and more and more plans were made, Henry couldn't quite believe his good fortune. He was grateful for his friends' forgiving hearts, both new and old, and most of all, he was grateful that he'd found such a woman as Evelyn.

When she slipped her hand in his and linked their fingers, he wished he could be alone with her yet again. To hold her in his arms, to kiss her, to cherish her. But he knew that would come soon enough. First, they had an ancient temple complex to explore.

"Would you like to hear about Cleopatra and her son Ptolemy?" he asked Evelyn. "There's a carving of them both just around this corner."

She squeezed his hand, meeting his gaze with her dark eyes. In them, he saw a satisfactory gleam. "I would love to."

Heather B. Moore is a four-time *USA Today* bestselling author. She writes historical thrillers under the pen name H.B. Moore; her latest thrillers include *The Killing Curse* and *Breaking Jess.* Under the name Heather B. Moore, she writes romance and women's fiction. Her newest releases include the historical romances *Love is Come* and *Ruth.* She's also one of the coauthors of the *USA Today* bestselling series: A Timeless Romance Anthology. Heather writes speculative fiction under the pen name Jane Redd; releases include the Solstice series and *Mistress Grim.* Heather is represented by Dystel, Goderich & Bourret.

Heather's email list: hbmoore.com/contact
Website: HBMoore.com
Facebook: Fans of H. B. Moore
Blog: MyWritersLair.blogspot.com
Twitter: @HeatherBMoore

Made in United States
Orlando, FL
27 September 2023

37330290R00159